# American Indian Story
## The Adventures of Sha'kona

BY

*Jana Mashonee*        *Stephan Galfas*

wampum
books

# American Indian Story

## The Adventures of Sha'kona

*Creative Direction by Stephanie Duckworth*
*Art Direction & Design by Don Wedge III of*
*stimulantd.com*
*Interior Illustrations by P. S. Lott of*
*The Ambulance Factory Studios*
*Cover Art by Peter Hale of Four Directions Media*
*Back Cover Photograph by Stephan Galfas*
*Cover Concept by Jana Mashonee and Stephan Galfas*
*Editing by Teresa S. Stevens*

wampum
books

*~~ To Emmitt ~~*
*We have never forgotten your beautiful spirit - our unconditional love for you carries on in our hearts forever.*

# ACKNOWLEDGMENTS

We would like to thank these special people that helped make this book possible:

First of all to Stephanie, for her passionate commitment to the story of Sha'kona and her unwavering support of the project. Thank you for the incredible concept of Taylor Mashonee and for helping us bring her to life. We have just begun our journey with you, and we look forward to the next chapter in our lives together. Thank you, sweet sister, for your wonderful beauty inside and out.

To all of our friends and family (Mom, Dad, Jamey - Jana loves you!) and (Mike, Jade - Daddy loves you!), who continue to support and love us no matter what - and that's why we love you all so much.

To David L. Boyle and family, who have made all things possible for us to accomplish our dreams - we thank you for this, David, and we will never forget your belief in us.

To Michael Galfas for his invaluable input in making this book an enjoyable read.

To Michele Slater for her dedication and endless hard work on this project - thank you so much.

To Ray Halbritter and Chuck Fougnier of the Oneida Indian Nation, The Men's Council and Clan Mothers, thank you for your support.

To Alex Salzman for his talent and friendship for so many years and his extraordinary role in the making of American Indian Story. We thank you.

Last but not least, thank you, Eswa, for being the most amazing little furry monster ever...we love you even though you are the weirdest creature alive.

*Jana & Stephan*

# *Foreword*

Truth is stranger than fiction, as the old adage goes. Except in this case.

In our story, thousands of years of history are compressed into three years of a young girl's life. Could this actually happen? Absolutely - in this book.

The inspiration came from Jana's GRAMMY nominated album, "American Indian Story." It is an album born from her Native roots, portraying her culture in a unique and positive way. Instead of individual songs that didn't connect with one another, we decided to have the music flow continuously from one song into the other, telling a complete story from start to finish. Sha'kona became our heroine and her adventures became our story. With the help of our gifted friend, Alex Salzman, a beautiful album was created.

A couple of years later, a wonderful relationship began between us and author, educator, and Wampum Books founder, Stephanie Duckworth. With Stephanie's amazing help and guidance, this story became a reality and our exciting adventure began into the magical world of books.

We would like to mention that this is not an historical book by any means. Throughout the pages there are culturally relevant facts (in our opinion) that have been sprinkled here and there, but its soul is pure fantasy. We hope you will be engaged by this epic tale of a young girl's remarkable journey, and through Sha'kona perhaps even discover similar feelings of self-discovery and adventure in your own life. It is our desire for you to look within yourself for personal enjoyment, enlightenment and fulfillment.

We look forward to sharing Sha'kona's heart with you.

*Jana Mashonee & Stephan Galfas*

# Table Of Contents

*Prologue*

*T*aylor Mashonee had just turned thirteen and wasn't ready for her great-grandmother's death. Only three days ago Taylor was sitting on the front porch of her house listening to her Nonie's tall tales and sipping sweet tea under an unusually hot September sun. Now she was standing by her great-grandmother's grave at the end of a funeral that felt like it would go on forever.

Taylor's tears had run out. She was feeling numb, unable to focus on anything that was being said. People were speaking to her, but their words would just float by and disappear. Her throat was too dry for her to even attempt to speak. That was okay, she didn't really want to talk. She wanted to be left alone to try and figure things out on her own, as she always did.

Ever since she woke up this morning Taylor had had the weirdest sensations that seemed to reach right down into the pit of her stomach. The smell of burning sage at the service wasn't helping. The acrid smoke irritated her eyes and turned her already dry throat raw. Her insides were doing cartwheels. When she closed her eyes things got worse, as if the strangest movie of all time were playing in her head in Technicolor and 3D. Images so real she felt she could reach out and grab them danced across landscapes that might as well have been from another planet.

It reminded her of the crazy stories Nonie would tell about the time before time. Taylor would sit for hours, spellbound, almost believing they were true. Of course, Nonie said they were totally real, that she had actually seen them happen with her "other eyes." Her "other eyes" were famous in the family. She knew about things before they happened or when she wasn't there, like what the weather would be in a week or if someone got in trouble at school. She also knew if a baby was going to be a boy or a girl months before it was born.

Taylor was so lost in her own thoughts she didn't even notice her mother walk up next to her.

"Hey, Sweetpea, it's time to go home. Everybody's gone already," she whispered. Taylor was startled. She had never heard her mom speak so softly, cracking with the emotion of the day.

"In a minute. You go ahead, I'll catch up," Taylor told her.

"Okay, but don't be long. Your grandma is making dinner. You know how cooking always takes her mind off things and makes her feel better." Her mother turned and headed up the hill for the short walk to their house.

As her mom slowly moved away, Taylor closed her eyes. A deep chill coursed through her body and a bitter wind shook the leaves on the azaleas and sycamore trees around her. In a heartbeat the temperature eerily dropped below the freezing point and the air became oppressively heavy. She shivered and wrapped her arms around herself to keep warm.

Almost against her will, Taylor's eyes snapped open to a bright light screaming down from above. She looked up to see a thick drape of black clouds cut the beam off and turn the late summer afternoon into a winter's night. Everything was happening so quickly she wasn't sure what she had seen.

No one was around. The last of their friends had left. Her mother was already at the top of the hill where their house stood, hurrying to get inside. Taylor's heart was beating a mile a minute as she turned to race home. Before she could take a single step, a flash of lightning lit up the sky, thunder roared in her ears and snowflakes the size of silver dollars began to fall faster than she thought possible.

What was going on? It wasn't fall yet, and even in the middle of winter they didn't have weather like this. It was definitely time to get home as quickly as her feet would carry her. Taylor started running up the hill toward the warmth and safety of her room.

The wind chased her, howling as if it were alive and in pain. Her feet slipped on the icy blanket that covered her ankles and swallowed her shoes. The snow had only started coming down a few minutes ago, but already everything she could see was being buried beneath a thick layer of frozen white crystals.

Every breath was a struggle, every step a battle against the downpour of snow doing everything in its power to slow her down. Half-running, half-sliding, she finally made it to the top of the hill onto the short path to her front porch. The rage of the storm was frightening.

"Taylor!" Her mother shouted above the roar of the wind, rushing out of the house to help her daughter inside. Drifts of snow blew through the open door as the two struggled into the house. It took all of their strength to close the door on the fury of the sudden storm.

"What is going on out there?" Her mother's voice had lost all of the calm from earlier. "I've never seen anything like this." A trail of snow and ice led from the front door to the living room where they were standing.

"This is more than just a snowstorm," Taylor answered, slipping out of her damp jacket. "Weird stuff is happening. I saw some kind of strange light shoot down from the sky right before the weather went nuts. Then it just disappeared. Or at least I think I saw it. Everything happened so fast I'm not sure." She stomped her feet to get the snow off.

"One thing I'm sure of, I ruined my favorite shoes," she added, looking down at what was left of her best moccasins.

"Don't worry about your shoes. They will dry out and be fine." Her mother was trying to make her feel better. "And that light was probably just lightning playing tricks on your eyes because of all the snow. You need to go upstairs to your room and get out of those wet clothes. Try to be quick, Grandma is going to have dinner ready before you know it." A sudden blast of wind rattled all of the windows. "I don't think this storm is letting up anytime soon."

"This is way beyond crazy weather," Taylor replied, as she wiped frozen strands of long black hair away from her face. "Labor Day was only last week and we have the Perfect Snowstorm going on. Where is all this global warming they keep talking about? I'm cold to the bone and I don't have any feeling in my fingers or toes."

"All we can do is ride it out. Now hurry it up. I'll call you when dinner's ready." Taylor's mom headed into the kitchen to help prepare the meal.

Taylor slipped off her soggy shoes and socks and bounded barefoot up the stairs to her room. Once there, she closed the door, took off her soaked blouse and skirt, put on jeans and her cousin's Davidson sweatshirt and climbed into bed. She pulled up the pinecone patchwork quilt her great-grandmother had made for her and snuggled against the huge stuffed bear she had won at the state fair a few years ago.

The wind was shaking the house and making all kinds of ominous sounds. Outside her window the world had turned ghostly white. In her room, however, under Nonie's quilt, Taylor always felt safe and warm. She stared up at the glow-in-the-dark stickers of the moon and stars she had put on her ceiling. They made her feel like she was sleeping outside under the great open skies. Tonight that probably wouldn't be such a good idea, but she still loved them. She could stay in bed all day looking up at her own little planetarium, if her mom would ever let her. That was highly unlikely. Right now she just wanted to be by herself for a while.

From the moment she'd gotten up this morning, it had been a really strange day. Taylor had felt oddly disconnected and really in touch at the same time, kind of how Nonie used to say she felt when her "other eyes" were on duty. Taylor didn't need "other eyes" to know how bizarre this day had been and she had the feeling it wasn't over yet. It was amazing how much things could change in the blink of an eye, when you least expected it. Even at the best of times she didn't like change, and this definitely wasn't the best of times.

"Sweetpea, time for dinner!" her mom announced loudly enough to be heard from the kitchen. Taylor hated that nickname, but couldn't bring herself to tell her mother. It was one of those "mother things," keeping her a little girl even though she was now a teenager. If it made her mom feel good, Taylor could let it slide.

"Okay," Taylor answered. The last thing she wanted to do was be with anyone right now, even her mom and grandma. She could hear them talking in hushed tones, probably discussing how they could make her feel better. She didn't want to have to talk about how she felt. Her mom was always trying to get her to "open up," to discuss her feelings. "You know you can tell me anything," she would say. Yeah, right.

Taylor dragged herself out of bed, stepping into her fuzzy bunny bedroom shoes. They might look funny, but they were as comfortable as it gets. She steeled herself for the family consolation dinner and made her way down to the kitchen.

"Hey girl, let's eat before the food gets as cold as it is outside." Her grandmother spoke in her "I mean business" voice.

Taylor didn't need any coaxing. The smells of Nana's cooking were like a magic potion that switched on the part of your brain that made you instantly famished. Taylor realized she hadn't had anything to eat since breakfast and all she had then was a sweet biscuit and a glass of milk.

Nana had laid out a feast. It looked as though twenty people would be eating instead of just the three of them. There was succotash and string beans, cornbread, hominy grits, fried catfish and ham steaks and, for dessert, homemade pecan pie. Everything was Taylor's favorite. Something was up. She never got all of that at one meal.

When Taylor went to sit at her regular place, her grandmother stopped her in her tracks, saying, "Why don't you sit at the head of the table tonight and say the blessing?"

Now Taylor was certain the world was out of whack. Her Nonie always sat at the head of the table and Nana absolutely always said the blessing, usually in her Native language.

"Are you all right, Nana?" Taylor questioned.

"I'm fine, honey. Why would you ask that? Today started out as a special day celebrating your Nonie's entering the spirit world, and with this storm it has gotten even more special. Very peculiar, but special nonetheless. I thought it would be the right thing for you to take your great-grandmother's place at the table. After we eat will come the most special part of the day."

Nana sat down at the other end of the table and Taylor's mother sat in the middle.

"What are you talking about?" Taylor had had enough "special" for one day. She just wanted to go back to bed and have it be tomorrow.

"You're just gonna have to wait and see, child. Now say the blessing so we can eat. I don't want all of my hard work to go to waste." There was never any point in arguing with Nana. No matter what you said or did, she would somehow end up having it her way. Taylor bowed her head and repeated the traditional blessing as her great-grandmother had done at every meal ever served in this house.

"Creator, thank you," her mom and grandmother said together as Taylor finished saying grace. Right away, they began to serve themselves. It was obvious they were all hungry; it had been a long day.

"What did you think of the ceremony for Nonie? I thought it was exceptionally beautiful. We were lucky to have our tribe's chief lead the service," Nana said in an unusually peaceful tone.

"It was good, but it seemed really long," Taylor replied.

"Sometimes our traditional ceremonies last for days. My father's went on for a week." Nana was beginning to speak in her "Indian voice." She had a lot of different voices.

"A week!" Taylor said. "I don't know if I could handle that." The idea that they were supposed to be celebrating was a difficult one for Taylor to grasp. She couldn't seem to get past the sadness and

7

emptiness she felt.

Her mom always knew when to change the subject. "I spoke to Aunt Wanda while you were in your room. She made it home before the storm hit but says it's real bad where she is." As if on cue, a gust of wind hurled a huge drift of snow against the big picture window in the dining room. They all gasped. For a moment it seemed the window would shatter from the force.

Taylor looked drained. "I hope this doesn't go on all night. I'll never be able to sleep and I'm exhausted."

"I'm sure it will slow down soon," her mother reassured her. "How long could Mother Nature keep this up? Now finish eating. I'll clean up tonight. Nana wants to talk to you."

When her mother volunteered to do the dishes by herself something big had to be going on. A sense of dread filled Taylor. The last time Nana had wanted to talk to her, she learned she couldn't have a dog. Nana didn't believe in indoor animals and Taylor wasn't going to have a puppy tied up outside all the time.

Nana got up and walked toward her bedroom. Taylor slowly pushed away from the table, stood, and followed with obvious hesitation.

"Sit on my rocking chair and get comfortable," her grand-mother said, gesturing at the old, familiar piece of furniture. "Your great-uncle made that for me when I was your age. I've rocked through more problems and done more thinking on that chair than I care to remember. I guess it's a kind of therapy for me. Go ahead and try it out."

Now Taylor was certain the end of the world was at hand. Nobody sat in Nana's chair. Ever. She did as she was told and tried to relax but was petrified with anxiety over what might be coming.

Nana didn't seem to notice. She had shuffled over to her closet, opened the door and pulled out a big cardboard box. She carried the box back to where Taylor sat, put it on the bed and sat down next to it.

"When you were born, your Nonie told me she had something I was supposed to give you once she had passed on," Nana revealed with a hint of mystery. "She also told me you would be thirteen when that happened. You know how she was with her 'other eyes' - always seeing and knowing things nobody else could. She didn't tell me what it meant or what it was for. She said you would know."

Taylor's mind was reeling. That feeling in the pit of her stomach was back. She was afraid to close her eyes, afraid that crazy movie would start to play again. From deep within the box Nana pulled out a huge, impossibly black, ancient book that seemed to be falling apart at the seams. She cradled it in her arms the way you would hold a little baby.

"This is for you. That's all I can tell you. I don't know any more." Using both hands, she gently placed the old book in Taylor's lap.

To say Taylor was confused would have been an under-statement.

"Go ahead, open it." The gentleness in her grandmother's voice brought on another surge of emotion. The moment Taylor put her hands on the book it began to glow like a firefly in the night. Her body tingled as if electricity were running through her veins. She was not afraid even though she knew she should be. Gently, she took hold of the cover and opened the old book on her lap.

"Nana, there's nothing in here!" she gasped. "The pages are

completely blank! I don't understand what..."

Before she could finish what she was saying, the pages began to vibrate, slowly turning transparent and disappearing. Without warning, a fierce wind blew out from where there had been pages a minute ago, carrying a dense cloud of snow into the room.

"What's happening, Nana?" Her grandmother was about to answer but stopped. Taylor looked into the blowing snow and saw deep within the book a girl who looked exactly like her, wearing animal skins, signaling her to follow...

## Chapter One

## The Great Storm

*"When you are in doubt, be still, and wait; when doubt no longer exists for you, then go forward with courage. So long as mists envelop you, be still; be still until the sunlight pours through and dispels the mists -- as it surely will. Then act with courage."*

*-- Ponca Chief White Eagle --*

*I*n another time, in another place…

Sha'kona could have sworn she saw a girl who looked just like her, dressed in extremely odd clothing, off in the distance staring back through the swirling snow. Or maybe her eyes were playing tricks on her. She couldn't be certain. The wind was blowing so hard and the snow was coming down so heavily that everything was a white blur.

She waved toward where she thought the other girl might be. Before there could be any response, a gust of wind shook the pine needles high on the trees above her, dumping a curtain of snow everywhere. Sha'kona covered her head with her arms to protect herself from the downfall. By the time she looked up again, the phantom figure was gone.

Very little had been normal since this morning. Sha'kona's entire family had gathered to celebrate her great-grandmother's life and say goodbye to her spirit as it passed on to the next world. The celebration part had gone well, but as soon as the farewell part had started, so had the snow. Everyone dismissed it as a freak flurry. It was much too early in the year for a real snowfall; they hadn't even harvested the crops yet. In fact, it had been extremely warm that morning when the ceremony began.

Sha'kona had known right away this was more than a flurry.

Much more. Though she had only been on this world for thirteen winters, she sometimes thought she had more sense than some of the elders. Plus, she had a bit of her great-grandmother's special gifts, the way she just knew things no one else did, her "other eyes." Not as intense, but there nonetheless. Her great-grandmother always did things in a really big way. Today was no exception. The weather was proof of that.

"Sha'kona!" Wowoka's voice thundered. He was her father and chief of the tribe. "What are you doing out in this storm by yourself? Your mother could use your help preparing dinner. Walk back with me. I'm hungry."

"What are we going to do Father?"

"I just told you. We're heading home."

"I mean about this cold and snow." Sha'kona offered, her brow wrinkling in worry.

"What is there to do, little one? It will soon pass and melt away as quickly as it came. Winter is a long way off." Wowoka put his arm around his daughter and they began to walk through the ever-deepening snow.

"I don't think so," Sha'kona said in the politest way possible. She knew it was not a good idea to contradict her father. "I have a strange feeling about this."

Wowoka stiffened ever so slightly at his daughter's comment and then responded, "You worry too much for someone so young. I know you see more than most, but sometimes snow is just snow. Your great-grandmother's passing has touched all of us, you probably more than anyone else. She was an amazing woman, but I don't think even she could make it snow like this. Your strange feeling will disappear soon. A good meal might make that happen."

Maybe he's right, Sha'kona thought. Her father had a way of knowing what was on her mind. She had been thinking her great-grandmother might have had something to do with what was happening. Maybe some food was the answer. She was kind of hungry - in fact, starving. The last time she had eaten was early that morning. She pulled ahead of her father and led the way through the ancient forest where he had found her.

*B*y the time they reached their camp on the wide open plain that neighbored the dense woodland, the snow was up to Sha'kona's knees. Their home, made from a wood frame covered with wool felt and animal skins, was the largest of the round tent-like structures that comprised the small village. She pushed aside the heavy sheepskins that covered the doorway and embraced the warmth.

Though the wind pounded against the sides of the dwelling, it felt safe and secure. A fire blazed in the center of the big open space where her mother, Makawee, her grandmother and her aunts were busy preparing mutton stew with noodles and rice. The irresistible aroma of her family's cooking filled the air.

"Are you all right, Sweet Potato?" Makawee asked with tender concern.

Sha'kona would never understand why her mother insisted on calling her by a name that belonged to a vegetable.

Makawee continued, soft-spoken as always when speaking to her daughter, "Come over here by the fire so you can get warm and help your grandmother squeeze out the yogurt and finish the rice pudding."

Rice pudding was one of Sha'kona's favorites. She moved close to the fire and started stirring the thick mix of rice, cream and honey that would be dessert.

"I'm fine," Sha'kona finally replied. "It's been a long day. First, great-grandmother's ceremony, then the bizarre change in the weather, and to top it all off I feel like I'm seeing things through her 'other eyes.' I just want to eat and get some sleep. My brain hurts." She began spooning the hot food into the clay bowls her grandmother had made a long time ago.

"There is a little work to do before you can rest," her father interrupted. "You have to bring the sheep and goats inside after we eat. The storm is getting worse; it's too nasty for them to stay out all night. It will be better by morning and then things can return to normal."

Sha'kona groaned. Herding all of the animals into the tent wasn't "a little work." Her younger brother, Kewa, would probably insist on helping, which meant it would take twice as long. She was only two winters older than him, but a lot of the time he seemed like he was still a baby, even though he was already almost as tall as she was. To be fair, once in a while he was fun to spend time with, but those moments were few and far between.

The women served the meal and Wowoka led the blessing. As soon as he was finished, everyone attacked the food with extraordinary enthusiasm. It was clear how hungry they were from how quiet everyone suddenly became. They devoured the main course in just minutes. When the rice pudding was passed around, Sha'kona did not take any. She had lost her appetite for dessert. She scraped off her bowl and put on her heavy coat. The older women were already cleaning up so they could make room for the family livestock's overnight stay.

Kewa hurried to get ready to help his sister. Dressed in so many layers he could barely move, he was all set to brave the elements.

"Come on, 'Sweet Potato,' let's go!" he taunted, knowing how much Sha'kona hated that name. Being annoying to his older sibling came very naturally to him.

Resigned to her fate, Sha'kona followed her brother out into the night. They were not prepared for what they encountered. The blizzard was in its full fury. Snow flew in every direction and the wind shrieked as if in protest to the mayhem. A mysterious glow turned the sky an ominous deep purple that added to the unnerving feelings Sha'kona had been experiencing all day. Kewa pulled close to her and she noticed his ever-present smile had been replaced with a look that could only be called dread.

"We should get the animals inside as fast as we can," Sha'kona shouted as she grabbed her brother's hand and pulled him toward the pen holding the family's sheep and goats. Only the heads of the herd were visible above the tall drifts. "Go around behind them and drive them toward me. I'll open the gate and lead them back to the tent. Once they start moving, don't let them stop or they might get stuck, or worse, get frightened and try to run away."

Kewa plowed his way to the far side. When he was in position, Sha'kona moved aside the rickety piece of fence that served as a door to the makeshift corral. The normally docile animals bolted from the enclosure in a sea of fur and horns, panicked by the cruelty of the storm. She barely had time to get out of the way as they rushed past her. It was foolish of her to try and move them without the help of the dogs. Luckily the snow and ice slowed them down and she was able to get ahead of them to lead them toward safety.

"Stay close to them and help me steer them in the right direction!" Sha'kona instructed her brother. Kewa hurdled the stockade and herded them forward. They stumbled and slid like one uncoordinated creature up the path to the opening of the tent. Sha'kona pulled aside the skins that served as the door and let the animals into the shelter of their home for the night. Wowoka and his brother Tokanosh settled the anxious sheep and goats on one side of the living space where they were lulled to sleep by the calm and warmth of the indoors as soon as they laid themselves down.

"What about the horses? We can't leave them out there!" Sha'kona exclaimed. Her horse, Tasunke, was her most prized possession. He was pure white with a black diamond on his forehead and was the smartest of all the horses. The thought of him frightened and shivering from the cold brought tears to her coal-black eyes.

"Your uncle and I led them to the shelter of the cave by the summer grazing land before I came and found you. They will be safe there," her father responded in the same loud voice he used to address the whole tribe. "The storm is getting much worse than I expected. We need to check on the rest of the tribe south of the river. Tokanosh, will you go and see how things are there? We might have to head that way tomorrow if this keeps up. Their camp is in the lowlands of the valley and will be more protected."

"No! We can't go that way! That would be the end of us. We have to head north. I see only bad spirits south. You don't know what you are saying!"

The words exploded from Sha'kona's mouth. She had no idea

where they came from. All she knew was that a frightening vision of what might happen had popped into her head. She looked up at her father, afraid of his response to her spontaneous outburst. No one ever spoke to him that way.

Wowoka glared at her and chose his words carefully.

"I am your father but I am also the leader of this tribe. It is up to me to make the decisions about our future. You will learn to hold your tongue and speak with respect to your elders. Tokanosh will head south to check on the rest of the family and prepare for our stay there and you will go to bed and conjure up a vision of the appropriate behavior for a chief's daughter."

Sha'kona had never heard her father speak to her with such authority. A chill ran down her spine. She wanted to apologize, but words would not come. It was all she could do to hold back the tears that threatened to flow for the second time that night.

What had come over her? Her emotions were overwhelming her and flashes of the disturbing sights that had inexplicably appeared to her would not stop. Too much had happened today. Her father was right. She needed to go to sleep and leave it all behind. If only she could convince herself that tomorrow would be better. With a heavy heart, Sha'kona crept off to bed.

It pained Wowoka to speak to his daughter so harshly, but it was his duty to be strict about the discipline of the family. Their survival depended on it. He watched Sha'kona crawl under the covers in her sleeping space and then turned to his brother.

"You must go now while you can still make it," the chief ordered. "If things are not better when the sun rises, we will leave as soon as we can to meet you."

*Chapter One*

*T*okanosh did not reply. He was an enormous man of few words. Grabbing his shearling coat, his spear and his snowshoes, he headed out into the rage of the storm. The snow stung his face like angry ice bees, but he ignored the discomfort and pulled the sled away from the side of the tent. He knew the dogs would be buried in the snow, huddled together and curled up in tight circles around themselves to keep warm. Sticking two fingers in his mouth, he whistled the signal for them to come. At once the snow erupted as all eight massive dogs responded to the familiar sound in an outbreak of excited energy. They were ready to play.

"Come, my friends. It's time to have some fun. We are going to the other camp to visit your brothers and sisters. Let me hitch you to the sled."

Tokanosh had no problem speaking to animals. People were a different matter. The dogs seemed to understand his every word. Quivering with anticipation, they lined themselves up in front of the sled and waited as he tied them into their harnesses. When he was finished, he knelt down in front of the lead dog and spoke to him in the gentlest of tones.

"I need your help tonight, Mingan. I can't see my hand in front of my face in this mess. You must guide us. I'm counting on you. Can you get us there, boy?" Mingan put his huge paws on Tokanosh's shoulder and licked his face. That was all the answer Wowoka's brother needed.

They took off at a breakneck pace. It seemed that Tokanosh

and his team only moved at full speed. The trees tore past them as the surefooted animals raced through the night. Their instinctive desire to find out what lay ahead, coupled with their incredible strength and stamina, assured him of a swift journey. The dogs never let him down.

It required all of Tokanosh's considerable strength to control the sled as it carved a path through the deep snow. The further south he traveled, the worse conditions became. He couldn't help but think of Sha'kona's words to his brother. Perhaps she had inherited some of her great-grandmother's gifts. A sharp turn by the dogs shook the thought from his head.

The sled snapped to one side, tilted up on a single runner and threatened to tip over. He could not afford to crash now. He would never be able to make it back on foot. Putting all of his weight on the high side, he twisted the sled in the opposite direction of the turn. The strain on the old snow cart was more than it was built to withstand. Just as he thought it would buckle and splinter into useless firewood, Tokanosh threw out the brake hook, slowing them down enough to somehow regain control.

"Mingan, stop!" The faithful dog reacted instantly to his master's voice and brought the team to a halt. Tokanosh realized how lucky he was and said a heartfelt prayer of thanks. He took a moment to rest and compose himself before carefully checking the sled for damage. Everything seemed to have survived the ordeal. He eased the sled back onto the trail and headed up the final hill before the camp. The dogs proceeded cautiously. They sensed something was wrong.

Once they reached the peak of the incline, Tokanosh looked down toward the camp in shock and disbelief. There was nothing left of the makeshift village. It was deserted.

The storm had flattened most of the tents and buried the rest. Ice covered everything, bending the trees like distorted bows with what were once the highest branches frozen upside down to the ground. Fearing that the dogs and the sled would not make it back up the steep slope, he left them, grabbed his spear and headed down on foot.

When he arrived at what was once the peaceful encampment of his extended family, he was met with only devastation and desolation. There were no signs of life. Everything was gone.

"Can anyone hear me? Is there anyone here?" Only silence answered. "I said, is there anyone here? It is Tokanosh, your brother from the north!" To be heard above the roar of the icy tempest he had to shout at the top of his lungs.

Just beyond the collapsed form of the main dwelling he thought he saw something move. With caution he crept forward. Wolves were the only creatures that would be roaming outdoors on a night like this. He respected all creatures but feared none.

Raising his spear to the ready he exclaimed, "Show yourself in peace or be prepared to travel to the next world!"

Two small figures stumbled into sight. "Tokanosh, is that you?" The voice was frail and trembled with age and cold. "It is Migisi. Help us!"

Though the heavy snow clouded his vision, he recognized the tiny woman. She was the oldest person in the tribe, his grandmother's sister, and had been blind for as long as he had known her. Next to her, holding on for dear life, stood Chepi, the daughter of his brother, Hakan. Chepi was born the same year as Sha'kona but was nearly a head shorter and almost as pale as the frozen landscape.

Tokanosh rushed to them, taking off the gigantic bearskin he wore on top of his coat and wrapping it around both of their shaking bodies.

"Where is everyone?" he asked, not sure if he wanted to hear the answer.

"I don't know," Chepi replied in a half whisper and then started to cry.

Tokanosh put his huge arms around both of them. "Calm down. You are safe now. Tell me what happened."

"In the time it takes a crow to flap its wings, the air froze and the sky dumped the snow of ten winters on us all at once," Chepi said. "Our homes were crushed and the animals went wild. My father told everyone to grab what they could and follow him to the other side of the ridge where we would be sheltered from the intense wind. Migisi said she was too blind and too old to go; she wanted to stay in her tent. We tried to convince her to come, but she wouldn't listen. You know how she is once she's made up her mind; it's useless to try and change it." Chepi raced through her story without stopping to even take a breath.

"All the rest of us went. We made it to the top of the mountain but on our way down to what we thought would be safety, a gigantic wall of snow came crashing over us, sweeping away everything in its path. It knocked me down but somehow passed me by. When I was able to stand up there was no one in sight. I started to look for them, screaming for my father, but no one answered. The only thing I could think of to do was to go back and find Migisi."

Deep furrows of concern formed in Tokanosh's brow. "I will go and see if I can find them. You wait here for me."

"No! Don't leave us!" Chepi cried. "It's no use! On my way back another avalanche threw itself down on top of the first and completely blocked the way. It's not possible to get there. I should have stayed and tried to help." Sobbing with guilt, she buried her face in her uncle's heavy coat.

"There is nothing you could have done," Tokanosh told her firmly. "You made the right choice. As bad as it seems, I trust that your father will take care of everyone with him, as I will take care of you. We must get back to my camp to join the others and let them know what has happened." Tokanosh scooped the two of them up, one in each arm, and headed back to the sled and the waiting dogs. Once there he carefully placed them in the sled's basket, the old woman cradled in the young girl's arms for warmth, and began the trip home.

*Sha'kona could not sleep despite how exhausted she was. She lay in bed tossing and turning, the events of the day replaying in her head. The storm had not let up; if anything, it had gotten worse. Somehow the rest of the family had managed to sleep. The only sounds came from beyond the walls of her home.

Without warning, what felt like an earthquake rocked the tent. The ceiling on the far side above the supplies came crashing down, followed by a mountain of snow. Frigid air rushed in. Everyone woke up in a flash, scrambling into their coats and boots while checking to make sure no one was hurt. By sheer luck, they were all unharmed.

Wowoka took charge immediately. "The snow has become too heavy for the tents to support the weight. Gather up only the belongings you need. We must seek shelter. Our camp is too exposed here. Liwanu, check on the other tents. Then take a few men and go bring the horses; we will need them." Liwanu was his younger cousin and one of the tribe's council. Along with Tokanosh, he cared for their animals and often led the hunts.

The family went to work right away, checking on the supplies and packing only what was absolutely essential. They would have to travel very light. The conditions were too treacherous to carry heavy loads.

There was very little Sha'kona felt she needed. The necklace her great-grandmother had left her and the doll her grandmother had made for her were all she took. Kewa was having a much more difficult time deciding. There was his bow and his spear, of course, but also his games and puzzles and his collection of bones and the special rocks piled next to his bed and...

"Kewa, what are you doing! You can't bring all of that, you won't be able to carry it," his mother chided as she noticed him filling his bag to the brim. "You must leave room for supplies in your bag as well. Choose two things and leave the rest behind."

Two things? How was he supposed to do that? It wasn't fair, but he knew his mom meant business. He looked to Sha'kona for help.

"You can always find more rocks and bones," Sha'kona told him as she packed supplies into her bag. "Take your bow and arrows and your favorite puzzle. I have a feeling we won't have much time for games."

The women quickly finished gathering all the necessities and headed out to salvage any of the crops that might still be edible. Only root vegetables like potatoes, onions and carrots could have survived the sudden freeze. Still, anything was better than nothing. They needed food and had no idea how long they might be gone.

Sha'kona left her brother still trying to decide what to take and went to help the women. She joined them in digging through the snow and yanking the vegetables from the frozen ground. Half of what she pulled out was already ruined and had to be thrown away. Her hands went numb but she would not stop until they had all they could carry.

The sun had risen but was not visible through the dark, menacing clouds. It did nothing to relieve the brutal cold.

Her mother was right beside her, and, like all of the other women, was totally focused on her work. Makawee hated the cold but did not complain. Sha'kona turned her head toward her mother to see if she was all right. As she did, she noticed a moving cloud of snow in the distance. The cloud drew closer and she could make out the shape of a team of dogs pulling a sled. She recognized Mingan and realized who it was.

"Father, Tokanosh is back!" she called out. Wowoka was with the other men getting the dogs hooked up to the sleds. When he saw his brother approaching he hurried to greet him. Tokanosh pulled his sled up next to the other teams. Wowoka saw only his young niece and the old woman in the basket.

"Where are the rest? Are they behind you?" the chief asked, reaching to help Migisi and Chepi.

"They're gone," Tokanosh replied. "An avalanche overtook them and buried the pass south in snow up to the trees. There is nothing left of their camp. We cannot go that way."

Wowoka was stunned. There had been too much misfortune for one day. He could not lose another member of the family. No ice storm would defeat his tribe. His daughter's warning from earlier no longer seemed like a tantrum from a spoiled child.

"Sha'kona, I need to speak with you alone." He led her away from where the family had congregated to hear what had happened to the rest of the tribe. "Tell me what it was that made you so afraid that you raised your voice at me."

"I am so sorry. I was very wrong," she said as she looked at him, wanting only his forgiveness.

"Do not apologize. Maybe it is I who was wrong. Did you see something that our eyes could not see?" Wowoka wondered.

"I'm not sure what happened," Sha'kona disclosed. "I thought I saw something. It seemed completely real and then it was gone. Mother Earth came to me and lifted me high into the sky. She told me to look to the south. When I did, I saw only a frozen wasteland where nothing lived and nothing would live for a very long time. It was as though the whole world had died. Then she turned me to face the north and I saw a bright light far, far away, like a signal fire beckoning me. I had no idea what I was looking at, or if I was really looking at anything at all. I was scared to death. Before I had a chance to question her about it, she let me go. Instead of falling, I started insulting you and telling you what to do. Falling would have been a better idea. What nonsense." She was relieved to be able to let her father know what had happened and let him know she was sorry. It seemed so foolish as she heard herself tell the story.

"I wish it were nonsense," her father responded. "It is I who must apologize to you. Apparently, your great-grandmother left her 'other eyes' behind with you. Her whole life she saw things no one else did and helped guide us as a family when we needed it most. I believe your vision was a message to us. We will head north."

Wowoka had made a decision that would change the course of their world in ways he might never understand.

Liwanu arrived with the horses and the tribe mounted up. The sleds were loaded and the dogs were anxious to go. Hearts were heavy and spirits uncertain. They were leaving all they knew. Or maybe all they knew was leaving them.

"Bring your horse up here, Sha'kona. I want you beside me," Wowoka requested rather than commanded. Sha'kona had never ridden next to her father when the family traveled. No woman had. She didn't understand what was happening.

Wowoka addressed the tribe, explaining their situation.

"We must leave our home in search of a new place to live. We cannot survive in this cold and I don't think this change is temporary. Mother Earth is giving us a warning. Sha'kona has inherited her great-grandmother's gifts and has had a vision that will guide us." Sha'kona squirmed as all eyes shifted to her.

"Do you think you can lead us to the fire you saw?" Wowoka inquired of her in front of the whole family.

Before she could speak, the bright light she had seen in the distance reappeared for an instant. This time she wasn't afraid.

"I think maybe I can." Sha'kona turned her horse into the bitter wind and took the first step into what would be the journey of her life. Wowoka was beside her and the rest of the family followed. As they began to move, Kewa rode up next to her.

"Sha'kona, Sha'kona, where are we going?" her brother demanded impatiently.

She looked at him with her first smile in some time.

"Home."

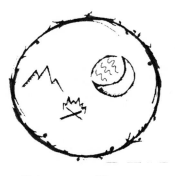

## Chapter Two

# The Journey - Part I

*"We will be known forever by the tracks we leave."*

*-- Dakota --*

*A*ll day Sha'kona and her father led the tribe north, fighting the angry wind and unrelenting snow. By nightfall they needed to make it through the pass known as One Horse Way to the other side of the hills that marked the boundary of their land. She was still basking in her father's approval but wished she had the same confidence in herself that he did.

Where was she going? Everyone was trusting in a daydream she had that somehow had been endowed with magic powers by her father. It was hard for her to believe she could see the future of her family and lead them to some light that was only visible to her. Sure her great-grandmother could do that, but she was an old woman who had all kinds of powers. Sha'kona was just a child who still liked playing with dolls when she could. Yes, the vision had seemed very real, but how could she know for sure? She had to believe in her father's judgment and hope that she could indeed guide them to that beacon she had seen so far away. Her family was trusting in her. No way could she let them down.

Wowoka had his own concerns. The lives of the eighty members of the tribe were his responsibility. Had Mother Earth really chosen his young daughter to receive a vision? Had his grandmother left her gifts behind for Sha'kona to learn to use to protect the family? He believed there was a purpose and a plan for each and every person. Was this Sha'kona's special place in the sacred circle of life? He struggled to find the answers within himself but knew they would only be revealed when the time was right. Yesterday she was his baby girl. Now she moved forward with purpose, driven by unseen spirits, and everyone followed her without question.

*M*akawee pulled up next to her husband and daughter. "How much further before we rest?" she questioned. "Some of the children and elders are getting tired. The cold is taking its toll."

"And I'm hungry!" Kewa complained. He had come from behind as well; he wanted to be up front with his father instead of with the women and children.

"Why does Sha'kona get to ride with you and I don't?" he asked his father, obviously annoyed.

"I need you in the back to watch after your mother and to protect the young ones," Wowoka answered, displaying the diplomacy that made him such a good chief. He turned to his wife, "We must make it past the bluffs before dark. Then we can stop for a while."

Sha'kona had heard the conversation and picked up the pace just a little, focusing on the narrow gap between the low peaks just ahead. She was curious about what was on the other side. Soon enough she would find out.

The snow got deeper as they got closer. When they reached the mouth of the pass she pulled back on her reins and brought Tasunke to a full stop. She now understood why it was called One Horse Way. There was only enough room for one horse to go through at a time. She wondered if it was wide enough for the heavily loaded sleds. Though exceptionally cramped at the bottom, the passage opened up as it rose to an immense space completely covered by a canopy of ice that cut off the light from above. It was dark inside and only going to get darker as night closed in.

Wowoka was beside her. He addressed the clan.

"We will have to go through single file, eight riders at a time, then the sleds one by one. After what happened to our tents I am worried about the passage caving in on us. Try to be as quiet as you can. I will lead the first of us. I don't know what waits on the other side or what lies within. If there is trouble I want it to meet me first. When we get through, I will give this signal for the rest to come." He made the distinctive sound of an owl then spoke directly to his daughter. "Sha'kona, wait here to make sure everyone gets through then you follow with Kewa and your mother."

All those on horseback lined up behind their chief, followed by the dog sleds. Wowoka and his group headed into the passageway. Once they got beyond the opening, it was nearly pitch black inside. They moved slowly. Everything was covered with ice, making each step treacherous. The trail got even narrower as they inched forward, the riders' knees almost scraping the sides. With the top closed over, it felt like a tomb.

Since he was a child, Wowoka had hated the feeling of being closed in. He prayed that the other side was not too far. Whatever was waiting there would be better than this. Just when he thought he could take no more, a blast of cold air hit him in the face and the trail became broad enough for all of the horses to stand side by side. They had made it through. Relief swept over him.

Wowoka trilled the owl signal then called into the darkness from which he had just exited, "Send the next team and keep them coming. Be very careful. I don't want anyone hurt. It is a tight fit and very slippery."

The rest of the tribe followed Wowoka. All of those on horseback joined him first, then the sleds and the dogs followed. They barely fit, constantly knocking into the walls as they navigated the constricted pass. Sha'kona heard strange groaning sounds coming from the blackness that swallowed the family. Anxiously she waited with her mother and brother for the all clear signal. The noises grew so loud, she barely heard her father's call.

"Time to go! And cover your heads! Pieces of ice are falling," Makawee told her son and daughter as she pushed her timid horse forward into the passage.

The two children pulled their coats over their heads, hugged their horses and rode toward the gap. Kewa followed closely behind his mother, looking around nervously. Sha'kona was the last to go.

The ice was moaning as she entered the narrow path. In spite of knowing the others had made it safely through, she had an uneasy feeling. She shivered.

Without warning, Tasunke stumbled and they both toppled into the snow.

"Sha'kona!" her mother screamed.

She got up as quickly as she had fallen and began to help her horse up.

"We're fine, Mom," she said quietly. "The snow was soft. Take Kewa and move as quickly as you can. I will be right behind you." Makawee took hold of her son's reins and the two quickly disappeared into the pass.

Sha'kona remounted and followed. Looking up, she saw icicles as tall as a man hanging like crystal spears. As she watched, one broke off and knifed itself into the snow next to her. All of the movement had loosened the frozen covering above. The sound of cracking ice joined the rumbling pouring out at her. Digging her heels into the sides of her horse, she bolted for the other side.

She could see nothing, but she could hear the ice above groaning and chattering and feel frozen slivers slicing through the air. Tasunke moved as rapidly as he could in the confines of the space. The slivers became chunks, smashing into her. A roar like thunder assaulted the young girl as the roof behind her fractured and collapsed. Instinct drove her forward faster than caution demanded. Everything was caving in, chasing her and trying to bury her before she could escape. It seemed the journey was going to be over for her before it had really started. Sha'kona hoped her mother and brother had gotten out in time.

Suddenly a small globe of dim light appeared, floating in front of her, illuminating the path. Everything seemed to be moving in slow motion. Tasunke's ears perked up and he slowed down as well. Silence surrounded her and she was filled with a strange calmness. She sat up straight and tried to focus on the sphere suspended in mid air. Was it really there? Before she had a chance to figure out the answer, the orb ignited with the brilliance of the sun. Sha'kona slammed her eyes shut and felt herself propelled ahead as if she were flying.

When Sha'kona opened her eyes, she was galloping out of the pass to where her family stood staring in disbelief. Snow and ice had completely filled in the crevice from which she had emerged, yet she was unharmed. In fact, there was not a mark on her or her horse, not even a flake of snow.

"Are you all right? What happened in there?" her mother asked, almost desperate with concern. Makawee was frantic but elated that somehow her daughter was there beside her. "Just as we got out, the mountain fell in on itself. I thought you were gone, sealed in that tomb. Then you just appeared out of thin air, careening at us at full speed."

Sha'kona was at a loss as to what to say. She didn't really know what had happened. It was all a bit of a blur. If she told what she did remember, people would think she was even weirder than they already did.

"I'm fine. I guess I got lucky. It was pretty scary."

Wowoka listened skeptically. He knew Sha'kona was still deep within the passage when the top and sides violently caved in, sealing off the way back forever. And yet, somehow, she was here beside him. This was more than the spirits watching her. He decided not to press for answers. When and if she felt like talking about it, she would.

"I am happy you are here with us, that we all are here," he said. Now we should rest. Tomorrow will be a long day as I'm sure they all will be for a while. We will make camp. It is too dark to see what is on this side beyond our lands. At first light we will continue on."

The tribe was physically and emotionally drained. They set up in the shelter of the bluffs through which they had just traveled. There they were protected from the incessant wind. No one spoke. They were all too tired. After a meal of dried meat and beans, Wowoka said the evening prayer and they retired for the night. Sleep came quickly.

*S*ha'kona thought the "light" was back. Her eyes burned from the brightness that clawed at her closed eyelids. She squeezed them tighter shut, petrified of what she might see this time when she opened them. The last thing she wanted right now was another hallucination masquerading as one of her great-grandmother's "other eye" experiences.

"Wake up, sleepy face. You have to check this out. I think you brought us to the moon. Remind me not to use you as a guide when I start going out on my own hunting trips," her brother taunted her.

Against her better judgment, Sha'kona opened her eyes and was attacked by the brightest sunlight she had ever seen, the kind of bright that hurts. It took a moment for her eyes to adjust. Once they had, all she could see was a surreal landscape of pure, flat ice stretching uninterrupted to the horizon. Kewa was right. This could be the moon. The snow had stopped and the wind was still. There wasn't a tree or a plant in sight, just a totally white panorama under a sky so dark blue it looked fake, as if it were painted with crushed blueberries.

All around, the tribe was preparing to move out. The horses and dogs were refreshed and full of energy. The dawn of a new day was enough to lift everyone's spirits. Sha'kona got up and went to greet Tasunke. She rubbed his nose and fed him some of the carrots she had pulled from the ground before they left. The young horse nuzzled her and pranced, excited to see her. As soon as she moved to his side, he quieted down and she climbed on him ready to take the lead again.

"Let's get a move on! We may have to ride a long way today and I want to make use of every bit of daylight we can. Are you set, Sha'kona? Can you see where we must go?" Wowoka spoke with authority. His questions seemed more like commands.

Sha'kona scanned the featureless tundra, hoping for some sign to point her in the right direction. Everything looked the same, endless plains of ice followed by endless plains of ice. Before she could decide, Tasunke turned northward and took off with certainty toward some unseen destination. She wished she knew where she was going or had something to guide her, like the peculiar floating light had done last night.

*T*okanosh rode just behind Wowoka and Sha'kona. His dog was in back helping pull the heavily loaded sleds. When Tokanosh traveled by horse, Mingan would normally run alongside him exploring every new smell that came his way. He missed the dog's company. He had no one to talk to.

By midday they had traveled quite a way, always due north. Though all seemed peaceful, Tokanosh stayed alert. Trouble never announced itself. It was his job to keep the tribe safe. The sun was high in the sky, exaggerating the monotony of this barren land he was seeing for the first time. It would be easy to let the boredom cause your mind to drift.

A slight movement to his right caught his eye. He turned his head and saw in the distance what looked like a moving ball of snow. Then it stopped. All he could see was whiteness. Was it his imagining it, or worse, was he seeing things like Sha'kona did? Tokanosh wasn't sure if he should say something to his brother or not. That's just what Wowoka needed, another member of the family thinking they had his grandmother's supernatural powers.

More motion. Now he knew something was out there, big

and almost invisible. The hair on the back of his neck stood up. He concentrated on the giant form. Was this a shapeshifter? Tokanosh had heard stories of these strange beings since he was a little boy. They could change their shape at will and appear and disappear before your eyes. Or maybe it was the elusive snowman, half human, half animal - another fable passed down from the elders. His imagination danced wildly in his head.

This was no fantasy. A colossal beast reared up on its hind legs and roared louder than thunder in the night. The tribe stopped dead in its tracks. The creature looked like the bears from their homeland but stood taller than two men and its fur was colorless. The absence of color was dangerously mysterious, whiter than a cloud but with a frigid sheen spun in a rage of frozen clouds.

Sha'kona's eyes locked onto the creature. Never had she seen anything so beautiful and so terrifying at the same time. The huge animal stared straight back at her with an unsettling intensity. She was mesmerized but for some reason did not feel threatened. She pulled away from the startled members of the tribe and rode toward the gigantic bear.

"Sha'kona! Stop!" Even as Wowoka screamed and drove his horse toward his daughter, Tokanosh was racing the same way. "That is Nanuk. He will tear you limb from limb!"

Many years ago Wowoka's father had told him the legend of the great white bear, Nanuk. When he was a child, he had believed all of his father's tales. This was one he wished his father had made up. It was said that Nanuk could outrun the fastest horse and defeat an army of warriors. With its enormous size and razor sharp claws, Wowoka didn't doubt it for a moment.

The chief's daughter stopped and got off her horse, never taking her eyes off the bear. Her father's warning had fallen on deaf ears. She began to walk toward Nanuk as though lost in a trance. Wowoka jumped down and went after her. Had she lost her mind? The girl was headed for certain death.

Tokanosh pulled up behind his brother, dismounted and ran to where Sha'kona was standing with his spear held high. As he moved, the bear dropped down on all fours and charged. Wowoka raised his spear and backed up next to his brother, but Sha'kona held her ground. Less than ten paces away the animal came to an unexpected halt and again stood up, towering over them. The two men drew back their weapons, ready to strike. Nanuk opened his mouth, baring fang-like teeth the size of small tusks, but no sound came out. He froze in place, prepared for their attack.

Lifting her arms high above her, Sha'kona stepped between the massive creature and her father and uncle. She turned her back to the bear and faced them.

"Please put down your spears. We must not hurt him. He has come to us for a reason. I can't explain how I know, but I do. I think maybe that 'other eye' thing is happening again." She paused, and then went on.

"We need him. He is here to help us. If he feels he is in danger, he will do what comes naturally to him, he will defend himself. Go back to the others and leave me alone with him." The words coming out of her mouth seemed crazy to her even as she spoke them.

Nanuk remained motionless. The brothers kept their attention on him, their gaze not straying for an instant. Wowoka had to make a decision. His daughter's life was on the line.

It was Tokanosh who made the first move and lowered his weapon. He trusted and related to animals much more than he did to people. There was something about the giant snow bear that inspired respect. That, and the confidence in Sha'kona's voice, told him he was making the right choice.

"We must do as she asks." Tokanosh had already begun to back away, but he stayed focused on the precarious situation.

Wowoka was not so sure. This was not only his child, but also the person responsible for guiding them to wherever it was they were going. Nothing bad could happen to her. He held himself accountable not just for her but for all of the family's well-being. Though he certainly had faith in the spirits, as a father and the leader of the tribe, he could not throw caution to the wind. He pointed his spear down but held his ground, ready to take action at the slightest hint it might be necessary.

Sha'kona had returned her gaze to Nanuk. His eyes shifted from her father to her and his mouth closed as he dropped back to the ground. He stayed still for a moment then warily began to approach. When he was right in front of her, the bear quietly laid down, stretched his neck out and brought his face right up to hers. Wowoka tensed, but there was no need.

Nanuk gently nuzzled Sha'kona then began to lick her nose. She cradled his head in her hands and softly stroked his ears. He responded by rolling onto his back and letting her rub his chest. All the while she spoke to him in hushed tones that only the two of them could hear. The whole tribe had been anxiously observing everything that was going on. Their dread was replaced by awe at the immense creature's extraordinary behavior.

The unlikely pair of a gigantic, snow-white bear and a fearless little girl continued to play together for quite some time, a magical bond forming between them. Everyone watched in silence and utter disbelief. The only sounds were Sha'kona's secret whispers and the contented purring coming from Nanuk. After a while, he rose onto all four legs and waited as she strode over to Tasunke and climbed on.

Wowoka and Tokanosh dashed for their horses as well, mounted and pulled up alongside Sha'kona. Not a word was spoken. There was nothing to say. They had put their faith in her. She knew the great white bear had been sent to show the way. Nanuk lumbered off, headed east. Sha'kona followed, leading her family toward their destiny.

*F*or many days they trailed Nanuk as he led them in the direction of the sunrise. From dawn to dusk, without let up, he traveled ever eastward. Sha'kona rode beside him, the tribe not far behind. Each night, precisely at sunset, Nanuk would stop and wait for them to make camp. Once they were settled, he would disappear into the darkness, not to be seen again until precisely at first light the next day.

One morning Nanuk arrived well before the sun came up and nudged Sha'kona awake. She sat up, surprised at his early appearance. Something was different about him. Normally when he showed up he would come up to her and lick her face then sit and wait for her to get ready so they could go. Today, he pushed her with his nose and moved away, returning to push her with his nose and move away again. He was trying to tell her something. She got up. Once more he pushed her and moved even further away. This time he just waited. She realized he wanted her to come with him.

"Nanuk, it's still dark and everyone is sleeping. Let me wake them and we will leave right away," Sha'kona whispered, as she always did when she spoke to him. Before she could take a step, he jumped in front of her, blocking her way. Now she was confused.

"What do you want?"

He ran off then came right back and lay down in front of her, reached out with one of his giant paws and pulled her onto his back. He wanted to take her somewhere, but where? Sha'kona held on tight to Nanuk's fur as he lifted himself to his feet and sped off into the darkness.

The sensation of riding this amazing animal was unlike anything she had ever known. With every move he made she could feel the incredible power of his muscles. He carried her across the ice faster than she had thought anything could move. She felt like the wind.

In no time, they came to a place where the ice rose gradually above the flat frozen plain. Nanuk slowed down and carefully climbed the shallow slope. As they reached the top, the sun was just beginning to peek out over the horizon in front of them, spreading its golden glow, pushing the night away. From her vantage point on top of Nanuk, Sha'kona looked out onto a spectacular sight.

The ice and snow came to an abrupt end in a sea of dark water divided by a narrow strip of earth that extended into the sunrise. Covered with low grasses and purple wildflowers, the land-bridge connected to what seemed like another world way in the distance. This was where she must take her people. She understood that Nanuk would not be joining them there.

The magnificent bear cautiously descended, his precious cargo on his back, and returned to the camp. The tribe was still asleep. No one knew that Sha'kona had ever left.

Nanuk stopped and lowered himself to the ground so his companion could get down. She slid off, wrapped her arms around his neck, and hugged the mighty beast.

"Goodbye, my friend," Sha'kona said softly in Nanuk's ear. She let go and stepped away. The great white bear rose to his feet, roared one last time and left, racing into the west. She knew she would never see him again, but his spirit would be with her forever.

*G*ood morning. You're up early. Did you sleep well? As soon as Nanuk gets here we should get started," Wowoka said, as he walked up to Sha'kona and greeted her with a kiss on her forehead. She was stunned. Her father never kissed her when anyone was around and they were surrounded by the whole family. What was that about? Her brain was on overload.

"He won't be back. He has gone as far as he is supposed to go and I have seen what I need to see," she replied, still reeling from Nanuk's departure, now compounded by her father's public display of affection.

It was Wowoka's turn to be confused. "What do you mean? Have you been seeing things with your 'other eyes' again? Without that bear, how will you know where to go? This is no time for us to be lost and wandering. Our supplies won't last forever." He was not happy.

"I saw with my own eyes. Nanuk showed me. I know exactly where to go." Sha'kona spoke with a confidence Wowoka had never heard from her. "You can depend on me. I will not let you or the family down. We should go as soon as we can."

Before he could respond, his wife came running to him pointing and shouting. "Look! Coming from the south! People on horseback!"

Wowoka looked but they were still too far away to tell who they were. "Everyone get ready to leave. Sha'kona, take the women and children and go ahead. I will stay behind with the men in case those approaching are not friends. Who knows what they may do if they are in need of supplies." They all scrambled for the horses and sleds.

"My brother, wait," Tokanosh cried out, already on his horse with his spear in his hand. "I'm not sure who is on it, but I think I know the horse up front." It would be like Tokanosh to recognize a horse and not a person.

The chief mounted his horse and trained his eyes on the approaching band of riders. He couldn't believe what he was seeing. It was Hakan and the rest of the family, forty men, women and children, from the southern camp. How could that be possible? They had been swept away by an avalanche. Wowoka's heart nearly jumped out of his chest with joy. In a mad dash, he and Tokanosh tore off to meet their younger brother and those with him. Right on their heels sped Hakan's daughter, Chepi.

"Daddy! Daddy!" she shrieked, tears of happiness streaming down her face. She had been living with the grief of believing her father had been killed in the great storm and now he was back. Without even slowing down, she flew off her horse into his arms.

The reunion of the two branches of the tribe was an emotional one, filled with tears and laughter, questions and answers, story after story, and lots of hugs. Hakan explained how he had heard the first foreboding rumbles of the mountain. Before they could move to safety, a large mass of snow broke away from high above them and slid down the mountain, pushing them to one side and separating them from Chepi. She was swept the other way. They fled to shelter under an overhang far down the other side of the trail. When it was over, Chepi was nowhere in sight. There was no way to climb back up and search. They tried calling for her, but the howling winds made it useless.

Going south was not an option so they headed north following the trail on the eastern side of the mountains. They came upon the remains of One Horse Way and followed the tracks they found leaving the collapsed pass. Hakan had been certain they belonged to Wowoka's clan. When the trail turned east, he noticed extremely large bear tracks mixed in with the dog and horse footprints. This bewildered him. If they were chasing the animal, hunting it, why was it taking so many days?

Wowoka told him about Tokanosh finding Chepi and Migisi, about encountering Nanuk and finally about Sha'kona's gifts. Hakan and the rest listened in wonder. These tales would be handed down for many generations to come.

*S*ha'kona was eager to get started. The return of the family was an unexpected and much appreciated surprise. They had faced quite a few challenges already, with considerable success. It was time for some reward. In her mind, the sooner they got where they were going the better. She didn't know exactly where that was, but she was ready to find out.

"We will follow Sha'kona! And she will follow her heart. Let us give thanks for unknown blessings already on their way," Wowoka said, with great pride in his daughter and his family.

Retracing the path she had taken earlier that morning, Sha'kona brought the tribe to the land-bridge across the sea of dark waters. Where the ice ended they stopped to unload the sleds and unhitch the dogs. The sleds would no longer be of use. They put the supplies on the spare horses, remounted and once again were under way. Their mood lifted as they left behind the now frozen world that had been their home and marched across the thin strip of flower-covered earth into a new reality of lush landscapes, vibrant colors and limitless possibilities.

Chapter Two

The Journey - Part II

*"Take only what you need and leave the land as you found it."*

*-- Arapaho --*

*T*he tribe continued traveling through the winter and into the spring. With each day that passed Sha'kona felt more confident that the family's trust in her had not been misplaced. Though their journey was not over, with the help of her great-grandmother's spirit she had led them to this land of plenty. So many wonderful sights, sounds and smells abounded in this exciting place, just waiting to make themselves known. Each discovery brought the promise of yet another, even more awesome than the last. Somewhere in this New World was the place they would call home. She just had to find it.

She appreciated the faith the tribe had in her but felt more than a little uneasy that she had become directly responsible for their lives. A lot had happened in such a short time, with many changes in and around her, but she was still so very young. Looking over at her brother, she couldn't imagine what he must be feeling about his older sister. All of a sudden she was not there to play games with or just while away the hours on one of his imaginary adventures. Now she was leading a real-life adventure, riding next to their father like she was a grown-up.

It was hard enough for her to comprehend. For Kewa, it had to be impossible, but she didn't feel sorry for him. For as long as she could remember, their mother had coddled him no matter what, and he had gotten and done whatever he wanted. Sha'kona envied that just a bit and thought about how much easier it would be if she didn't have all these new abilities and the burdens that came with them. She had only just passed her fourteenth winter. Why couldn't she be a normal girl?

"This might be a good time to stop for a while. Migisi is in one of her moods," Hakan called out, clearly annoyed at the old woman's antics. "She refuses to go even one step further until she has had a foot rub and something besides dried meat to eat."

Wowoka was ahead of him, taking in all of the marvels of this unique, new place.

"I hear you," he said to his brother, then looked to his daughter. She had been solemn-faced for a while. "Maybe we should take a break now. Migisi is about to become a handful. Besides, you've been pushing yourself pretty hard. I think we could all use some rest."

"I'm fine," Sha'kona replied. "I think there's a clearing just ahead. I finally see some light through the trees. If we're lucky, there will be fresh water nearby where we can all clean up. We can stop there if you want."

She had been deep in thought for too long and welcomed the interruption. Since yesterday they had been traveling through an overgrown forest of evergreens. It was a perfect place to think. The deep covering of pine needles on the ground muted every noise, bringing a special kind of serenity to the place. However, she had done enough thinking for one day - in fact, probably for a whole season. A break was a good idea.

"Old woman!" Wowoka yelled back to Migisi. "We will stop

so you can rest but I won't be rubbing those feet. When was the last time you washed them?" he teased.

Hakan smiled, but Migisi didn't seem to find it funny. "Go ahead, make fun of an old, blind woman. You are some warrior," she scolded.

Sha'kona ignored their bickering. As she got closer to the clearing, she heard the sound of running water but not like you would hear from a stream or a creek. It was much too strong for that. In fact, she wasn't sure she had ever heard anything quite like it. The peculiar noise tickled her ears with curiosity and she moved ahead of the group to find its source.

Her interest turned into amazement as the woods opened to reveal the most incredibly beautiful sight she had ever seen. Millions and millions of tiny liquid droplets were suspended in the air, creating a thick web-like mist that floated above a crystal clear pond teeming with fish. Rushing water cascaded down from atop a tall mountain that had been hidden by the trees, crashing unmercifully upon a bed of rocks rising majestically from the lagoon below. Over hundreds and hundreds of years the force had polished the black stone to a mirror-like finish that illuminated the glade with an unearthly glow. Sha'kona couldn't believe the spectacle of it all.

The high-speed approach of an overly excited Kewa brought her back to reality in a flash.

"Sha'kona, Sha'kona, Sha'kona!" he cried out.

If he wasn't calling her some obnoxious vegetable's name, he seemed compelled to repeat her real name endlessly. That never made her respond any faster, but it did cause her to think about a name change.

"Sha'kona, look at that waterfall! That has got to be the tallest one in the world! Come on, let's put our feet in the water. Mother, can we?" Kewa was so bored with the incessant traveling he couldn't think of letting this opportunity to play pass by.

Wowoka and the tribe joined them, ready to enjoy this miracle of Mother Earth. Makawee was delighted by what she saw. Maybe they could stay here for more than one night. It had been a long hard stretch of being on the move non-stop. She looked over at her husband, hoping he felt the same.

"This is just what we need, Wowoka," Makawee suggested. There is fresh water to drink, fresh fish to eat and a perfect place to set up camp. You and I might even get a minute to be alone. What do you think?" She had learned a long time ago how to get him to decide what she wanted.

His mind was already made up. "Sha'kona and the spirits have led us to a great place. We will stay here for a while."

"Go ahead, Kewa. Have some fun," his mother told him. "But stay close to your sister. I don't want you falling in." Makawee knew it would be good for both of them to have time to just be children. A lot had been put on Sha'kona's shoulders and Kewa needed to be Kewa.

Brother and sister jumped off their horses at the same time and ran to the pond. Chepi and the other children were right behind them. When Sha'kona got to the edge of the little lake, she knelt down and splashed water on her face. It felt silken and the coolness tingled her skin.

"Look at all these crazy pink fish. There are millions of them and they're jumping so high they're almost flying. I'm going to catch one!" Kewa yelled with pure joy as he tried to grab one out of the air with his bare hands. They seemed to anticipate his moves and managed to stay just out of reach. Soon the rest of the young ones and the dogs were in on the act. In the mayhem that followed, everyone and everything got soaking wet, but not a single fish was caught. The family looked on laughing as they had not done since they left their home. Satisfied with this new place, they began to unload the horses and settle in.

*T*he young chief's daughter walks alongside the speeding *river to the edge of the cliff. She stares in silence as she looks out. A path unfolds below her, cloaked in darkness. She must take the next step to save her people, but she cannot see where that step will take her. She cannot stay where she is. She knows what she must do. She asks the Great Spirit to protect her and steps off into the darkness, following the racing waters into the unknown beyond...*

*S*weat poured down Sha'kona's face as she bolted upright from a sound sleep. Her hands were clammy and her heart was pounding. She was completely disoriented and took deep breaths to calm down. What had happened? She looked around and saw everyone sleeping peacefully. It must have been a bad dream. No, it was more real than that, and worse. Even nightmare wouldn't describe it. Though she didn't want to, she remembered every detail. The girl in the dream was her exact double, and the cliff where the girl had stepped off was at the top of the mountain where the waterfall they were camping next to began.

What did it mean? Was it a sign? A vision? A message? Or maybe just the random craziness of a nightmare. It was bad enough seeing things with her "other eyes." Trying to figure out what they meant was more than she could handle.

Sha'kona shuddered and lay back down on the cool ground knowing she would not be able to go back to sleep. Her mind wandered and battled with itself as she tried to make sense of what she had seen, or dreamt, or whatever it was called that she did. What was she supposed to do? She struggled with her thoughts.

The answer came, but not the answer she wanted. They must continue their journey. They had not reached their final destination.

She knew how much her family liked it here. For the first time since they had started this odyssey, everyone was happy, especially her mother and brother. It was indeed a special place of beauty but it was not to be their special place. That was yet to come.

She knew what she had to do but was filled with dread at the thought of telling her father and the rest of the tribe they had to move again. The tangerine colored glow of the morning sunlight warned her of how little time she had to prepare for that conversation.

"*G*ood morning, Daddy. I brought you some of the sweet red fruit we found growing on the trees. I thought you might be hungry," Sha'kona said as she woke her father. She thought it was a good idea to give him something to eat before she let him know about her latest revelation.

"Are you feeling all right, girl? Since when have you started gathering food for breakfast? And I can't remember the last time you called me 'Daddy.' With everything else going on in your head, this is very unexpected," Wowoka replied. Suddenly he noticed the worried look on her face. "Uh, oh. Now I understand. It's happened again, hasn't it? I'm almost afraid to ask." His tone had changed dramatically.

"Yes, Father. I saw something and I don't think you're going to be happy about it," Sha'kona said, all too aware of how unsettling her next comments would be. "I know how much everyone likes it here, but I saw something last night, the special kind of seeing. We must move again. This is not the end of our journey."

Wowoka listened intently and responded with concern, "I can't say this is something I wanted to hear. Our people are tired and feeling displaced. This has been very hard on the children and the old ones. Staying here would be good for them. I need to know you are absolutely sure before I tell the others."

The image of the young girl stepping off the cliff into the darkness flashed inside Sha'kona's head, even more real than it was before. For a moment, she was shaken to the core but quickly regained her composure. She knew what she had to do.

"I am sure," Sha'kona replied. "I was given a sign, a kind of warning, while I slept last night. It woke me up and scared me at first, but now I understand what we have to do. I'm sure it sounds insane. This is a lot for me to even begin to comprehend. A new home - our final destination - is waiting for us and it's up to me to take us there.

"We must travel south on the river fed by the waterfall. When the time is right, I will know what to do after that. I need for you to believe me. If we don't leave soon, terrible things will happen."

His daughter's words were those of a grown woman and he could almost see their weight bearing down on her shoulders. His child was growing up. It pained him to see his little girl carrying this burden. He would not let her do it by herself.

"If this is what has been shown to you, we will go," her father acknowledged. "You have my trust and my love, always. You do not have to do this alone. We will lead the tribe together wherever your spirits take us."

Wowoka put his arm over Sha'kona's shoulders and gave her a little squeeze, then sighed dramatically. When she looked up at him, his eyes were twinkling.

"Your mother is not going to be happy about this."

*W*hen the family had all eaten their morning meal, Wowoka assembled everyone and addressed them.

"Very soon we must leave this beautiful spot," he announced. "Mother Earth wants us to continue our journey. She has picked out a very special place for us to call home and it is time to make our way there.

"Not far from here, the creek that flows from this pond joins a great river going south. That is the way we will go. We will need to build rafts large enough for all of us and the animals. We must start right away. The sooner we can go the better. It will be a long trip, but the hardest part will be getting ready. Once we leave, we can relax and let the river do the work."

The reaction of his people surprised even him. He had

expected serious grumbling, if not outright arguments. Instead, they immediately began to divide into teams, organizing themselves for the work ahead.

The next few weeks were grueling as the men built the rafts that would carry the clan and all of their animals and supplies. It was a massive undertaking. To cut down the red cedar trees, they made axes of stone, ground to sharp edges and fastened to hardwood handles with deer sinew. All the branches and bark from the trunks were stripped off and the fibers from the bark and the roots braided together to make rope. With the rope, they bound the logs together, creating huge floating structures that would take them to their new land. With special stone and bone tools, they carved out the largest cedars to form canoes. These smaller boats would be easier to handle and could be used to lead the voyage.

Kewa and some of the older boys figured out how to catch the pink fish that had avoided capture so well the first day. Using nets the older women had woven from milkweed stalks and sedge grass, the novice fishermen hauled them in by the basketful.

Makawee and the younger women cleaned the fish and dried them on racks out in the sun, while even the smallest children helped gather fruits and berries from the forest. They would need as many supplies as they could carry in the boats. They had no way of knowing what might be available along the way.

Finally, their preparations were done and they were ready to start this new adventure.

Sha'kona woke up early on the morning of their departure, before anyone else was even stirring. She had been doing this a lot lately. A sense of urgency she could not escape tugged at her insides, like she was being pulled in four directions at once and had no idea which way to go. It had something to do with the young chief's daughter from her dream.

Sha'kona could not stop thinking about her. Why was she so troubled? What was she doing on top of the mountain? Sha'kona understood what the girl must have felt as she looked out from that fateful cliff and stepped off into the unknown. Today Sha'kona would be doing the same thing. Was it brave or foolish? She realized that sometimes they were one and the same. The young princess had shown great courage, faced her fears and taken the step she knew she must. The meaning of the dream was suddenly perfectly clear.

The deep emotions Sha'kona felt surprised her. The girl from the dream had left a lasting mark on her heart. Tears filled Sha'kona's eyes. She slipped silently from the middle of the camp to the edge of the falling waters and sat on the shiny black rocks. Their polished faces were just beginning to ignite the surface of the pond with reflections of the waking sun's morning rays. The dancing light drew her attention to a small blue stone with a pointed tip nearly hidden in the shallows. She reached into the water and picked it up, thinking Kewa might want it for his collection. As she rolled it back and forth in her hands an idea came to her. She would leave her mark here, honoring her people.

Very carefully, she began carving shapes and lines into the polished stone with the blue rock she had found. She created images and symbols that would tell their story for generations to come.

When she was finished, she felt at peace. She got up slowly and walked away, never looking back. Sha'kona had said her goodbyes. It was time to go.

*T*he day had finally arrived for the start of the tribe's voyage and the camp was a beehive of activity. The clear skies and warm sun were a great relief after the constant rain of the past few days. Wowoka and Hakan gathered the animals and began loading them on the rafts while their cousin Liwanu and the other men tried to find room on board for the tents and the overabundance of supplies.

Sha'kona went to get Tasunke. Wanting to be sure her horse was relaxed for the long ride on the river, she brought him his favorite treat of carrots and the new red tree fruit she had found. Tasunke greeted her with even more enthusiasm than usual, punctuated by snorts, grunts and animated prancing. She rubbed his nose and lovingly stroked his neck before walking him to the river.

Tokanosh woke up bleary-eyed from a restless night. He was worried sick about the river journey and the dangers they might face. His fear of water and the fact he could not swim did not help how he was feeling. These were two secrets he had never revealed to anyone. How could he explain that someone as big and powerful as he was got weak in the knees when confronted by even a shallow stream? He was obviously going to have to deal with his phobia. There was no backing out. Where the tribe went, so did he.

Two furry paws on his chest followed by a coarse, wet tongue licking his face pushed his worries out of the way.

"Mingan, my friend! You can get off me now, and leave some skin on my face. I can see that at least one of us is excited about our boat ride." Tokanosh jumped up, pushing the dog away.

The two of them began playing their own crazy game of

chase-around-the-camp. Soon they were joined by the rest of the dogs, disrupting everything and everybody as they tried to finish last minute preparations before getting underway.

When things finally calmed down, Wowoka called for all the members of the tribe to come together. After forming a circle, they asked for the Great Spirit's blessing, that they be given strength and their voyage made a safe one. Then Liwanu sang a song of thanks and left an axe on the rocks by the falls as a gift for anyone who might come this way after they had left.

Their stay in the clearing by the pond was over. The women collected the last of their personal belongings and herded the children onto the rafts. After taking a last look around to make sure nothing they needed was left behind, the men followed them down to the river. Hakan and Liwanu were already there, pulling their canoes across the muddy shore and launching them into the water.

Sha'kona, Kewa and Chepi were on the first raft along with Tokanosh and Migisi. Hakan had put the old woman there so his brother could look after her. Behind them rode Wowoka and Makawee, keeping an eye on everyone. The vessels were heavily loaded with people, animals and all of the family's possessions.

"Do you think we might be taking too much with us?" Makawee asked. She was concerned about the enormous amount they were carrying.

Wowoka sensed how anxious she was. "We will be fine. Don't worry. If the boats are too heavy, we'll just unload some children. No problem in that, right?"

Makawee chuckled and gave him a kiss on the cheek. He always knew how to calm her nerves.

They pushed off and set sail. The river was as smooth as glass, the air crisp and fresh, filled with the aroma of cedar and pine from the trees lining the gently sloping banks. They glided across the water so effortlessly Sha'kona was beginning to think they were flying. The breeze massaging her face as they traveled slowly southward only added to that sensation. Everywhere she looked were new and different kinds of animals, and plants with flowers sprouting colors more vivid than she ever imagined existed. She didn't need her "other eyes" to see the exquisite beauty surrounding her.

For many days and nights they drifted with the current. Even in the cramped confines of their floating homes, everyone was relaxed and content. The peaceful pace of the river seemed to be rubbing off on the tribe. The weather was perfect, water was everywhere and food was abundant. Fish almost jumped into their nets and fruit and berries were always close at hand. They had barely touched the supplies they had packed anticipating the worst. Life was good.

*T*he tranquil, easy ride would not last. Late one afternoon the clouds gathered above them and the wind whipped the surface of the water. The gently sloping banks suddenly became steep canyon walls and the river began rushing down an incline that grew steeper and steeper. The waters picked up speed, pushing the rafts forward at an alarming pace. Large, jagged rocks reared their ugly heads above the torrent, splitting it in a hundred directions and turning the once calm surface into a mad rage of whitewater.

In an instant, panic set in. The rafts were being tossed around like rag dolls. Wowoka feared they would capsize or be smashed to bits. Both Hakan and Liwanu had managed to bring their canoes alongside and come aboard to help.

"Everyone get down as low as possible and hold onto each other. Liwanu, see to the animals, but don't fall over. And Hakan, try to tie the rafts together. I don't want us getting separated!" Wowoka bellowed out his orders over the roar of the river. Liwanu scrambled to take care of the frightened livestock while Hakan grabbed several coils of rope and jumped from one unsteady floating platform to the next, securing them to each other as well as he could.

Balancing herself carefully on the rocking platform, Sha'kona went to make sure Migisi was okay. Migisi's response was as expected. She muttered under her breath about how she never wanted to get on this crazy river in the first place and how an old blind woman should be at home, warm and dry, not on some wet thrill ride with a bunch of children. Water was for fish. Sha'kona was used to Migisi's rantings. She put her arms around the old woman and held on tight.

Meanwhile, Wowoka and several of the other men had grabbed their spears to try to push away from any rocks they might crash into. Before they had a chance to use them, a voice screamed out from in front of them.

"Kewa, no!"

It was the voice of Tokanosh. Kewa was leaning way over the edge of the lead raft, trying to retrieve his bow, which in the turmoil had slipped from his hands and fallen over the side. That bow was his most prized possession, one of the two things he was allowed to bring when they left home during the great storm. He wasn't going to lose it. Before Tokanosh could get to him, the boat lurched violently to one side and Kewa tumbled off the cedar logs into the churning waters.

Without thinking, Tokanosh leapt off the raft and plunged in after Kewa. Kewa could not swim and neither could Tokanosh. Instinct drove him to act, to try and save the boy. He had no idea how he was going to do that but knew he had to try. As soon as he hit the water, Tokanosh grabbed his nephew with one arm and began to flail wildly with the other to try and make it to safety.

"Please, get my baby!" Makawee wailed as she watched the horror unfolding. Her only son was at the mercy of a very angry river.

The rafts were caught by the full turmoil of the rapids and swept past Tokanosh and Kewa as they fought for their lives amidst the rocks and whitewater. All those on board clung to each other, fearing the worst. They helplessly rode the convulsing waters further and further away from the struggling pair.

Tokanosh paddled frantically, trying to keep himself and Kewa afloat. They gasped for air as their heads bobbed in and out of the water. Fighting the current, the big man desperately kicked his feet, attempting to navigate around the rocks that threatened their every move. He had only been in the rapids for a few minutes and already was exhausted.

"Kewa, hold onto me! I need both hands." Tokanosh was strong, but, with one hand holding the boy, he was losing the battle against the river's fury. Kewa wrapped his small arms around the big man's neck, allowing Tokanosh to grab for an oncoming boulder. With all of his might, he reached out and took hold of the stone. The riverbank was close but not close enough. He looked around searching for a way out, unsure of how much more of this they could endure.

Just ahead, a tree branch hung low over the water. If they could get to it, Tokanosh could use it to pull them both out. Between them and escape stood an obstacle course of deadly rocks being pounded by the explosive power of the river. To make it to the overhanging limb, Tokanosh would have to let go of his safehold and survive the rapids dragging them through those rocks. If they tried to go for it, there was a good chance they would be crushed, but if they stayed they would surely drown. Not much of a choice. One thing was certain: he hated the water. No way was he going to drown. He looked into Kewa's frightened eyes.

"Hang on, little man!"

Tokanosh released his grip and wrapped his enormous arms around the boy. He would use his own body as a cushion to protect Kewa.

The current instantly grabbed them and shot them downstream. Time and time again they crashed into the half-submerged boulders with unbelievable force. Tokanosh's body was punished by the impacts, but he held on to Kewa, keeping his head above the water. When the branch was finally above them, Tokanosh stretched one arm as high as he could and, kicking his feet like a madman, pushed himself upward out of the rapids. He seized the limb with his one free hand and, in an almost inhuman show of strength, pulled them both from the turbulent waters.

Tokanosh slowly and painfully worked his way along the branch, hand over hand, until they got to the small strip of rock and sand on the edge of the river. Kewa wouldn't let go of his uncle's neck.

"I am so sorry. I didn't think I would fall over. I just didn't want to lose my bow. It was all I had to remember home. How will I become a warrior without a bow?" Kewa was crying, barely able to speak, trembling like a leaf in the wind.

The older man was not good at dealing with emotional moments like this. He awkwardly patted the boy on his head. "You don't have to explain. And you just proved that you don't need a bow to be a great warrior."

Meanwhile, Tokanosh was not sure whether what he had just done was courageous or stupid. Or if that mattered. He had faced his greatest fear but did not feel any different for it. He still hated the water.

With a shake of his head, he pushed those thoughts away. Right now there were much more important things to worry about.

Like, where was the rest of the tribe?

$O$nce the rafts left Tokanosh and Kewa behind, they were hurled down the river at a dangerously fast speed, forcefully thrown about like so many twigs. No one knew how they would ever survive. All they could do was hang on. Just when they were sure the end was near, the river made a sharp turn to the west and emptied out into an enormous lake. There the water was eerily still and silent. It was as though the madness of the day had never happened.

Except for one thing.

Kewa and Tokanosh were missing.

Though bruised, badly shaken and completely soaked, everyone seemed all right. Wowoka wanted to get them to dry land as soon as possible to make sure. He asked Hakan and Liwanu to untie their canoes and use them to pull the rafts to shore. They made quick work of it and in no time the tribe and their animals were off the rafts.

Sha'kona helped her father carry Migisi. The old woman was drenched and her long silver hair was matted to her head. She was not happy and she wasn't feeling well either. Never at a loss for words, she couldn't wait to unleash her feelings.

"Put me down! I'm old, not crippled. I want my tired feet to feel solid ground. The next time somebody has a brilliant idea like this, I hope they forget to tell me," Migisi whined. A hacking cough racked her body.

Sha'kona felt horrible. This was all her fault. Why did she ever think she knew what she was doing? Her "other eyes" seemed to lead them to trouble - like what they just went through. If they were a gift, maybe she should give it to somebody else. Her great-great-aunt did not look well and Sha'kona was responsible.

"Migisi, do you feel all right?"

"No child, I don't. I am an old woman. When do old women ever feel good?" Migisi sighed with a forced, half smile. "I would be a lot better if you would stop thinking you're to blame for what has happened. I don't need my sister's 'other eyes' to see what's going on in that pretty little head of yours. All you can do is your best and you have been doing a lot more than that. Now leave me be and go find your brother." Another spasm rocked her frail body.

Sha'kona left Migisi and was walking toward her father when Mingan erupted in a frenzy of barking. The rest of the pack joined his outburst and they all took off into the woods like they were after a wild rabbit. Sha'kona started to chase after them but stopped at the sight of the apparition in front of her. Tokanosh was walking triumphantly out of the woods with Kewa on his back. They were a mess, covered with cuts and bruises, their clothing torn and filthy, but they were alive.

Mingan was all over his master, so excited he was vibrating. There were kisses and hugs and barks and howls. Makawee and Sha'kona waded through the sea of welcoming dogs to greet the returning members of the family. As soon as Makawee reached them, she took her son in her arms like she did when he was a baby. Sha'kona wrapped herself around both of them. Happy couldn't even begin to describe how she felt. If she had lost her brother or her uncle, she didn't know what she would have done. The whole tribe swarmed around them.

"This little man is quite the warrior," Tokanosh announced proudly. "'Giving up' are words he doesn't understand." On hearing this, Kewa beamed.

"You can let go now, mother. I'm not a baby. I am a warrior," Kewa declared as he broke free and ran to share his adventure with the other children. Mingan took off at the same time but headed to the edge of the river. When the dog returned, he had Kewa's bow in his mouth. The boy couldn't believe his eyes. He took the bow from Mingan and held it high over his head. At that moment, he was indeed a young warrior.

Once again the tribe had been spared from tragedy. Perhaps the spirits were watching after them. They set up camp beside the quiet lake, swapping stories as darkness fell. With each telling the tales got taller and taller. Nervous energy finally gave way to exhaustion and sleep overtook them all.

*S*ha'kona was the first to hear and see them. Strange, high-pitched noises woke her from a deep sleep. At first she thought it was another one of her weird dreams, but as they kept occurring, even with her eyes wide open, she realized that the sounds were real. She got up to search for the source of the disturbance.

Circling gracefully overhead was a flock of earth-brown birds with pure white heads and matching tails. Their enormous wings barely moved as they soared high above, crying out with the peculiar voices that had awoken her. As they glided through the air, their beautiful feathers billowed in the soft early morning breeze. Others in the camp were roused by the birds' boisterous presence and they too were entranced by what they were witnessing. None of them had ever seen anything like these winged creatures; another surprise from this new land.

One of the birds broke free from the formation, swooped down and flew so close to Sha'kona its wing feathers nearly touched her face before it turned away to rejoin the rest of the flock. Twice more it repeated the same pattern, punctuating each flyby with its unique squeaky call. On the fourth pass it sailed by and landed on the branch of a nearby tree. The bird fell silent and stared at her from its perch, ruffling its wings and shuffling its feet in some kind of cryptic dance.

Oh, no, Sha'kona thought, it's happening again.

Out loud to the bird she asked, "Are you trying to tell me something? Is this some kind of message I'm supposed to understand? If it is, my 'other eyes' must not be working so well, because I don't have a clue as to what you want!"

"Now you're talking to animals. You are definitely losing it, Sister." Kewa had walked up beside her with their great-great-aunt, Migisi for a better view of what was happening. He found the situation a bit ridiculous and very amusing. His sister was trying to have a conversation with an overgrown bag of feathers.

"Get out of here, Kewa. You're going to frighten it!" she shouted.

The white-headed bird reacted to her outburst by flapping its wings and taking off to join the rest of the flock still circling above. As soon as it reached them, they all flew down and landed together in the same nearby tree. Now there were seven birds staring at her, doing seven very peculiar little dances.

"Sha'kona, what is going on? Who or what are you talking to?" Migisi's voice was very weak and she looked worse than she had the day before. Her skin was almost gray in color and her hands were shaking.

"There are some birds making bizarre noises and doing really unusual things. They were circling above, and then one flew down, did a dance, and flew back. Then all of them flew down and now they're in the tree right next to you, just staring and dancing. I was trying to talk to one of them." It was just one more time Sha'kona heard herself explaining something and realized how abnormal she sounded. More than abnormal. Seriously odd.

"Are they brown with white heads and tails and are there seven of them?" Migisi asked.

Sha'kona turned around to look at Migisi in disbelief. "How did you know that?"

"I have lived a long time, but I never thought I would live long enough to find out they still existed." Migisi smiled as though remembering a sweet secret from her past.

"Many years ago, long before even I was born, these birds lived in our land," she continued. "In fact, I was named after them.

Migisi means "eagle" and that is what they are called. One day they just disappeared. When I was a little girl, my sister told me if I ever got lost they would come back. There would be seven of them, one for each direction: north, south, east and west, above, below and within. She said if I followed them I would find her."

As Migisi spoke, all of the eagles lifted off as one and flew straight and true toward the east.

Everything was clear. Sha'kona understood the message she had been sent. Their journey would be over soon. They would follow the eagles and Migisi's heart.

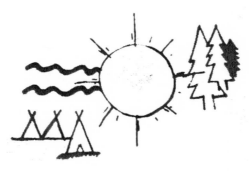

## Chapter Three

# The New World

"*Listen to the voice of nature, for it holds treasures for you.*"

*-- Huron --*

*T*ime passed quickly as Sha'kona and the rest of the one hundred and twenty members of the tribe trekked through a forest of unimaginably tall evergreens. Sunlight barely peaked between the slender trees, projecting a hazy glow tinted green as it filtered through the leaves. On this day as they walked across the ivy-covered ground, the faint light began to get brighter and brighter, drawing them to the edge of the woods. There, it was as if someone had drawn a finish line marking the end of their journey. Beyond that line a panorama of overwhelming beauty opened before their eyes.

The eagles stopped their eastbound flight and formed a perfect circle directly overhead. They had done their job. They had led the way to this place. Sha'kona knew this would be her family's home. It was where they were meant to be. They had found their New World.

What the weary travelers saw as they looked out exceeded all expectations. Vast open plains were adorned with pristine lakes that shimmered like precious jewels in the morning sun. Bordered by majestic purple mountains and rich woodlands, this fantastic landscape was an unspoiled paradise. Animals, so spectacular that legends would be created about them, freely roamed the open spaces.

"Father, our trip is over. This is where we are meant to stay. Everything we need is here," Sha'kona said, absorbing every sight and sound and smell.

Wowoka, Makawee and Kewa stood next to Sha'kona in awe. Everywhere they turned was another magnificent discovery.

"The Creator has truly provided for us. From this day forward, this will be our home. You used your new gifts with wisdom and brought us here. I am very proud of you. Our family will grow and fill this land. We will live in peace and harmony with all of the abundance that surrounds us." Wowoka's voice resonated with joy as he spoke to his daughter. He had been blessed in more ways than he could count.

Tokanosh walked up to them carrying a very frail Migisi. He carefully set her on her feet and, with great effort, she shuffled over to Sha'kona.

"I can see everything! The fields and the mountains and the lakes and the animals. Everything! I never knew such beauty existed," Migisi exclaimed. "Thank you, Sha'kona for bringing me here. This is my place of celebration.

"Do I look pretty? I must look pretty today if I am going to see my sister again," Migisi explained, her voice strong. "The seven sacred eagles can take me to her now. I am happy. I am with my family on this special day. Now I must rest. I don't want to be tired. I still have a long way to go." She gently touched Sha'kona's face then lay down on the soft grass.

"Migisi, what are you talking about? We are home. You don't have to travel anymore. Your feet will never be tired again." Sha'kona was confused by what her great-great-aunt had said.

"The spirits will always be with you," Migisi said softly. "Though many will stay here, your journey, like mine, is not yet over."

As the old woman spoke, the seven eagles came down from the skies and landed all around her. She looked straight at Sha'kona and smiled, then closed her unseeing eyes. As soon as she did, the sacred birds flew off, disappearing into the perfect azure blue skies above.

"Migisi! Migisi!" Shakona shouted, dropping to the ground next to the old woman. Migisi lay motionless, a look of tranquil contentment on her face. She was gone.

Sha'kona could not contain her feelings. She began to weep, sobbing uncontrollably.

"It's all my fault for bringing her here, for all she had to go through. I should have known she was too old and weak. I am to blame for this."

Her family gathered around and knelt down beside her. Wowoka cradled his daughter in his arms. Sorrow, regret, anger and frustration poured out through her tears. He let her cry, wishing he could take the pain away.

"Migisi chose this day to move on to the spirit world as she chose everything in her life," Wowoka told his daughter, wanting to comfort her. "You had no part in that, Sha'kona. The old woman always did things her way. You brought her to the place she had to be, so the eagles could take her. This day had been foretold many years ago by her sister, your great-grandmother. This was her doing, not yours." The Great Chief embraced Kewa as well and Makawee put her arms around all of them.

"I don't know if I can handle these gifts anymore. Maybe I'm not ready." Sha'kona looked up at her mother and father.

"It is best to not question what has been given to you,"

Wowoka admonished. "You must accept your gifts with honor and dignity as we now accept Migisi's death by honoring her life with the dignity she earned."

When Wowoka finished speaking he fell silent and leaned over to kiss the old woman on her forehead. As he did, he noticed a feather tucked neatly in her hand. It was from one of the eagles that had guided them here. Gently removing the feather from her grasp, he held it up to the darkening sky then stood before the tribe. They were stunned with grief. All of them gathered in a circle around Migisi's lifeless body and Wowoka offered up a prayer. The words were simple and true.

"In her passing, we are given a new life full of prosperity in this place we will now call home. Migisi would want that for all of us and for those who will live after us and after them. She was a blessing to us all. The spirits that watched over her brought us here. They took the shape of the seven eagles. Her last gift to us was this feather from one of them. In honor of her and those spirits, the eagle feather will forever be sacred." It was all Wowoka could do not to break down, for this was a woman he had known his entire life, a woman he cared for and deeply respected. The oldest member of the family was no longer with them.

Wowoka turned to his daughter. "You will be the keeper of this feather. For the rest of your life you must take care that it is safe. It is meant to always fly high, so you can never let it touch the ground. The power of the sacred eagles and Migisi's spirit have been entrusted to you. Never doubt their strength or your own." With this, he took her hand and placed the feather on her open palm.

Sha'kona struggled to keep her emotions under control. She was certainly grateful and honored by this new gift, but it was yet another responsibility on top of all the other ones she had been given. Grief confused her feelings even more than they had been. She closed her hand tightly around the feather, afraid that if she let go she might lose all that she believed in.

Time passed and the light faded into sunset. The prayers had been said, the chants had been sung, and the tears had all dried. Migisi's burial place was prepared at the very spot from which her spirit moved on. Wowoka, Tokanosh, and Hakan tenderly put her body in the soft, cool earth and covered her with rocks they found nearby. When this was done, the family solemnly walked away. In the tradition of their people, they knew that none of them would ever visit there again.

*W*owoka directed the men of the tribe to start work on their homes. Though their mood was still somber, they labored tirelessly to create a permanent place to live. First they laid out a plan.

In the center would be a meeting house and surrounding that would be the individual dwellings. Areas for planting crops and keeping the animals were also part of the overall design. They adapted the techniques they brought with them, using the materials that were at hand, and began building. The structures each family would live in went up quickly. They were round and framed with wood as in their old homeland, but stone and bricks made of sun-baked clay were used to make low walls that served as a foundation. The large rectangular meeting house was built of cedar logs and planks lashed to a wooden frame. Here they would hold their tribe's gatherings and spiritual ceremonies.

While the men were occupied with construction, the women did their part, staying constantly busy. Not only did they care for the children and prepare the food, they also tended to the livestock and readied the land for planting. It was already late in the season and they would need a good harvest to make it through the next winter. Bowls and pots were crafted from clay and personalized with intricate painted designs, while utensils were crafted from bone and wood. New clothing and footwear had to be made and herbal medicines collected. There was never a free moment.

Almost miraculously, the work was soon finished. Feelings of satisfaction and accomplishment filled the entire family as they completed the first village in the New World.

"Sha'kona, wake up!" Kewa whispered in his sister's ear and thumped her on the head, rudely waking her from a deep slumber.

"Kewa, it's not even daylight outside. What is wrong with you?" Just the sound of Kewa's voice could grate on Sha'kona's nerves. Getting her up in the middle of the night took this to another level. Especially since this was the first night in a long while that vivid dreams with incomprehensible plots had not interrupted her rest and she was actually getting some real sleep. Her brother had better have some extraordinary reason for this disturbance.

"I heard something outside. At first it seemed far away, but I think it's getting closer to us." Kewa actually sounded upset.

"It's probably just some animal roaming around out there. That's what they do at night. Now go back to bed," Sha'kona said, not wanting to deal with her brother's childish fears.

Kewa's voice rose with concern. "No, I don't think it's just an animal. There's something else out there."

Sha'kona rolled over and gave him a scathing look. "This had better be for real. If you make me get out of bed for no reason at this hour, I will make your life miserable. I'm not in the mood for your games."

"I'm not fooling around. I just don't want to go out there by myself," Kewa responded, a worried look on his face. "What if it's one of those monsters you're always dreaming up? Please, just this once, come with me."

Sha'kona relented. "All right, but if there's nothing out there, you have to feed all the animals for the next five sunrises by yourself. Except Tasunke, of course."

She meant business.

"Deal!" Kewa stood up quietly and crept to the door. "Come on."

They tiptoed out, leaving their parents sleeping. Clouds concealed the moon. The resulting darkness was oppressive. Though the air smelled sweet there was an eerie stillness about it. Sha'kona and Kewa held hands as they made their way through the night.

A sound. At first muffled, then again, clearer. Kewa was right. It didn't sound like a wild animal foraging in the dark. They climbed to the top of the hill above their home. From there they could see the edge of the forest they had come through on their way to this new land. The sound became sounds and grew louder.

"I think it's horses," Shakona whispered.

It was horses. It took her a moment, but she thought she finally knew what was going on. "Did you let the horses out? Is this some big practical joke of yours? If it is, I'm going to kill you!" she shouted at her brother.

"No! I didn't! I swear!" Kewa looked like a scared puppy.

More sounds. This time voices she did not recognize. Sha'kona's heart skipped a beat. She stopped Kewa in his tracks and yanked him to the ground, covering his mouth with her hand. A small hill covered with sumac bushes in front of them made it impossible to see where the voices were coming from.

"Keep your head down. Don't move and don't make a sound. I'm going to go see who it is." Staying low to the ground she crawled up to where she could peer over the shrubs. She was shocked speechless by what she saw.

"Sha'kona! What is it?" Kewa sounded very afraid. He slid up next to Sha'kona, but keeping his head down as she had ordered made it impossible for him to see out.

"What do you see? Say something!" the boy demanded.

She still couldn't speak. Kewa finally lifted his head to find out what was going on and froze. Right in front of them, too many people to count were coming out of the woods on horseback.

"Let's get out of here right now! We've got to tell Father. He will know what to do," Kewa blurted, then ran as fast as his legs would carry him toward home. Sha'kona stayed, unable to take her eyes off the strangers.

Who were these people? Where did they come from? They looked different from anyone she had ever known.

The leader was a giant of a man, almost as big as Tokanosh, on a horse so black it was almost invisible in the darkness. He wore loose-fitting clothing that mimicked the colors of the rainbow. Next to him was a boy about her age. He was dark with long brown hair and fine features, wearing clothes like the big man.

But it was his horse that really shocked her. It was so white it looked like a ghost and on its forehead was a black diamond exactly like Tasunke had. The two could have been twins.

*K*ewa crashed through the door of their home and, without slowing down, raced to his parents' bed and began shaking them both awake.

"Mom! Dad!" the boy shouted. "There are millions of people riding out of the woods! I heard noises and Sha'kona and I went to see what it was 'cause we thought it might be animals but we weren't sure and we didn't want to wake you up for nothing and I wasn't afraid but I ran back and Sha'kona is still there and…" Kewa was rambling faster than his mother or father could follow in their half-asleep state.

"Kewa, slow down. What are you talking about? What million people? And where is your sister?" Wowoka asked. He barely moved, opening up one heavy eye to look over at his son. He knew that Kewa occasionally had nightmares. His wife was the one who usually comforted him and the groggy chief did not want to take that job from her. "Were you dreaming?"

"This is no dream! There are strange people on horses outside at the top of the hill and Sha'kona is up there with them. You have to hurry, Dad. She's by herself. I ran to get help because I run faster. We're going to need the whole tribe!" Kewa was so on edge he was vibrating.

Either his son had gone crazy or there was serious trouble brewing. Neither possibility was good.

"There is no 'we' anything. You will stay here with your mother. I will get the men together and we will find out what is going on. Makawee, wake the women and children and take them to the meeting house. Do not leave there until I come back for you." Wowoka was already up and dressed and headed for the door. He grabbed his spear and his bow as he left.

"Tokanosh!" Wowoka shouted, ready for action.

Sha'kona shifted her weight to get a better view of the good-looking boy and her foot slipped from underneath her. She regained her balance, but her movement caused pieces of the loose gravel she was standing on to roll loudly down the hill. Afraid the sound might alert them to her presence, she ducked as low as she could, but it was too late. The boy heard the noise and turned her way before she had a chance to hide.

Enapay saw her. From a single glance he knew she was prettier than any girl in his family. And different. Her skin was lighter and her hair was long and as straight as straw. What was she doing out here by herself? Girls from his tribe were not allowed out alone at night. Where did she come from? Was it the trail left by her people that they had been following for so long?

He wanted to say something to his father but he was afraid of how he might react. Strangers were always a threat to him. Enapay didn't want any harm coming to the girl even though he knew nothing about her, hadn't even met her. There was just something about the way she looked at him.

As chief of their tribe, it was his father's job to protect them. He admired his father, always had, but he knew that his father could sometimes get out of control. Act first, ask questions later; that was how the older man led his life, and the clan. It was something about the history of his people.

Generations and generations of chiefs had been born into his family and their roots ran deep. In order to be a true leader you had to have a special strength. Sometimes it involved making sacrifices and sometimes it involved hurting others. It's the circle of life, his father would say, and Enapay believed that to his core.

Except this time.

He didn't want the mystery girl hurt or even frightened. The look on her face made him hold his tongue. Enapay didn't know where these feelings came from but they were strong enough for him to risk crossing the mighty chief.

"*W*owoka, what is happening?" Tokanosh asked. "You sounded ready for battle." He had come running when he heard his older brother calling. Hakan, Liwanu and the rest of the men were right behind him, armed with spears, axes and bows. From the sound of their chief's voice they knew something was very wrong. They always stood together as one when the family was in jeopardy.

"Strangers have come and Sha'kona is up on the hill with them. Alone," Wowoka announced, the gravity of the situation evident in his voice. "I don't know where they are from or how many there are. If they are from nearby, they may have come to defend their land as some tribes do. If they have come from another place, they may need food or supplies.

"Because they have come at night I have to think it's because they want to surprise us. They would come during the day to greet us. We must be prepared for anything, but we will not start trouble. It is not our way. If they are hungry we will share. If they need help, we will help. But if they have harmed Sha'kona, they will pay."

Wowoka was more serious than the family had ever heard him – deadly serious.

*O*hanko had spotted the young girl. What kind of people sent a child to scout for them? Certainly none he knew of. Her thin, muscular body and lighter complexion were a sharp contrast to his family's dark skin and stocky builds, but he had to admit she was attractive in her own way. He wondered how something so little could survive.

His son, Enapay, did not know he had seen her, but to be a truly worthy chief and protector of the tribe you had to be aware of your surroundings at all times. You had to notice every little thing. Your life and the lives of your family depended on it. Enapay would learn this someday. He was still young, but one day he would be a warrior and chief like his father. Until then, he would continue to follow his father's lead. And that would be for a long time. Ohanko planned to stay in charge until the spirits came to take him, and even then he would not give up easily.

If the girl was here then the rest of her tribe would follow.

Ohanko had a feeling that would be very soon. If she was his daughter, he would have already been here. Though he sensed their camp was nearby, he could not tell for sure because of the darkness and the hill just ahead that blocked his view. Judging from the tracks they had followed, there would be many of them - not as many as in his family but more than enough to cause problems.

Ohanko thought about how he had come to this place.

Once the bad weather came, his people were forced to travel north from their land. The passage south had been blocked. When they stumbled upon the path some other tribe had taken he decided to go the same way. They seemed to know where they were going, whereas he had no idea which direction would lead his clan to safety. Ohanko was at a loss as to how they knew which way to go, but they did. Their guide must have had a direct connection with the spirits.

First they went north, then east to the dark waters which they crossed on a thin strip of flower-covered earth to arrive in this new land. The trail from there was easy to follow until they came to the waterfall and the big river where it stopped cold. He reasoned that they must have taken the river south. That course was too dangerous so he continued along the shoreline reconnecting with the other group's tracks by the wide lake and ending up here.

Now fate would determine where his journey would go next. He would be prepared for the worst.

"Ready yourselves for battle, my brothers!" Ohanko ordered.

The men spread out on either side of him, spears and shields in hand. Their shields were made of thick animal hides stretched over circular wooden frames and would protect them from all but the worst assaults. Lined up in front of the forest, the warriors were an imposing sight. The women and children hurriedly took cover back in the woods. You could almost taste the tension.

*W*owoka could just make out the shape of Sha'kona lying on her stomach at the top of the hill behind some sumac. She did not know he was right behind her. Her focus was on the strangers. Under the cover of the night, Wowoka had led his men almost all the way up the hill to where he could see the other tribe as they took up a fighting formation. There were many of them and their intentions were obvious. Though their dress was somewhat comical, this was no welcoming committee. He was relieved to find Sha'kona unharmed. If she did not move, she would stay that way for the moment.

"Hakan, get up beside Sha'kona," Wowoka commanded. "As soon as you can, take her and a few of the men back to the meeting house. Stay there and guard our families. The rest of you will sneak up the hill and spread yourselves along the ridge. Stay low and unseen behind the bushes with your bow ready and an arrow nocked until my orders. Keep your spears and axes close to you." His words demanded immediate action.

Only Tokanosh hesitated. "What are you going to do, brother?"

"I am going to introduce myself and ask them who made their clothing," the chief joked. "Now, go with the others and don't move until I say so." Tokanosh was not amused. Had his brother lost his mind?

Once the men were in position, Wowoka dropped his spear and walked through the tall shrubs, exiting directly in front of the big man on the black horse.

Ohanko had been expecting a swarm of warriors to come charging over the hill on horseback, spears in their hands and war cries on their lips. Instead, one man without a weapon strolled silently out of nowhere as though he did not have a care in the world.

"I am Wowoka. Welcome to my village."

"Welcome to your what?" Ohanko asked rather sarcastically. "If by village, you mean you and that scrawny girl who thinks she is invisible because she is behind some scraggly plant, I accept your greeting. I don't know how it is with you, but among our people we don't send little girls out to scout for the men."

Ohanko was relieved and disappointed that all he was up against was a child and this man of questionable sanity. Who would come alone and unarmed against eighty warriors on horseback? His troops visibly relaxed, laughing at their leader's comments.

"I am not scrawny!" Sha'kona shouted, jumping up from her hiding place. Her hands were on her hips and she was furious. Hakan was vainly trying to pull her back down.

"Sha'kona, hold your tongue!" Her father cut her off before she could continue her tirade.

"Someone should teach that girl some respect for her elders," Ohanko added.

"That would not be your concern. But speaking of respect, I hope you come in peace with respect for my people." Wowoka's tone had hardened.

"I think 'your people' need to get out of our way. In case you haven't noticed, I have many warriors and you are two men and a child. I have no more time for this nonsense," Ohanko said and

91

signaled for his men to move forward.

"Neither do I. Say hello to my family." As Wowoka spoke, the men of his tribe rose as one, their bows in hand, aiming straight at Ohanko's horsemen.

Ohanko froze and his men followed suit. Their spears were pointed upward, useless against the bowmen on the ground. He had underestimated this man before him.

"Put your spears down and you and I can talk. I don't want anyone hurt. We came in peace and I want us all to leave in peace," Wowoka declared firmly. His patience had run out.

Ohanko knew it was time for diplomacy. He put his spear down. So did the rest of his men.

"I am Ohanko, chief of this great tribe. We have been following your tracks for many moons from the old lands to here. I have acted disrespectfully and I apologize. We are tired and would like to set up camp here. You have stumbled upon a great treasure. This New World is a gem. How did you find it?"

"This 'scrawny girl', as you called her, led us here. She is my daughter, Sha'kona." Wowoka did not take his eyes off of the other chief.

"You are a smart girl, Sha'kona, but you should not go out at night alone. You never know what you may run into," Ohanko smirked and then nodded at Enapay. "This young man you were staring at is my son, Enapay. One day he will be chief. Hopefully, not too soon. Now that we have all been introduced, we would like to settle in next to where your family is. It will be safer in case there are others out there."

Sha'kona wondered how the leader of the strangers knew she

had glanced at his son. Did he have "other eyes" too? The boy kept trying to steal looks at her. She pretended not to notice. His dress was a bit funny but she had to admit that he had a certain way about him that was different from any of the boys in her tribe.

Enapay wished his father had not seen the girl, then maybe he wouldn't have been so rude to her. She was pretty courageous standing up to his chief the way she did. And, she led her people here. How did she do that? There was something special about her. For some reason, his hands were sweating. He tightened his grip on the reins.

Wowoka spoke. "We have made our permanent village here. There is plenty of room on the other side of the lake, so there is no need for us to be crowded together. It is quite safe. As you can tell, we have no problem taking care of ourselves."

"It is late and my people are exhausted," Ohanko replied. "I cannot ask them to travel anymore. We will stay here for a while. Our people believe that no one owns the land. It must be shared by all. So if there is nothing else, ask your warriors to put down their bows and let us through. We can talk more another time." He locked his eyes on Wowoka, challenging him to stand in their way.

"The land here is plenty and we have no problem sharing this great lake with you," Wowoka countered. "But where we are living is sacred to us; it has a special meaning for our tribe. If you must, you can stay for the night but you cannot build your homes here." For Wowoka the discussion was over. With one motion of his hand, his warriors lowered their weapons.

"Very well, then. I will see to it that we do not get in your way." Ohanko gave his horse a light kick and started down the hill. Half of his men went with him and half, including Enapay, held back allowing the women and children who were still hiding in the forest to go before them. As he passed, the Dark Chief did not even look at Wowoka.

Ohanko knew what he said and what he did could be two very different things. He felt no threat from this man Wowoka or his smaller tribe. Ohanko had been caught off guard once. It would not happen again. He planned to do what he always did. And that was whatever he wanted.

Tokanosh was ready to explode. He had been struggling to control himself since the big, ugly stranger first opened his mouth. How dare he speak to Wowoka that way? And the way he addressed Sha'kona was outrageous! Who did he think he was? Tokanosh did not care what size that pompous chief was. He could take him down.

"I don't trust him, my brother. We cannot let them walk all over us!" Tokanosh stated angrily. He was not good at hiding his emotions. His blood was boiling. Wowoka saw the intensity in Tokanosh's eyes and tried to calm him down.

"The man does not fool me," the Great Chief asserted. "We will extend our hospitality for now but we won't let them get too comfortable here. This will be a very temporary situation. If he gets out of line, I'm sure you can think of ways to reel him back in. Now let's go home. We need our rest. Tomorrow will be a long day. Planting begins." Wowoka patted his brother's back and went to collect Sha'kona.

As Enapay waited for the women and children to ride down the hill, he looked straight at Sha'kona and smiled. She turned away as quickly as she could but felt a warm flush come to her cheeks. She didn't dare look at him. She had heard her father and uncle talking. It was not difficult to tell when Tokanosh was upset. Though she was curious about the boy, it was obvious from their fathers' reactions to each other and the look on her uncle's face that even thinking about Enapay was not a good idea. But it was not going to be easy to push that smile out of her thoughts.

"Sha'kona, Sha'kona, what am I going to do with you?" Wowoka put his arm around his daughter and they headed for home. Tokanosh had gone ahead to make sure Ohanko and his men stayed out of trouble.

She wondered what it was about her name that caused her family to say it more than once when they wanted her attention.

"Going out with your brother in the middle of the night was not a good idea. You know better than that. And though I admire your strong will, I think I can handle talking to another chief on my own." Wowoka spoke with kindness. There had been enough stress for one night.

He was not looking forward to the next part of the conversation.

"What is it your mother calls you? Sweet Potato? I'm not exactly sure how to say this, Sweet Potato, so I'll just say it." Wowoka was feeling very awkward. He could lead his men on a hunt or into battle but he was stepping into unfamiliar and uncomfortable territory. "I know you are becoming a young woman and that as a young woman you are beginning to have certain feelings. I understand those feelings. Believe it or not, I was young once myself.

"One day you will start to think about young men. I just don't want that one day to be today. I couldn't help but notice the looks between you and Ohanko's boy or that smile he gave you. Those people are not our friends and Ohanko is not a good man. In a few days they will be gone. You are a chief's daughter and you must act like one. You need to put that boy out of your head. Now, my little girl, let's try and get whatever sleep is left in this night. There is a lot of work to do tomorrow."

Sha'kona had never been so embarrassed. She wondered if everyone now had "other eyes." Even though it was dark and she thought she was hidden, it seemed that half the world had noticed that for one second she might have glanced at Enapay. And so what if he smiled - who said it was meant for her? Her father was making such a big deal out of it. How humiliating. She had absolutely no intention of thinking about that boy.

Except for maybe that smile.

*Chapter Four*

# The Sacred Gifts of Mother Earth

"The Great Spirit is in all things, he is in the air we breathe. The Great Spirit is our Father, but the Earth is our Mother. She nourishes us, that which we put into the ground she returns to us."

-- Big Thunder (Bedagi) Wabanaki Algonquin --

*M*other Earth had truly blessed this land. Life-giving waters, trees, plants and animals were there for the asking. Sha'kona, like all of her people, had been raised to honor these sacred gifts and never take them for granted. Ever since her great-grandmother had passed on, she had felt a strong connection to all of nature's wonders, especially the animals. She had always loved them and been really good with them, but it seemed that since Nanuk she had almost been able to read their minds. Not all the time, but often enough that she was sure it wasn't something she was imagining.

Like yesterday, when Mingan came up to her and somehow she knew he had a burr in his paw. Or last night, on her way home from all the excitement of the encounter with Ohanko and his tribe, she got a feeling that Tasunke needed her help. It was as if she could see that he had gotten his hoof caught in a gopher hole. More of her "other eyes" at work. Strange stuff, but she was getting used to it. Strange was becoming more normal to her every day.

With the plants it was a little different. They didn't send her messages, she just had a certain sense about them. She knew which ones were good to eat, which ones were for healing and which ones were poisonous. Sometimes she had her unique style of dreams about them.

In one, a raven came to Sha'kona and led her to a dark cave where a beautiful spirit known as the Corn Woman was tied up and being held captive by the evil spirit Hunger. With the raven's help, she set the Corn Woman free and drove Hunger out of the cave into the sunlight where he melted away and disappeared.

In gratitude, the Corn Woman showed Sha'kona where to find corn, also known as maize, from which she could take seeds and how to use every part of the plant. Nothing was wasted. The corn could be eaten or ground into meal to make bread and cakes and the husks could be braided and woven into moccasins, sleeping mats, baskets and cute little cornhusk dolls. The corncobs could be used for fuel or turned into rattles for their ceremonies.

When Sha'kona awoke, she went straight to where the Corn Woman had shown her the corn would be, in a cave in the woods not far from their home. Sha'kona brought the plants back and picked the dried kernels off the cobs so that they would have seeds to plant. Today was the day her mother and some of the other women would join her to sow this new crop. Along with beans and squash, corn would become one of what would be known as the Three Sisters, the most important foods her family grew.

Hakan was in charge of the farming. When he saw the size of the stalks that Sha'kona had found, he decided to use the field farthest from the village to try growing this "spirit plant." Normally they would alternate rows of crops, but this corn plant grew too large and would block the sunlight from anything it was next to. It would be best for the squash and beans if it were far away.

Hakan accepted Sha'kona's story about how she found the odd looking plants, and what they were, without blinking an eye. He no longer questioned how his niece came up with the things she did. He just went along with it.

*T*he women started their day of planting just after sunrise. Between the tools, seeds and supplies, they had so much to carry, they decided to take their horses. That made Sha'kona happy. She loved to ride and it gave her a sense of freedom to have Tasunke with her. Because of the events of the night before, Wowoka sent several of the tribe's best warriors with them. Though he didn't anticipate any trouble, it was better to be safe than sorry.

As soon as they reached the land the men had cleared over the last few days, the women went to work. Using pointed sticks, stone hatchets and bone shovels, they dug furrows and made rows spaced far enough apart to accommodate the plants when they were fully grown. Many hands made the work go faster and soon they were ready to start putting the seeds in the ground.

"Sha'kona, do you know where Chepi is?" Makawee asked. "We could use her help now."

"She just got here. She said she had to see her father before she could come. I don't know what took her so long." Sha'kona wiped the sweat from her brow and stood up. She had been on her knees digging since she got there and needed a break. As she did, Chepi walked up carrying a large bag. Before she was even close, an overpowering smell assaulted Sha'kona and Makawee.

"Don't you say a word, Sha'kona! Not a word!" Chepi was not happy. "My father made me carry these disgusting fish heads all the way here. I'm going to smell like dead fish forever. Who came up with the crazy idea to use these to grow food anyway? I'll never eat anything that these foul things were even near. This is like something you would come up with, you weird cousin of mine!"

Sha'kona and her mother were trying to be serious but were not very successful at it. They both started giggling, then burst out in laughter.

"I would say you should take a swim in the lake, but I'm afraid you might drive the fish away." Sha'kona couldn't stop herself from teasing her cousin, but Chepi did not find it amusing.

"All right, girls, enough," Makawee interrupted. "Let's start planting. Chepi, you can go behind us and put a fish head in with each seed, then Sha'kona can cover it up with dirt. We have a lot to do, so no more fooling around." With that she grabbed the seeds and started moving quickly down the rows, jabbing a pointed stick into the ground and placing a single kernel in each hole.

At once the girls started their assigned tasks. When Makawee had worked herself away from them, Chepi leaned over to Sha'kona.

"So, what happened last night? Did you really tell that other chief off?" Chepi asked under her breath so as not to be overheard. "I hear he's a really mean looking character."

"I kind of opened my mouth when I shouldn't have," Sha'kona answered without looking up from what she was doing. "My father came down on me pretty hard for that."

"I also heard you had something going with the chief's son. I saw him walking around in their camp this morning. He's gorgeous! Silly looking clothes, but gorgeous." Chepi added.

"What do you mean, 'you heard'? Nothing's going on! Doesn't anybody have anything better to do than talk about me? And what were you doing spying on Enapay?" Sha'kona stopped putting dirt on top of fish heads.

"You know there are no secrets in this family. If nothing is going on, why are you getting so upset?" Chepi wasn't going to let it go. "And for your information, I wasn't spying. Some of the girls and I happened to be near their camp this morning and we glanced over and there Mr. Gorgeous was. So, it's Enapay is it? When did you start calling him by his name? Come on, cousin, give me the dirt and I don't mean the kind you're scooping up off the ground!"

"Okay. So he might have noticed me last night and maybe smiled a little at me," Sha'kona divulged. "But I didn't do anything! Except blush. My father made it very clear, in no uncertain terms, that I'm not allowed to even think about Enapay." She paused for a breath. "He is kind of cute though. Even with the clothes."

"What are you going to do?" Chepi was digging now.

"What do you mean what am I going to do? Nothing. I can't disobey my father. Besides, I doubt Enapay even remembers who I am. He is a chief's son with a lot more important things to do than think about me." Sha'kona went back to work.

"Are you serious? Have you checked out your reflection lately?" Chepi questioned, not really needing an answer. "You are stunning. I doubt he's thought about anything else since he first laid eyes on you!" As she finished, Makawee walked over to them.

"More work, less talk." Sha'kona's mother ordered, in one of her all business moods. "We have to be finished long before sundown. Wowoka wants all of the adults at the meeting house tonight to discuss what we should do about our visitors. They were supposed to stay one night and it doesn't look like they're even thinking about moving on. That awful man Ohanko is just looking for trouble.

"Sha'kona, we need some more water. Load the big pots on Tasunke and ride over to the pond on the other side of that stand of trees. You can fill them there then come right back. I mean, right back!" Makawee returned to sowing the kernels of corn.

*C*hepi helped her cousin put the clay jugs on Tasunke and Sha'kona took off to get the water. Because of the extra weight, she went slowly, enjoying the break from working in the field. As much as she tried not to, she couldn't help thinking about the boy with the long hair and the great smile. What was wrong with her? When she got to the pond she slid off her horse and started to remove the heavy containers. A voice from behind startled her.

"Can I help you?"

Sha'kona turned around to see Enapay on the same white horse he had been riding last night. She had not heard him approach. A swarm of butterflies took flight in her stomach and she could feel herself shaking. She tried to speak, but words wouldn't come to her mouth. Excitement and fear battled for control of her feelings. She had to calm down.

What was he doing here?

"I'm sorry if I scared you," Enapay apologized. "I didn't mean to. We are taught to be silent on our horses from when we are practically babies." He dismounted and stood by his horse. He had more confidence than she had ever seen in a boy. "I was in the woods collecting firewood and I saw you ride this way. I thought I should say hello and properly introduce myself. I am Enapay, son of the Dark Chief Ohanko."

He bowed ever so slightly and then...that smile again. Sha'kona thought she was going to lose it. She was acting like a complete idiot, her mouth hanging open, her hands trembling, unable to make a sound.

"I can't blame you for not wanting to talk to me after the way my father spoke to you," he continued. "Please accept my apologies. He can be overbearing sometimes, even terrifying, but deep down he has a good heart. Taking care of his family comes first to him. He will do whatever is necessary to accomplish that. Manners and diplomacy are not things he is very good at. Neither is compromise."

Enapay delivered his words like an adult and Sha'kona hung on every one of them. His eyes were as dark as hers and filled with sincerity. All she could do was stare at him.

What was wrong with her? She couldn't move a muscle or respond to him at all. It was as if she were paralyzed. Up until he appeared, she had never been at a loss for something to say. Now she seemed to have completely lost the power of speech. She couldn't even imagine what he must be thinking about her. This was way beyond embarrassing. This was mortifying.

"You don't have to say anything," the boy offered with unexpected compassion. "Listen, I couldn't help but notice how much our horses look alike. I thought I had the only white horse with a black diamond and there yours does too. I saw how well you ride him. If you can forgive me and my family, maybe you would consider meeting me here later and we could go for a ride together. The adults of my tribe are meeting tonight so I could slip away. I have to be honest, my father doesn't want me even thinking about you so I will have to sneak out. If you don't want to see me, I understand.

"I have to get back to work before somebody notices I'm missing. I really hope you'll be here later." He bowed again and in one graceful move mounted his horse and rode off. Still silent, Sha'kona couldn't take her eyes off of him until he disappeared into the woods.

$A$s soon as Enapay was out of sight, Sha'kona regained the use of her faculties. She felt like she had been in some kind of trance.

"Tasunke, what in the world just happened?" She addressed her horse and at the same time hurried to get the pots filled with water. She decided the jugs would be too heavy to move when they were full, so she left them on her horse and used a smaller pot to fill them with water from the pond.

"I just made a fool out of myself." Sha'kona continued talking to Tasunke as if he understood every word. He cocked his ears and watched her inquisitively. "He caught me off guard, but that's no excuse. I wasn't even polite, in fact, I was downright rude. I just stood there like a statue, frozen and speechless. He must think I am the biggest loser ever. I could have at least said hello and introduced myself like he did. What was I thinking? I wasn't. That's a problem.

"And not the only problem, there's more. What do I tell my father? The whole time he was here, my father's speech was in the back of my head like some spirit haunting me. I'm not even supposed to have a single thought about Enapay and here I was alone with him. And, he asked me to sneak out and go riding with him! What should I do? I have never disobeyed my father on anything big, and this is big.

"Enapay did apologize. It seems like he wants to get along

with me. Maybe if I did see him, we could figure out a way to make peace between our tribes. If that worked, our fathers couldn't say anything about us going against their wishes. My dad has always told me that being a chief sometimes means making difficult decisions and that I needed to learn how to do that even though I would never be a chief. This is certainly one of those times.

"One more thing, like there aren't enough issues already. Do you think my father knows about Enapay's family's meeting tonight? How can I tell him about it without letting him know I saw the boy? Is it important for him to know?" Tasunke looked back at her with a puzzled expression.

"Boy, you're a lot of help." Sha'kona stroked Tasunke's neck as she spoke. "Where are my 'other eyes' or my supernatural visions that have all the answers when I need them?"

She had gotten as much water as her horse could carry. She grabbed the reins and started walking back. If she rode, the load would be much too heavy for Tasunke.

"I don't know what to do."

$B$y the time Sha'kona arrived back at the field, it was getting late in the day. Everyone was working as hard as they could to finish up so they could make it to the meeting on time. Chepi came over to help her cousin with the water.

"What took you so long?" she asked.

"Everything," Sha'kona replied.

*T*he women went straight from planting to the meeting house where the men were already assembled. Everyone was anxious to discuss what should be done about the uninvited guests. They had reached the end of their welcome and were showing no signs of leaving. No one in Wowoka's family wanted trouble, but they had not traveled this far, to such wide open spaces, to feel crowded and disrespected.

"Please sit so we can get started. We have a lot to talk about." Wowoka had to raise his voice to be heard above the hub-bub.

The tribe settled themselves in a circle while four men from the family gathered around a large ceremonial drum. The chief and his two brothers made their way to the center of the crowd where the drummers were seated and waited for the noise to subside and calm to prevail. Then Wowoka spoke.

"As is our custom, we will begin with a prayer from our drum group. The drum is the heartbeat of our people. Through it we are given the songs that are our prayers. This is the first drum made from the bounty of our new home."

The drummers began playing a steady pulse, adding vocals and then accents that followed their singing. They told the story of the family's journey and struggles and gave thanks for their blessings. They prayed for wisdom and guidance that they might always honor Mother Earth and her sacred gifts. When they finished, there was a time for silent personal reflection.

"We have received the first visitors to our village," Wowoka began without introduction. "As you all know, they too come from far away. Though we met under less than perfect circumstances I invited them to rest here for one night. It is our practice to welcome those in need. They had been traveling a long time and were exhausted. Perhaps that is why they were less than friendly. Weariness can cause people to be on edge.

"Their chief is a man named Ohanko who is arrogant and not trustworthy. I came to him in peace and he disrespected me and my daughter and thus our whole family. It took a show of force from our warriors before he apologized, but he has since proven his words to be hollow. They were supposed to have moved on already but are showing no intentions of doing so. Now we must decide what we should do about the situation. I want to hear what you think before I make my decision."

Though hesitant to speak in front of the tribe, Tokanosh was still outraged over Ohanko's behavior.

"We should go to their camp tonight and 'help' them pack up and get out," Tokanosh stated, leaving no doubt as to where he stood on the matter. "When I say 'help', I mean with spears and axes. We cannot let them walk all over us and show such disregard for your words." There were many shouts and nods of approval.

"Thank you, Tokanosh, for your very subtle 'Tokanosh solution.' Does anyone else have something to say? Hakan, what about you?" Wowoka knew that his youngest brother kept a cooler head and often had very practical solutions to problems. His input would be valuable.

"This has been on my mind, as I'm sure is true for everybody," Hakan said in a very soft voice. He was almost as uncomfortable speaking in public as Tokanosh. "There is an expression, 'You catch more flies with the sweetness of honey than with the bitterness of dandelions.' Perhaps this is how we should act.

"Ohanko's tribe is tired and hungry after their long journey and, I am sure, eager to settle in a permanent place of their own. As a gift for them to use in their new home, we could provide them with food and supplies and then host a farewell ceremony to wish them well. We would make a big deal out of their departure. They would have to leave then." The tribe listened attentively. Tokanosh was confused.

"Hakan may have a good idea," Wowoka commented. "It would almost be like shaming them into leaving, a huge hint that they need to go. If they don't get the hint, they just might get Tokanosh." His words brought smiles and a few laughs to the crowd. Tokanosh looked embarrassed. It didn't take much for that to happen.

Wowoka continued, "Tomorrow morning we will hunt the great beasts that roam the plains south of here. We will offer Ohanko's tribe our first kill. By tomorrow night they will be long gone. One way or another.

"There are a few other matters we need to discuss..."

*O*hanko and the elders from his family gathered around the fire in the middle of their camp. He had summoned them to inform them of his plans. The Dark Chief had seen all of the adults from Wowoka's tribe file into their big community house. It did not take a genius to know what they would be heatedly discussing. Did that fool Wowoka really believe that the great Ohanko would bow to his commands and leave because he was ordered to? Ohanko obeyed no man.

"I have decided we will stay in this place for a while," Ohanko announced. "I have a proposition to make to Wowoka. As soon as their meeting ends I will go see him and let him know what I have in mind. If he does not accept it, there could be trouble - for him." When Ohanko spoke, no one responded, they knew only to listen.

"In the meantime, I want everyone to stay separate from them. We were told to be out of here by tonight and quite evidently we have not done that. Nor do I intend to. I cannot predict their reaction, but we must be prepared for anything. They are weak but think they are clever. If they try anything, they will find out they are not so smart.

"Now, let's eat some of the fine game our women brought us and talk about more pleasant things." Ohanko grabbed a piece of venison that was roasting in the fire and began to tell the men with him one of the many stories of his amazing accomplishments, not that they had not heard it many times before.

"Sha'kona, snap out of it! It's your turn!" Kewa shouted, extremely annoyed. He had just about had enough. His sister had not been paying attention since they started playing his favorite game of bowl and bones. She seemed to spend most of the time drifting off into her daydream world.

The game was simple enough but both players had to be totally engaged or it just wasn't fun. There was a bowl and six small circular discs made of bone. One side of each disc was plain and one side was decorated with simple designs. You tossed the discs into the bowl trying to get at least five discs to land with the decorated side up. If you got five you won one stick, if you got six you won two sticks. Kewa's throw only resulted in four discs decorated side up. Not enough to win. The score was even with Kewa and Sha'kona holding seven sticks apiece. Whoever amassed ten sticks first, won the game. Kewa was anxious to go again, but Sha'kona was taking her sweet time. She had not even watched his last toss; she was too busy staring into space.

"What?" Sha'kona replied as if in a haze. She had not heard a word of what Kewa had said. She had just been going through the motions of playing the game. Ever since she had seen Enapay earlier, she couldn't concentrate on anything, especially not bowl and bones. Her every thought had been preoccupied by the not so chance encounter. She could not get him out of her head. The harder she tried, the more impossible it was. Why did things have to be so difficult sometimes? This would be a perfect time for one of her visions to come along and wipe out everything else in her brain. But, of course, no such luck.

What would her father say to all this? He made it perfectly clear that she wasn't supposed to even think about the boy. She certainly wasn't obeying that order. When her father gave her a comforting hug and kiss on the forehead before he left for his big meeting, she was consumed with guilt. She had never kept anything from him. It had been her intention to tell him everything right then, but before she got the chance, Tokanosh arrived and took off with her father for the community house.

One thing was for sure, she was not going to see Enapay tonight. As soon as her father got home, she would let him know exactly what had happened. He would understand that it wasn't her fault. In fact, she had not said a word to the boy.

"That's it, I'm done. You're no fun," Kewa ranted. "You've been weird the whole time we've been playing. I mean, the whole time I've been playing. I don't know what you've been doing." He was upset and had no problem showing it. "Is it because I'm going to beat you or because you're too grown-up to spend time with me? You were so much better to be with when you were younger. I'm out of here."

Her brother's words jarred Sha'kona back to reality. She realized he was not happy. "Kewa, wait a minute. I'm sorry. I've got a lot on my mind and it wandered a little, that's all. Let's finish the game. I promise I'll pay attention."

"No, it's too late. I'm going to find someone else to play with!" Kewa stood up and stormed off, taking his game with him.

This was not good. She had planned to keep herself busy with Kewa so she would not be tempted to think about Enapay's invitation. She couldn't leave her brother by himself with her parents away, so no chance would she try to meet up with the Dark Chief's son. But now he was gone and she was all alone with nothing but her thoughts. Of Enapay.

Maybe she could just go close enough to see if he was there waiting. He probably wouldn't be. And if he was, and he saw her, she would formally introduce herself and let him know that she could actually speak. It would be the perfect opportunity to see if they could come up with a way to help the two families get along. Then she would never see him again and she could tell her father the truth. She had done it for the family. He would be proud of her.

"I can't believe I'm doing this." Sha'kona was speaking out loud to herself as she walked out of the house. She checked to see if anyone was watching. No one noticed her. Most of the adults were at the meeting house and the children were scattered throughout the village. Some of the young mothers were feeding their babies inside their homes. Sha'kona headed toward the corral where Tasunke waited.

"Come on boy, we don't have much time to spare. They will be done with their meeting soon and I want to be back before then." As always, Tasunke greeted her with his own unique brand of unbridled enthusiasm.

"Quiet, we don't want anyone to hear us." Silently they slipped out of the paddock on their way to the pond.

*H*e was there.

Sha'kona rode through the thick stand of trees that surrounded the pond and stopped in front of Enapay. He had been watching her make her way through the woods. For a moment, not a word was spoken. Neither of them had expected the other to show up. Hoped, perhaps, but not expected. Her nervousness began to take hold again, but she willed it away. She was determined not to be speech-less again.

"I am Sha'kona. Apology accepted."

Now it was Enapay's turn to be tongue-tied. He had not really believed she would come. Their first meeting was his doing, but this was different. She had chosen to be there with him. She looked even more exquisite than he remembered, and what he remembered was pretty amazing. His mind and his heart were racing.

Had she risked as much trouble as he had? If his father found out he was with her, the consequences would be severe. He had not told anyone where he was going, but instead had waited until his father left to meet with the council, then sneaked away. If he was caught, Enapay did not know what he would say. Going against his father's wishes was never a good idea, but lying to him would earn the kind of punishment the boy didn't want to even think about.

After a painfully long pause, he finally responded.

"She speaks!" He tried to cover his nervousness with an attempt at humor. "I was worried that you only communicated by shouting, especially to chiefs you haven't even met yet." Then he smiled.

Before that smile could have its previously devastating impact, Sha'kona replied, "Sometimes I act before I think. Sorry about that." She hesitated then added, "I'm glad you're here. How did you get your father to let you come?"

"I didn't. Unfortunately, he is not as understanding as your parents are."

"I don't know about that. My father has forbidden me to see you or even think about you as well. He doesn't like your father very much," Sha'kona disclosed.

"You shouldn't be here then." Enapay's expression became noticeably serious.

"Do you really mean that?" Now Sha'kona was confused.

"No, and yes. I want to see you, but I don't want you to have problems with your family because of me."

"I appreciate your concern, but that would be my choice, wouldn't it?" Sha'kona wasn't asking a question. "I'm a big girl. I can make my own decisions and take care of myself. I came here to see if you and I could think of a way to help resolve the conflict between our tribes so we can all have what we want but live peacefully with each other."

"That's a very noble cause, but I don't think it will be possible with my father involved. Don't get me wrong. I love him, but you have to really get to know him to feel that way." Enapay waited, then added, "Is that the only reason you came?"

"No, I wanted to see you to explain my behavior yesterday, but I don't think there is any explanation that makes sense. You took me by surprise and I didn't know how to react." Sha'kona was beginning to relax. "More importantly, I thought our horses should meet since they're practically twins. This is Tasunke," she said, patting him on the side of his neck.

"Whatever the reason, I'm glad you showed up and so is my horse. His name is Achak and obviously he likes Tasunke. I thought Achak was one of a kind, but these two look so much alike it's a little bizarre." Enapay was relieved at the change of subject.

"You may find that a lot of things are bizarre when you're around me," she said, and gave him a sheepish grin.

The two stallions nuzzled each other, neighing and snorting the whole time. They wanted to play.

Sha'kona continued, "They do seem to like each other - which surprises me. Tasunke rarely connects with other horses. He's a bit of a loner. I guess I am too when I get the chance, although that's not very often. I've got a younger brother who is always around. His name is Kewa and his greatest talent is annoying me."

"I don't have any brothers or sisters, but I have a lot of younger cousins, so I know what you mean." Enapay enjoyed talking to her and hearing her talk.

"I was supposed to be looking after him tonight, but I didn't do a very good job. He got really angry and left in a huff to find someone else to play with. I don't blame him. I wasn't very good company. I was trying to make up my mind about whether I should come meet you so I wasn't paying any attention to him. I wasn't even sure you would be here." Sha'kona had never confided like this in anyone before. Something about him made her feel at ease. What a change from the last time they were together.

"And I was worried you wouldn't come," Enapay admitted. "I didn't think I made a very good impression on you, just showing up like that without any warning. I know I scared you." He was trying to apologize.

"More shocked than scared," Sha'kona laughed.

The horses were getting antsy. They were excited about getting to know each other and tired of just standing around.

"We should let Tasunke and Achak have some fun. Would you like to go for a ride?" Enapay asked hoping she would say yes.

Sha'kona thought for a moment before answering, "I would like that, but it will have to be a short one. I have to be home before my parents get back."

Enapay gently dug his heels into Achak's side. Sha'kona did the same to Tasunke and the horses started walking away from the pond toward the open field beyond. They rode silently for a while, taking in all the sights and smells of the spring evening. There were colorful wildflowers everywhere and strange new animals peaking out from behind the trees. The sweet sounds of nature enveloped them.

Sha'kona found herself looking over at Enapay as much as she was looking ahead. He noticed every glance because he was doing the same to her. His hair and skin were darker than hers and up close she could see that his fine features were just beginning to take on the rugged edges of a man. The quiet between them was comforting.

"I want to know more about why you think things are bizarre around you. You seem pretty normal to me," Enapay interrupted her reflection as they slowly made their way through the wooded area.

"Let me see if I can explain without it sounding completely crazy," Sha'kona began. "Ever since my great-grandmother died I've been having weird dreams, actually more like visions, that tell me about things that are going to happen or things I should do. My family calls it my 'other eyes'. That's how we found this New World. We were kind of led here by what I saw with what my dad says is my gift. Oh yes, animals talk to me or guide me as well. All right, now I do sound crazy."

"I think it's pretty cool." He was enthralled by her.

"It's never boring, that's for sure!" A bright smile lit up Sha'kona's face. "I have a question for you. Why did you come here?"

"To see you. Ever since I caught the first glimpse of you hiding behind the sumac, you're all I've been able to think about." Enapay didn't know where those words came from. It was true, but he hadn't planned on telling anyone, especially not her. He could feel the blood rushing to his face.

Sha'kona blushed too. It was becoming a habit around him.

"I meant, why did your family come to this new land and end up where we settled?" she asked. "For us it's sacred. Someone very special from our tribe died here and blessed the ground with her spirit.

We can never leave."

"Oh, I misunderstood," Enapay said, embarrassed at his confession. "We just followed your tracks. I guess my father liked what he saw when he got here. There's no real reason we have to stay right next to your village. There's a lot of great space nearby that we could move to. Hopefully not too far."

"We'll figure a way to get our fathers together. I wouldn't like it very much if you were far away." The swarm of butterflies in her stomach took flight again as his disturbingly perfect smile returned in full force.

Enapay didn't know what the right thing to say was. He didn't want to put his foot in his mouth again. Conversation with this girl was different, as challenging as it was exciting. Maybe they should do something besides talk. When they reached the end of the trees an idea came to him. Ahead were open fields.

"How about we let our horses loose?" Enapay suggested, rubbing Achak's head. "We could race to that big boulder by the lake. I've seen you ride. You're pretty good, but I'll beat you easily."

"We'll see about that," Sha'kona said and with two swift kicks to Tasunke's midsection was off.

Enapay was right behind her, digging his heels into his stallion. Achak, like his rider, was a natural competitor and wanted nothing more than to catch up with his new friend. Soon they were neck and neck with Sha'kona and Tasunke.

As they flew across the flatland, the night air was filled with the sound of thundering hooves. The wind blew their hair back and whistled in their ears. With each stride, the stress of the last few days slid away. There was nothing like the feeling of freedom going full-out on a great horse could bring.

When the boulder was close, Sha'kona bent over low against Tasunke's neck and whispered in his ear, "Do this for me, my beautiful." He understood what she wanted and responded with all of the power he could muster. In a burst of explosive speed he lunged ahead of Achak and reached the finish line first.

Enapay pulled his reins tight, bringing Achak to a full stop right next to Sha'kona. She was beaming. This time the color in her cheeks was from the wind.

"I can't believe you won! Nobody ever beats me," Enapay told her in surprise. "That is an incredible horse and you are one of the best riders I have ever seen. You're amazing." Enapay was bursting with enthusiasm.

As he spoke, he reached over and put his hand on top of Sha'kona's. It was as if she were struck by lightning. Feelings she had never imagined swelled up inside her. It scared her and thrilled her. She sensed how dangerous those feelings could be. Even she was surprised by her reaction.

"It's late. I need to get home." Sha'kona's mood had suddenly turned somber. Enapay didn't understand what was going on. He had never been happier.

"What's wrong?" he asked.

At that moment Sha'kona made the most difficult decision she had ever made in her young life.

"We cannot see each other again."

Without another word, she turned Tasunke around and rode like the wind toward home.

*O*nce Ohanko saw the members of the other tribe exiting the meeting house, he took two of his strongest braves and rode up to find Wowoka. The Dark Chief's approach caused quite a stir in the village. Some of the men ran to get their weapons while others stood steadfast in his way. Hakan was already outside.

"To what do we owe the honor of your presence?" he asked, uncharacteristically sarcastic. "Are you coming to say goodbye?"

Ohanko looked down from his black steed. "On the contrary. I have come to have a word with your chief. I do not have to explain myself to you, my business is with him."

"What are you doing here?" Wowoka appeared at the doorway with Tokanosh next to him. The younger brother put both hands on his ever present spear and raised it menacingly.

"Is that any way to greet a guest? You can tell your man to put down his weapon. We are unarmed. I have come to make a proposal to you. Can we speak alone?" Ohanko was smug as usual.

"Anything you have to say, my family can hear," Wowoka replied.

"Very well, then. I have a plan that will allow us to live together in harmony." Ohanko's arrogance was almost unbearable. "Your people are farmers and mine are warriors. We will stay here and hunt and protect you while your family can raise crops for all of us. The rewards of our hunts will be shared by all as will your harvest. Everyone benefits."

"Our women take care of the crops. Our men are warriors, and good ones I might remind you, since you seem to have so quickly forgotten," Wowoka thundered. "We graciously received you and gave you sanctuary for a night. That time has passed. Your presence will no longer be tolerated.

"Tomorrow we will hunt the giant animals to the south. Our first kill we will bring back to you so you have fresh meat to take with you when you leave - our 'safe travels' present to you. You will accept our offering and immediately be gone. We wish you only the best. You should get back to your camp to prepare for your departure. My patience is wearing thin."

"I understand how you must feel. Obviously, you don't like my suggestion." Ohanko was unimpressed by Wowoka's warning. "Let us resolve our differences with a challenge. If your men are such great hunters let them prove it. Your best and my bravest will hunt that magnificent wild creature we call tatanka, or buffalo. Whoever brings down the biggest one will have the right to remain here and the other tribe must leave. Of course, if you are afraid of a little competition, I will just go back to our camp and start planning our village next to yours." Being antagonistic came easy to him.

The challenge had been made and Wowoka eagerly answered it. "Agreed, with one condition. Every full moon until the first snow, the losers must bring the winners a freshly slain buffalo."

"Done!" Ohanko exclaimed. "I guess we will be eating a lot of fresh meat." His two bodyguards roared with more laughter than the comment deserved. "I will see you in the morning, bright and early." The three of them turned tail and galloped off.

"My brother," Hakan said, "We have never hunted this buffalo animal before. Many things could go wrong. What if they win?"

"They won't. We have a secret weapon." With that Wowoka put his arm around Tokanosh. Tokanosh grinned.

Chapter Five
*The Hunt*

*"Every animal knows more than you do."*

*-- Nez Perce --*

*A*t first light, the leaves on the tall white birch trees outside the village were still holding onto the early morning dew. Tokanosh woke up in his cozy home with Mingan snuggled next to him snoring softly. The rest of the pack was scattered all around them, large, round fur balls purring in their sleep.

This is heaven, Tokanosh thought as he looked around at all of his dogs. They were his children. He smiled, content, wishing he could stay here forever with the rest of the world far away. When he passed to the spirit world, this is what he hoped it would be.

His smile faded as he thought of the challenging day ahead. Killing the largest buffalo was important, but his real mission was to destroy the pride and arrogance that flowed through Ohanko's veins. By the end of the day, that pompous fool would bow down before Wowoka, right before he packed up that hideous camp and moved far away. That was something to look forward to. The thought brought his smile back. He hurried to get dressed and out of the house. It was time to get Wowoka.

They had a competition to win.

*W*ake up, Sha'kona! It is time!" Wowoka shouted. Some

125

days her father's voice was as unwelcoming as thunder at a feast.

She had been tossing and turning all night, trying to shake the recurring images of Enapay out of her mind. It wasn't working. When she got home last night Kewa was next door with a friend, completely unaware that she had been gone. Thankfully, he had decided to sleep there. She was in no mood to deal with him this morning.

When her parents had returned to the house after the meeting, she had pretended to be asleep. She didn't want to talk to anyone or answer any questions. The fact that she was hiding something from them was eating her up inside. No matter how she thought about it, it was lying, and she had never lied to them before. She was disappointed in herself. Today she had to confess to her father everything about Enapay and her reasons for going to see him, valid or not.

Whatever the consequences.

The lack of sleep wasn't helping. Sha'kona was exhausted. Why was her father calling her so early? What was it time for? She wondered if he had somehow found out about her and Enapay. She braced herself for the worst as he came over to where she was lying down.

"I have something important to talk to you about, Sha'kona. Get ready as quickly as you can and meet me by the horses." He sounded serious.

This was not how it was supposed to be. If he had already discovered her disobedience, he would never believe that she had intended to tell him the truth. She was terrified. Consumed with guilt, she put her clothes on and walked outside to where her father was standing quietly.

"Good morning, my little sunshine," Wowoka said warmly. "You look tired. I guess spending a whole evening alone with your brother could do that. He can be a handful. Thank you for looking after him." Her father wasn't angry, but his trust and gratitude made her feel even worse.

"I met with Ohanko last night," he disclosed in his chief's voice.

Uh oh, here it comes, Sha'kona thought. I should tell him now before he can bring it up.

She was petrified with fear and shame. Before she had a chance to speak, Wowoka continued.

"As you know, we feel the other tribe must move. This is our sacred land and we alone are responsible for looking after it. Ohanko doesn't care. He has refused to find a new home. Rather than go to war, where no one really wins, we have decided to settle our differences with a challenge. Today both of our families will go to hunt the giant animal they call tatanka or buffalo. Whichever tribe kills the largest one will have the rights to this place and will decide what the other must do."

Sha'kona was stunned. "You met with Ohanko?"

"Yes," her father replied. "After our meeting he showed up with an insulting idea that we should become farmers and grow food for them and they would remain here and hunt for us. I don't believe he even really cares about this place, he just has to have his way. They think very differently than we do, and it's not good."

"Did you talk about anything else?" She had to know if Enapay's father knew anything about his son's rebellious actions.

"What else could we possibly say to each other? Isn't that

enough?" Wowoka demanded. "The fate of our family rests on the size of one buffalo and you want to know if we talked about what - the weather? What are you thinking? I would not have any conversation with him if I had the choice. And soon I will." He was getting perturbed by her complete lack of acknowledgement of the gravity of what he had just related.

"You interrupted me before I could tell you what I wanted to talk to you about," the chief continued. "Now let me finish. I have given it a lot of thought and have decided that I want you to come with us on the hunt today."

Sha'kona's jaw dropped. She was elated, her panic replaced with incredible joy. Her father had just asked her to go on a hunt with him. And not just any hunt, but the first one for buffalo and the one that would determine the future of her tribe. She had often thought about this day. Every time her father and uncles went hunting she begged to go but was always told that she was too young. Today, without even asking, she was being invited. She could hardly believe her ears.

A moment ago, her world was falling apart and now she was on top of it. She didn't know how many more of these enormous emotional swings she could take. They seemed to be happening a lot more frequently than she was ready for. Her brain was rattled. Though she wanted to, how could she tell her father about Enapay before the hunt? He had his family's future to worry about. This was not the time to add to the pressure he was under. She would have to wait until they won.

"Well, are you going to answer? Of course, if you don't want to, I can always go ask your brother," Wowoka said, and made a big deal out of pretending he was going to find Kewa.

"No! I mean, yes! Yes, I want to go, of course, and no, don't you dare ask him! Thank you more than you could know. You have no idea how much this means to me. This is a huge honor." Sha'kona hugged her father, barely able to contain herself.

"I had a feeling you might say yes." Wowoka grinned. "I want you to bring your bow and some of my game arrows. You won't be hunting today, but you should have them just in case. These could be very dangerous animals and I don't want you getting hurt. Today you will just observe and learn, I hope. If I am lucky enough, I will teach you how to kill the biggest buffalo!"

This kept getting better. Sha'kona knew that Kewa would be beside himself with jealousy when he found out that not only was she going with her father, but she was bringing her bow and real arrows, not the target ones they practiced with.

"Let's get a move on, the men are already at the meeting house getting prepared." Wowoka led the way.

*T*he village was awake in a flurry of frantic energy as the tribe anticipated the hunt of the tatanka. Men meticulously prepared their hunting weapons. The ends of long spears were carved to precise points and arrows were tipped with stone ground to razor-sharp edges while hand axes were chiseled into killing tools. No detail was left unattended.

Makawee directed the women to gather the ceremonial dyes made from berries, colored clay and special tree barks, that would be applied to the men's faces and their horses' bodies. The decoration was a ritual performed before every hunt, always unique to each individual and his mount. The warriors drew intricate designs on themselves as symbols of bravery and strength while the women painted the horses with perfect circles around the eyes to give them keen sight for the quest and bold markings on the legs and hindquarters to enhance their physical power and stamina.

Sha'kona was in the middle of trying to paint her own face when Tokanosh came over.

"Very frightening. You will definitely keep evil spirits away," he announced. Not exactly what a girl wanted to hear. Her uncle had a way with words. "Would you like some help?"

"After that comment, what can I say but yes," Sha'kona answered and handed him the small piece of deerskin she was using to apply the color.

"Your father discussed your coming on the hunt at the meeting," the big man continued. "Everyone felt it would be a good thing. Who knows, you may be able to find the biggest buffalo with your 'magic eyes'."

"'Other eyes'," Sha'kona responded. "Great-grandmother called them 'other eyes'."

"I don't care what they're called as long as they can help." Tokanosh was working on her face as he spoke. "Stay behind me. Don't be tempted to join in - you are not ready yet even if you think so. Next time you will be. Try to hear what I am saying. I know how pig-headed you can be. You are just like your father was when he was young, always dancing to his own drum."

"I hear you." Sha'kona had always listened to the few remarks her uncle shared with people. This was a long speech for him.

Tokanosh stepped back to admire his work and smiled.

"Better," was all he said.

When everything was ready, Wowoka gathered the family together in a circle just outside the meeting house. In the tradition of his people he offered up a prayer of thanks and protection.

"Great Spirit we are blessed by your presence among us. We thank you for the many gifts that Mother Earth provides. Today we are especially grateful for the opportunity to pursue these majestic animals we call tatanka. We also thank these great beasts and ask for their forgiveness, because in order to sustain our lives we must take theirs. Through their deaths we will be given all of our necessities of food, shelter and clothing. We honor them and commend their spirits unto you as they make it possible for the circle of life to continue for our family. Protect us and grant us a successful hunt that we may forever stay on this sacred ground."

Wowoka solemnly spoke those words and those words were true.

"How wonderful to see that you all got dressed up for me," Ohanko declared in the condescending manner that infuriated anyone he addressed. He and his men had barged into the village, rudely interrupting the ceremony that was under way.

"I like the face makeup, especially on the horses - but then again, they looked better than you to start with," the Dark Chief added obnoxiously. As always, tension ensued.

If verbal sparring was the combat preference of the moment, Wowoka would gladly oblige.

"I see that you have dressed as well. But surely you have made a mistake. We are going on a hunt and you are ready for a social dance," Wowoka replied with a large degree of mockery. He and his family tried not to laugh. Their uninvited guests had on their usual outlandish attire of ribbon-bedecked, multi-colored fringed leggings and bone chest plates. To their already ostentatious outfits they had added excessive amounts of ornate feathers in their hair and on their horses.

"I am sure that this banter is quite amusing to you, but I am bored by it," Ohanko stated, unfazed by the previous comment. "Shall we get started? There is at least one buffalo that will die today. Let's not keep it waiting."

"We are ready. The sooner we get started, the sooner you will be gone. Mount up brave warriors." As Wowoka spoke he climbed on his horse. Sha'kona did the same. Ohanko could not help but notice and comment.

"You are bringing the little girl with the big mouth? Is she going to disrespect the animals to death?" he asked, relishing his own sarcasm. "What mighty warriors you are! You must be eager to move. This is going to be easier than I thought."

Sha'kona opened her mouth to respond but was cut off by her mother's hand on her leg.

"Be careful," Makawee said with concern in her voice, but a smile on her face. She didn't want to show how worried she was. She knew how much this meant to Sha'kona and all of the women of the family. This was the first time a female had ever joined the men on their quest for game. Reaching up, she took her daughter's hand and kissed it.

"I am very proud of you," Makawee softly disclosed, then let go and turned away, not wanting the tears in her eyes to be seen.

Goodbyes were exchanged and Wowoka and his troops started their journey south. With a wave of his hand Ohanko directed his hunting party to follow as they made their way toward the plains where their unsuspecting prey grazed.

"I don't understand why she gets to go and I don't. I'm not a baby. And she's a girl! Even uncle said I was a warrior. It's not fair, not fair at all," Kewa whined. He had wandered up next to his mother to watch them all leave. His bow was in his hand and he had used some of the leftover dyes to color his face.

"Your time will come," his mother assured him, "sooner than you think. Being a true warrior is not determined by whether you are a girl or a boy, and most of the time it has nothing to do with hunting or fighting. These are things you will learn as you get older. This is Sha'kona's day. It is probably too soon for her as well, but there is no turning back now. Be happy for her. Now let's go get your bones and bowl game. I want to keep my mind busy until they return." Makawee put her arm around her son and ambled toward their home.

Sha'kona had not spotted Enapay until they were on their way. Catching up with her father at the head of the procession, she had passed right by him. He did not look at her or acknowledge her presence; he just stared straight ahead with a very grown-up look of determination carved onto his face. If he hated her, she would have to live with that and learn from her mistakes. Disobeying her father had been a bad decision. Embarrassed, she turned her head to focus on the trail ahead.

Tokanosh rode up alongside her.

"There are wild creatures out here much more dangerous than the tatanka," he remarked. "That boy you weren't staring at is trying like mad not to look at you." With that, he moved up next to his brother.

How could Tokanosh know what was going on? Did everybody in her family read minds? She wished Enapay hadn't come. It would have made things a lot easier.

*T*he two families traveled quickly and without conversation. Until they found the great buffalo, there was nothing to talk about. Everyone was keenly aware of how high the stakes were. After today, one tribe would remain on the sacred land and the other would leave in shame to find a new place to live.

Undertaking this competition had been Wowoka's decision and as the chief he accepted the responsibility of his choice. That was his duty. The alternative was going to war and he knew far too well the consequences of taking that road. He believed in himself and his family, they were skilled and fearless warriors. They would be victorious in this challenge.

Ohanko felt the pressure as well. Though outwardly he made a boisterous display of courage and self-confidence, he was smart enough to realize that he had an exceptional opponent in the person of Wowoka. The man had no fear and played by his own set of rules. His people loved him and would follow him into the jaws of death if need be.

To come out on top of this challenge, the Dark Chief knew he would have to use every skill he possessed. Had this conflict gone to battle, he would have suffered heavy losses even if he did manage to win, and he wasn't certain he could have been victorious against Wowoka. Ohanko's men were still suffering the effects of their long trip to this New World. It would be some time before they were at their full strength, both physically and mentally.

*T*he trail swerved sharply to the right and up a treacherously steep hill. Wowoka led the tribes' warriors to the top where two towering rock formations stood guard over the vast expanse of open country below. There he stopped and stared in awe at the breathtaking panorama that revealed itself.

Thousands of massive beasts with long, shaggy, dark brown coats grazed docilely on the seemingly endless grasslands. They had humped backs and huge heads topped with short, curved horns that announced danger to anything near. This was tatanka, the mighty buffalo. As far as the eye could see, the land was dark from their sheer numbers.

Ohanko and two braves made their way to the front where Wowoka and Tokanosh waited, mesmerized by the spectacle in front of them. When Ohanko took in the view, he too was stunned. It was one of the most magnificent sights any of them had ever witnessed.

"I have never seen anything like this. It is truly a wonder of nature." Wowoka's voice was filled with a deep reverence for this sacred gift of Mother Earth.

"Finally, we agree on something," Ohanko replied with a sincerity that caused both Wowoka and Tokanosh to turn their heads. Realizing that he may have shown a moment of weakness, he quickly continued.

"Before us are truly formidable animals. It will take all of the skills of the bravest warriors to take one down, even more so since we seek only the largest. I have an idea that could make this competition a little more interesting. You know how much you love my ideas," he chuckled, glancing at Wowoka. "Let us use only our spears - no bows, no axes, no fear. Do you think you can handle that? Of course, if you are afraid, we can all go armed to the teeth. Not very sporting or fair to the buffalo but much safer. Your choice, Great Chief."

Ohanko had made another mistake. The spear was Wowoka's weapon of choice.

"As you wish," he fired back. "So your men won't be tempted to stray from this rule, let us leave all of our other arms here."

"Now we have a real match," the Dark Chief quipped. "Let the challenge begin!"

*T*ime stood still as the two clans of hunters prepared themselves for what was to come. An intense silence seemed to change the texture of the air surrounding them, thickening and focusing all of their energy on a single goal: victory. Their futures hung in the balance. Today was not about killing an animal; it was about establishing order in this New World. Two extremes of spiritual and moral standards were pitted against each other. The destinies of both families would be determined by the resolution of this first conflict.

The calm before the storm ended as quickly as it began. Fueled by adrenaline and a frighteningly powerful single-mindedness of purpose, the hunters raised their battle-sharp spears high in the air and erupted in their traditional war cries: high-pitched rhythmic chants of pure emotion wailed at the top of their lungs. As one, they charged down from the butte toward the horde of buffalo beyond. Sha'kona stayed far behind, mindful of her father's command that she was to be an observer only, not a participant.

At the bottom of the slope, Ohanko veered off to the left toward a watering hole in the distance surrounded by hundreds of bison. Wowoka continued straight into the grasslands directly ahead.

"Our approach will certainly cause the beasts to panic and take flight. We must find our behemoth quickly and separate him from the rest, driving him to an open space where we can make the kill. Otherwise we may get caught up in the stampede and end up as their trophies. I don't want to find out what it feels like to be rammed by those horns," Tokanosh shouted to his brother as they rode.

Wowoka nodded in agreement and accelerated the onslaught toward the beasts. Sensing the impending danger, a sea of buffalo turned tide and scrambled in one dark motion away from the oncoming hunters. Thousands of hooves beat angrily on the earth's floor, provoking a dust cloud in their wake so profound the sun was obscured in a choking haze.

The bison were fast, but not as fast as the warriors on horseback. Wowoka, Tokanosh and the rest rode straight into the mayhem of frightened beasts. Up close, the size and strength of these extraordinary creatures was almost unfathomable. They were forged of solid muscle and crowned with two lethal weapons, the likes of which not one man out there had seen before. In this madness the hunters had to find the one colossal animal whose demise would secure their homeland.

Wowoka knew that if they were to succeed in this challenge, he would have to be dead on with his spear. There would be no second chance. If he missed his mark, he would surely be gored or trampled.

Tokanosh spotted it first: a buffalo so large it dwarfed all those around it, standing head and shoulders above the others. The beast snorted and grunted ferociously as it raced to get away, instinctively aware that it was the one the new enemy wanted. Maneuvering with startling agility, it rushed deeper into the herd to avoid capture or worse, its lethal horns ready to attack if it could not escape. This was the monster they were seeking.

"I see it!" Wowoka roared above the noise. The others saw it as well. It was impossible to miss.

"We must get that giant away from this horde." Tokanosh was vibrating with the anticipation of battle. "When it is in the clear you and the men can encircle it and drive it toward me. I will be on the ground waiting, ready for the kill. As I send its spirit to the next world I want to look it straight in the eye!"

"We are supposed to be hunting the buffalo not inviting the buffalo to hunt us," Wowoka shouted back, surprised by the foolishness of the plan. "You will only succeed in killing yourself. One man alone cannot defeat this animal."

"With all due respect, my chief, you are wrong," Tokanosh argued. "From above on horseback it will be difficult to pierce the heart. It will take many spears, with much risk to all of our men, to wear the creature down. And if he becomes enraged and decides to run, we will not be able to stop him. I will plant my spear in the ground and let him charge right into it as he attacks me. From below I can guarantee a mortal wound."

Tokanosh's idea just might work. It was extremely perilous, the potential consequences dire, but if timed right, the swiftest and surest kill. However, it would be Wowoka in that circle staring the mighty tatanka down. As chief and the one who made the decision to take on Ohanko in this challenge, it was up to Wowoka to take the responsibility and risk for his family. He could not put his brother in such a dangerous position.

"We will go with your plan, as crazy as it may be, but as leader of this tribe it is my duty alone to slay the beast. I know you are our finest warrior and feel it should be your life on the line, but I cannot allow that. This is my burden to bear and I will not fail. Are you with me?" Wowoka's words were final.

Tokanosh knew there would be no discussion. Though disappointed and concerned for his chief, he did not argue.

"I am with you."

"And Tokanosh."

"Yes, my brother?"

"I need you to watch my back as you always have. If I should fall, do not let that monster get away. I am counting on you. Now let's show Ohanko who he is dealing with!" Wowoka knew just what to say to his sibling to make things right.

"Now you're talking!" Tokanosh smiled.

*W*ith a fury that was contagious, Tokanosh led his tribesmen into the sea of bison. The monster would not get away. Quickly catching up to their prey, the warriors began forcing it away from the rest of the buffalo. Their adept horsemanship kept it moving in the direction they wanted it to go. Years of practice herding their own animals were paying off.

Soon the great beast was by itself, running frantically, not sure of what to do or where to go next. The riders kept it running helter skelter until at last, exhausted, it came to a stop. In an instant the hunters formed a circle around it with their horses and began to methodically close it in. The mighty creature was trapped and knew it. There would be no escape from the tight loop of horses and men without a fight. It began to pace, searching for a weak link to attack.

Wowoka and Tokanosh entered the ring. The chief dismounted, spear in hand, while his brother kept both eyes on their prey.

Sha'kona remained outside of the circle looking in, her heart in her throat. Her father seemed so small compared to the size of the animal in front of him. She was frightened for him. How could one man bring down something so enormous? Could he win? Soon enough she would find out.

"I want to hear your loudest war cries while you wave your weapons in the air. You must prevent the creature from getting out. He will then focus on me, the smallest target in sight." Wowoka addressed his men then spoke to Tokanosh. "When I give the signal, run it toward me. After that, it will be in the hands of the Great Spirit."

The warriors let loose their screams with a manic fervor, flailing their lances like madmen. The noise reached a fevered pitch, the atmosphere intense. Desperately seeking freedom, the huge bison went berserk. It was time.

"Send it to me, now!" Wowoka knelt down and stabbed the end of his spear into the ground, the razor-sharp point aimed at the enraged beast.

Tokanosh and his horse lunged at the buffalo from behind, slamming into it with all their might. It was like crashing into a huge boulder.

Shocked, in fear, and prepared to fight for its life, the animal lowered its head and charged, hatred in its eyes, foam drooling from its mouth, survival its only thought. The speed and immensity of the oncoming creature defied Wowoka's wildest imagination. He braced himself for the impact and prayed for the spirits to protect him.

In the flash of a firefly, at the last possible moment, Wowoka rolled out of the way and the massive beast ran full speed into his spear, impaling itself right through the heart. The great tatanka shuddered, not comprehending what had happened, and then fell on its side. Dead.

Wowoka let out what could have been his final breath. He had been holding it since kneeling in front of the animal that lay beside him. Relief and joy swept over the triumphant warrior as his family erupted in cheers of victory. Tokanosh ran to his side and helped him up.

"You got lucky, my chief. That wasn't a plan, that was a suicide mission! Whose hare-brained idea was that anyway?" Tokanosh grinned and gave Wowoka a Tokanosh bear hug. "Could you have cut it any closer? I swear, sometimes I don't know if you are brave or just plain crazy. Don't ever scare me like that again!" His grin turned into full-blown laughter and his hug got tighter.

"You can let go now!" Wowoka shouted, struggling to breathe. "I didn't survive an attack from that furry colossus to be crushed by an animal even uglier than the one I just killed." Now he began laughing. Tokanosh lifted his brother high in the air, set him on his shoulders and carried him to his horse.

Sha'kona had watched the ordeal fascinated and terrified. At the very end she had turned her head away, unable to witness the climax, afraid of the outcome. When she heard the cheers and saw her uncle grabbing her father, tears came to her eyes. He was safe. She rode as fast as she could to the center of the circle, arriving just as Wowoka climbed onto his horse from Tokanosh's shoulders. She leaned over and threw her arms around her father, squeezing as hard as she could. She hated being so emotional in front of the men but couldn't help it.

"With all the love I am getting, I will have to remember to go hunting more often!" Wowoka wrapped his arms around his daughter as he spoke. He saw the tears in her eyes. "Sha'kona, everything is good. It looked more dangerous than it was. Besides, I had a backup plan - your uncle." His soft words calmed and reassured her, as they always did.

Everyone had gathered around the giant beast marveling at its size. This was by far the largest animal any of them had ever seen, much less slain. There was no way Ohanko could find bigger. Wowoka knew they had won but this buffalo was more than a victory, it was a true blessing for his people, a symbol of life and hope.

Hakan had gotten down from his horse and was surveying the carcass.

"This is big enough to feed the entire tribe - as long as Tokanosh doesn't eat!"

Now the whole family laughed, the stress and tension over. This was an important moment for them and Wowoka wanted it to be recognized.

"We must give thanks to Mother Earth for the gift of this mighty creature and pray that its brave spirit has a safe journey back to her." The chief paused, allowing time for a moment of personal reflection.

"I am proud of each and every one of you," he continued. "Once again you proved yourselves as hunters and warriors with courage and skills that bring honor to me and to our tribe. All of you deserve credit for this conquest. Because of you, this sacred land we were brought to will remain our home. It will take a force far more powerful than Ohanko to make us leave. I am deeply grateful." Wowoka spoke as a great leader should, with dignity and respect. His family was moved by his comments, knowing they came from his heart.

Wowoka kept his speech short. There was much to be done and he addressed it.

"Hakan and Liwanu, take some men and drag our prize winner over to the trail we came down. You will stay there until Ohanko sees the proof of our kill. Then you can dress it and bring everything back to the village. Tokanosh and I will go scouting for the Dark Chief and his warriors and see what they have come up with. We should be back soon." Wowoka and Tokanosh left them to their work.

"Sha'kona, come with us. You might just learn what not to do!" Tokanosh invited her, trying to cheer her up. He wanted to keep an eye on her. She still seemed shaken up. She had not said a word since the hunt began.

Sha'kona nodded to her uncle, unsure of what she was feeling. She hoped it was nerves. The last thing she needed right now was another episode with her so-called "gifts."

The three of them rode off together, confident that the challenge was over.

"So what do we tell Ohanko?" Tokanosh asked.

"We tell him to start packing." The look on Wowoka's face was priceless.

---

*O*hanko and his men used a very different strategy from Wowoka's crew. They had approached the watering hole quietly so as not to disturb the bison who surrounded it. Once there, Ohanko rode to the top of a small hill overlooking the plains and from this vantage point searched for his target. It did not take him long to find what he was looking for. Just beyond the peaceful group of animals in front of him was the buffalo to end all buffalo, a creature of colossal proportions standing all alone.

His plan was simple. He would take on this foe himself, one on one. Man versus beast. From birth he had trained to be the greatest warrior of all his people. Now he would put those skills to the test. Ohanko had never been defeated and was not going to change that now. The fact that he had never come face to face with something so large unnerved him a bit, but he quickly shook those feelings off. Confidence bordering on cockiness ruled his life. Self-doubt had no place in it. He was invincible.

Ohanko rode down to where his warriors waited and gave them

their instructions.

"I have found what we came here for, a freak of nature, a beast from your worst nightmare, the biggest living thing you will ever lay your eyes upon. It is by itself just over the next rise. As silently as possible, I want you to take positions all around it to stop any of its relatives from interfering. And keep your distance so as not to disturb it. I want the element of surprise on my side when I go in for the kill. Now move it!"

The braves did as they were told, but Enapay held back. He wanted to watch his father in combat up close, to learn all he could. The Dark Chief was the best there was. Whatever failings he had were not as a warrior. Time and time again he had shown he could vanquish anyone or anything that dared challenge him. Everything he set his mind to he did, without fail. That was the part of his father's character Enapay admired most and what made him such a great leader.

"Enapay, go with the men. It will be too dangerous here with me. I must do this on my own." With that said, Ohanko spun his horse around and rode toward the unsuspecting king of the tatanka. It would be an epic battle as the hunter and the hunted met in mortal combat. Only one would walk away.

Ohanko rode straight to the top of the rise and assessed the situation. In front of him the chosen buffalo grazed peacefully, all alone, unaware of the impending danger. The Dark Chief's warriors were at their posts in the distance ready to turn back any curious bison who tried to become involved in the clash of the two titans about to occur. From the corner of his eye he saw Enapay take his place. All was ready.

Ohanko took a moment to mentally prepare, blocking every-thing from his mind except the death of his prey and what he had to do to make that happen. As he visualized every detail of his attack, he began to chant an ancient war prayer, getting louder and louder with every repetition until at last a shriek emerged that was inhuman in sound and intensity. At that instant he raised his spear above his head, reared up on his black stallion and exploded down the hill, his sights set on the soul of the beast.

Speed was everything now. As soon as the monstrous animal realized the threat screaming toward it, it would run for its life. Ohanko would have to race beside it and with deadly accuracy plunge his spear into its heart.

The oversized buffalo raised its head and saw death on its way. Anger flared inside it as it saw its territory invaded by the hostile two-headed peril coming its way. Instead of retreating, the animal let out a blood-chilling roar, lowered its head and charged as though possessed by demons.

Ohanko had not expected such an aggressive reaction but welcomed it, urging his horse on even faster, straight at the maddened monster thundering his way. He had already adjusted his plan to this unforeseen response. Just before they crashed into each other, he would veer off to one side and ram his spear deep into the flesh of the beast.

Before Ohanko could think another thought, the infuriated buffalo was upon him. He yanked his horse to the right and aimed his weapon at its mark. The Dark Chief never got the chance to strike. At the same instant he tried to turn to one side, the king of the tatanka swerved the same way and smashed against him with all of its mass and power. The giant bison's deadly horns stabbed deep into Ohanko's leg and the horse was slammed to the ground on top of him.

Wowoka, Tokanosh and Sha'kona arrived just in time to witness the catastrophe. They were horrified.

"Ohanko needs help now!" Wowoka exclaimed. "That is not a buffalo, it is a mountain, a mountain filled with molten fury! The fool is hurt and that crazed beast is already turning around to finish him off. His men are too far away to be of any use."

There was an urgency in his voice, the hatred for his opponent forgotten for the moment. He had to act quickly to save the man's life. He and Tokanosh bolted for the fallen warrior with Sha'kona close behind.

"We will never get there in time. Can you throw your spear that far, my brother?" Wowoka asked.

"We should try to get in as close as we can," Tokanosh answered. "I will wait until the last minute before that monstrosity tramples or gores him and then let it fly. It will still be a long way, but I might get lucky. What other choice do we have? If I don't try he will surely be killed." He had his weapon ready.

Ohanko was on the ground unarmed, his weapon knocked away by the impact. His horse had recovered from the fall and galloped off to safety leaving him totally alone. The last few moments were a blur to him, but he knew he was in grave danger. Bleeding profusely and in excruciating pain, he lifted himself up on one elbow to see just how bad of a situation he was in. It wasn't good.

The huge bison was eyeing him, pawing the ground, savoring the moment before it finished what Ohanko had started. The wounded warrior tried to move but could not, his legs were damaged beyond use.

What an ironic twist. The hunter killed by the hunted. Again he had misjudged an opponent. Maybe he was getting too old and it was time for his spirit to travel on without him. His fear turned to acceptance. With heroic effort, he sat up and extended his arms forward, beckoning to the mighty tatanka.

"Come and get me you useless bag of fur! You won't see me back down. Take your best shot!" Ohanko's voice was hoarse and weak, his chest heaving as he spoke.

The animal obliged, mercilessly storming at him with a savage rage that could only be satisfied by taking the life of its attacker.

"Now, Tokanosh, now!" Wowoka screamed above the noise of the horses' hooves.

Tokanosh launched his spear with a superhuman effort, using every bit of strength his body could summon. It sailed toward its target. Though he gave it his all, Tokanosh knew his weapon would fall short of its mark.

Thwack!

*F*rom out of nowhere an arrow struck the monstrous buffalo in the chest embedding itself up to the feathers. The animal stopped in its tracks and looked around in confusion, searching for the source of its sudden pain. It would never find it. With a bone-chilling howl, the defeated beast collapsed. Its lifeless body lay still on the grassland that had been its peaceful sanctuary for so long.

Wowoka and Tokanosh reined in their horses and came to halt beside Ohanko. Looking behind for where the deadly arrow had come from, the brothers were confronted with the sight of Sha'kona on her white horse, her bow in her outstretched hand. Wowoka didn't know what to think, but he would have to deal with it later. Ohanko's eyes were closed and he was not moving. His breathing was labored, in short gasps, and blood was everywhere.

*W*hen Sha'kona had seen the buffalo begin its final run toward Ohanko, time slowed down for her and she felt as if she were floating. This time she recognized the signs of her "other eyes" going to work and was not as bewildered or afraid as she had been before. She felt cut off from everything around her and yet extremely connected at the same time. Just watching Tokanosh ready his spear, she knew he would not be able to save Ohanko. It was up to her.

Even in her trance-like state, the young girl knew that she would have to go against her father's orders again. He had made it very clear before they left for the hunt that she was to be an observer only. That's what she had been up to this point, but that was about to change. She couldn't let a man die, even if that man was someone her father hated.

Galloping full speed behind her father and uncle, Sha'kona grabbed her bow and nocked an arrow. She felt a wave of unbelievable clarity rush through her body as she drew back to fire. At the same moment, Tasunke's ride became smooth and steady, the flying sensation she had experienced once before. The world closed down to just her and her target, an enraged animal trying to end the life of its tormentor.

Effortlessly, Sha'kona released the string and let the arrow go. As if guided by some unseen hand, it flew straight and true toward its fatal destination. Everything was moving in slow motion, the boundaries between the real world and the world of dreams temporarily blurred.

Then one chilling sound snapped her back to reality like a slap in the face.

Thwack!

*W*owoka jumped off his mount to see how badly Ohanko was hurt. The fallen chief was unconscious and not responding to Wowoka's voice or touch.

"Help me, Tokanosh," Wowoka told his brother. "We have to get him back to the village as soon as possible. His injuries are far more serious than I can take care, perhaps too serious for anyone to take care of. I wish our grandmother were alive, she would know exactly what to do." Wowoka picked Ohanko up off the ground and Tokanosh gently lifted the wounded man onto his horse.

"What are you doing with my father?" Enapay demanded. He and the other warriors had finally arrived at the tragic scene. The boy was beside himself with shock and fear. He had never seen his father hurt or even sick before. This was more than he could handle.

"He needs help and he needs it now. We don't have time to fight or argue," Wowoka snapped back.

"Father!" Enapay shouted. He had come alongside Tokanosh and was gently shaking his father to try and wake him.

"He can't hear you, son. We must go now," Wowoka said with

a great deal of compassion.

"Great Chief, please bring him to our camp," Enapay implored. "Our medicine woman is very powerful and my father trusts her. I will ride with you."

"We will take him there," Wowoka agreed.

Enapay knew he must take charge. Until his father recovered he would have to lead his family as chief. He spoke to his men. "I want you skin and field dress the carcass and bring it to their village. It belongs to them."

"Wait!" Sha'kona interrupted. She had ridden up next to her father.

"We can't. There is no time. As it is, it will take a miracle for Ohanko to survive," Wowoka said softly so only she heard what he said.

"I know, father. Look."

The herd of bison began to separate into two halves leaving a wide path between them. Not a sound was made as hundreds of the sacred creatures formed two perfectly straight lines on either side of that path and stood motionless. Both families watched in awe, unable to explain or understand what they were seeing.

In the open space between the two groups of animals a dense cloud formed. It hovered close to the ground, and from within its depths came a mysterious humming, like a multitude of birds taking flight at one time.

The strange noise stopped as suddenly as it had started and the cloud rose high into the air, revealing a buffalo so white it seemed to be lit from within.

## Chapter Six

# The First Celebration

*"If you see no reason for giving thanks, the fault lies in yourself."*

*~~ Minquass ~~*

$\mathcal{T}$he white buffalo stood immobile, a majestic spectral image, its iridescent blue eyes locked onto Sha'kona. Even from a distance it was clear the apparition was beckoning her to come closer. She got down from Tasunke and seemed to glide toward the phantom creature as if drawn by some supernatural magnet. An ethereal calm settled over every living thing.

Wowoka wanted to ask his daughter what she was doing, but he could not speak. He was riveted to the drama unfolding before him.

As soon as Sha'kona reached the hauntingly beautiful animal, she touched its face ever so gently with her fingertips. For the first time since it appeared, it moved, rubbing its head against her body. She felt the same connection she had had with Nanuk, only deeper and more intense. The white buffalo was trying to communicate with her. Letting her "other eyes" open wide, she understood everything.

The world around her came into view as if through a gossamer veil. Ohanko was still unconscious, barely breathing, limp on the front of Tokanosh's horse. With just one arm, Tokanosh was holding him up. The Dark Chief's body was dead weight. Enapay was beside them, his ashen face frozen in despair. Both families were motionless, stunned. In front of them all, her father anxiously watched her every move.

A stream of images suddenly appeared before Sha'kona's "other eyes," glimpses of what was to come. Ohanko would survive, forever changed, and Tokanosh would one day be a heroic leader in his own right. Though Enapay would give his heart to her, fate would demand a price from each of them. The two families would become as one and face a challenge they would never expect. And her father would lose something he loved more than life itself.

These things she saw clearly and knew them to be true.

An all-encompassing sense of tranquility washed over Sha'kona and she spoke in a voice that was not her own.

"The white buffalo was sent to us by the Great Spirit as a symbol of peace. We must always hold it sacred. It has given me answers to questions I did not ask and asked me questions I could not answer. From this day forward our tribes will live together in harmony and build a wondrous civilization that will spread to every part of this New World. Our differences will be our strength. Guided by the wisdom of the Creator and a respect for all things, we will honor this land and share it with each other and Mother Earth. Her gift of the first harvest will be bountiful. We must celebrate that as one people in remembrance of this day, and in thanksgiving for all of our blessings."

With that said, the fantastic animal knelt down before Sha'kona. After placing one hand on either of its horns, she touched her forehead to its nose. An indescribable energy shot into her and she recoiled from the shock. The sensation was startling but not unpleasant, its purpose clear. At once she made her way to Ohanko.

"Uncle, hold him so that I can touch his head."

As though under a spell, Tokanosh complied without a thought.

With a gentleness that belied his size, he lowered Ohanko to within Sha'kona's reach. She put one hand on each side of the Dark Chief's face, leaned over, and tenderly pressed her forehead against his. There was a blinding flash of light as a jolt of power surged from Sha'kona into the mortally wounded man.

At the same moment the dense cloud reformed around the magnificent white buffalo then lifted and vanished in the sky. As mysteriously as it had appeared, the phantom creature was gone.

Ohanko opened his eyes, nose to nose with Sha'kona. He sat up with a start.

"Don't tell me the spirit world is full of skinny young girls with bad tempers! If it is, I am not staying. And why does this vile bear have his arm around me? Am I being punished for the sins of my life? I could not have possibly done anything bad enough to merit this!" He was weak and delirious, his voice a raspy whisper, but he was alive. His foul humor was irrefutable proof of that.

Enapay reached over and grabbed his father's hand. The boy tried to blink away the tears in his eyes, but the flood of emotion was too strong to stop.

"Bring me my horse!" Ohanko demanded. He tried to move, but his injuries were so severe he could not even lift his leg.

"Stay still, you old fool!" Tokanosh ordered, tightening his grip on Ohanko. "You nearly died back there and you're not out of the woods yet. If it was up to me, I would have left you, but my brother took pity on you. I will take you back to your camp, but if you open your mouth once on the way I will throw you off my horse without a care in the world. And don't bleed all over me!"

The Dark Chief was in too much pain to argue. Drained by his outburst of bravado he passed out again in Tokanosh's arms.

"We need to bring him to their medicine woman now. He got the miracle he needed, but that won't keep him alive." Wowoka was in command. He turned to Enapay. "I have seen you ride; you and your horse are fast. Go ahead of us and find your medicine woman. Take her to our meeting house, ready to use all of her powers. We will meet you there." The boy obeyed without hesitation and lit out for home.

Wowoka then gave orders to all of the warriors.

"Some of you will stay here and work together to bring this animal back and some of you will go help Hakan and Liwanu with the other one. The rest will follow me to our village. Sha'kona, get Tasunke and ride with me"

As soon as his daughter was next to him, he took off, leading both families home from the hunt.

"*O*ur medicine woman, Wa'kanda, is waiting for you." Enapay reported to Wowoka as the combined force of tribesmen arrived at the village. Without stopping, they all rode on to the meeting house.

Ohanko was breathing but had not regained consciousness and he was pale, very pale. His leggings were soaked through with blood. Time was running out for him. The white buffalo had given him a second chance, but that alone would not save him.

A tiny woman, older than time, greeted them at the lodge. She was hunched with age and her skin was like dried parchment. Even with her cane she could barely walk, but there was a force to her presence that demanded attention. She wasted no time on niceties.

"Bring him in. Everyone but the girl must leave and stay out until I call you." Wa'kanda's sightless eyes wandered as she spoke and her frail voice had an uncontrollable shake to it. Her words were difficult to comprehend.

"How did you know I was here?" Sha'kona asked, aware of the old woman's blindness.

"I know a lot more than that because I don't ask stupid questions. Now stop talking and have them take my chief inside right now. And you come with him." She pointed directly at Sha'kona with a trembling hand.

"I want to be with my father," Enapay interrupted. He was trying to act bravely, but the frightened look on his face gave him away.

"That is not possible. You must wait with the others." The medicine woman dismissed the chief's son's demand and turned toward the lodge.

Tokanosh and Wowoka lifted Ohanko off of the horse and carried him into the meeting house. After gently laying him down in the center of the big room, they left. They said nothing. There was no need to.

Wa'kanda hobbled in behind them followed by a nervous Sha'kona. The old woman pulled the skins down over the doorway and made her way to Ohanko. He lay still in the darkened space, the only sign of life the sound of his labored breathing. Smoke billowed from a small ornately decorated bowl, blanketing the room with the spicy scent of burning sage. She picked up the bowl and carried it up and down the length of the Dark Chief's body, letting its vapors drift down on to him. As she did, she began to chant in a language known only to her, mysterious words that pushed through the walls of reality into a place of tranquility and healing energy.

Sha'kona was captivated by the ancient shaman's intensity. As she performed the ceremony, she seemed ageless, her hands steady, her voice strong. The wisdom and skills of a thousand generations of healers poured from her heart. Sha'kona had no sense of time. A moment could have been forever and forever passed in an instant.

Wa'kanda paused the ritual for a moment to take two bundles of herbs out of the goatskin pouches she wore around her neck. She crushed them and placed them in the burning bowl. As she did, she explained their meaning.

"These are two very special plants we use for healing. Cedar is from the south and is used to purify and cure physical ailments. Sweetgrass is from the north and is full of positive energy. We use it to restore emotional and mental health, without which no injury will ever truly heal." She took the new mixture and began to walk around Ohanko, waving her hand above the bowl, spilling the smoke on every part of his body. Her movements were suddenly as graceful as a dancer's and her once unseeing eyes restored with sight. They were focused on Sha'kona.

"I have been expecting you," she said gently. "I was told you would come and that you would be called Sha'kona. You are the chosen one. Powers have been given to you, but you must recognize them and learn how to use them. Until you do, they will be incomplete and not serve you as they should.

"That is why the great bear did not lead you all the way to the eagles, why the eagles took a spirit with them when they brought you here, and why you could not fully heal our chief with the force given to you by the white buffalo." The medicine woman spoke clearly and with a warmth that radiated from her as though a fire burned within.

"The bear gave you strength that you may always be victorious," she continued. "The eagle gave you direction that you may always know the way. The sacred buffalo gave you wisdom that you may always make the right choice. There is one more power you must find, the most important one of all. Without it all the rest have no meaning. When you have it, you will come back to me, for only then can your true quest begin."

Sha'kona listened with rapt attention but was unsure of the meaning of what she was being told. Wa'kanda carried on.

"Your great-grandmother left you her 'other eyes' to see the courage you were born with. Every time they open, you will understand more and your powers will grow stronger. There will be signs to guide you, but you must follow those signs."

Wa'kanda placed the bowl of smoking herbs on the floor and removed some leaves from the bag around her waist. She wrapped them around Ohanko's legs and put a wool blanket on top. From behind her she picked up a small pitcher and poured a thick, foul-smelling liquid into the chief's mouth.

"I have done all I can do." As she spoke, her eyes glazed over, all sight leaving them again, and her body hunched over, the dancer's grace replaced by the tremors of an old woman.

Ohanko stirred and opened his eyes.

"What happened? Where am I?" he mumbled. The color had returned to his face and he was able to sit up, but the pain in his legs was excruciating. One had been gored by the buffalo and the other crushed by his horse.

"You must rest," the old woman told him. Her shaky, frail voice had returned. "You have been badly hurt. I am afraid it will be some time before you fully recover. Little girl, go get your chief! There is much our two leaders need to discuss."

Sha'kona ran to get her father, her mind reeling from all that had taken place and all that had been said.

---

"*H*e's awake. Wa'kanda says he will live, but he is not in good shape. She wants you to come in and talk to him." Sha'kona was surprisingly calm. Wowoka was waiting outside with Tokanosh and most of Ohanko's family. He walked in with his daughter, unsure of what he would say.

Wa'kanda addressed Wowoka as he entered the smoke-filled room. "Our families are at a crossroad. If you and Ohanko can put your differences aside and choose the right direction, a future of countless blessings awaits us all." She eased herself down and sat cross-legged next to her chief.

Wowoka was surprised to see his nemesis sitting up.

"You are a tough old buzzard," he proclaimed. "I didn't think you were going to make it. That was some monster you decided to butt heads with."

"If you knew how I felt right now you wouldn't think I was so tough." Ohanko spoke softly, obviously suffering. "I don't remember anything after it rammed into me then turned and charged. How am I still alive? Did one of my men kill it?"

"No. Actually, your favorite big-mouthed scrawny girl from

my family killed it with a single arrow. She saved your life. I am sure your men will tell you the whole story.

"Is that why she is here, to claim the victory in our little challenge?" Until now Ohanko had ignored her presence.

"She is here because your medicine woman asked her to be. Who won our 'little challenge,' as you call it, is not important right now. I am more concerned about your health. Though I can't say you are my favorite person in the world, I don't want you dying in my lodge. There is not enough sage in the world to cleanse this place if that were to happen." Wowoka smiled.

"You have some bedside manner, Great Chief. Thank you for your concern, but I always honor my debts. My people will move as soon as possible and you can expect to be eating a lot of buffalo from now on. Every new moon a fresh kill will be delivered to your village." To Ohanko, honor was everything. He had lost, so he must pay the price.

"I don't think you are in any condition to move. Besides, while you were somewhere between here and the spirit world, a white buffalo appeared to our families and sent a message through Sha'kona. Both of our tribes are to remain here and become as one." Wowoka knew that directive may have been delivered by his daughter, but it was not from her. It could not be ignored.

"There can be no argument. It is meant to be," Wa'kanda added, her voice shaking more than it normally did.

"While I was drifting between this world and the spirit world, I had a very peculiar dream about what I must do," Ohanko admitted. "The white buffalo was in it and so was your child. They showed me images of a time of enlightenment when there was only one nation made of many different tribes. We will make our peace. But first, come close to me, Sha'kona."

Wowoka nodded his approval and she went to Ohanko's side.

"I am indebted to you," he told her. "You saved my life and perhaps the lives of all of us with your gifts. You have my eternal gratitude - on one condition. You must teach me how to kill a monster like that with one arrow." Ohanko laughed but the laughter was cut off by a coughing fit. When it subsided he continued.

"You are a true warrior, little one, and I am proud to know you." He reached into the pocket of his shirt and pulled out an arrowhead. "This was my father's. He gave it to me when I was about your age. I want you to have it. You have more than earned it.

"Wowoka, I am also extremely grateful to you, and to your family. You had every right to leave me to die. I was your enemy, yet you chose to help. I would be honored if you would accept me as your friend and ally." The Dark Chief offered his hand and Wowoka took it.

"Now if you don't mind, help me up and let us go outside. I want to speak to my people standing next to you."

"Are you sure you are well enough? Maybe it would be best to wait until you get your strength back," Wowoka said with grave concern.

"Even another giant buffalo could not stop me, at least not while your daughter is near." The Dark Chief smiled and began to pull himself up using Wowoka's hand for assistance. Together they made their way outside.

When Ohanko appeared at the doorway, the worried members of his clan began to cheer. Wowoka's warriors spontaneously joined them. Moved by the outpouring of emotion, Tokanosh stepped forward to help his brother support the injured leader. As Ohanko gratefully accepted the help, he whispered into Wowoka's ear.

"In my dream there was a wretched-smelling bear that had his arms around me like I was a baby." After a glance at Tokanosh, he added, "I have a feeling that was not a dream." Now it was Wowoka's turn to smile.

*S*tanding between the two brothers, Ohanko raised his hand to signal for quiet. The crowd responded immediately and he began.

"To all of you I offer my deepest thanks and highest regard. The finest warriors I have ever known stand before me, and before them stands an arrogant fool.

"I am humbled by my mistakes in judgment both on and off the battlefield. Here, holding me up when I least deserve it is a great man and an even better chief. Through my failings, we were defeated in our challenge, but he has offered us his home. I looked down upon him, but he treated me with dignity and respect. And when I fell, he picked me up. I have learned much from him. From this day forward he will have my friendship and allegiance.

"We have been invited to stay here and I graciously accept. As you witnessed, a sign was given to us and we will heed that sign. Our tribes will become one and Wowoka will lead us in all matters that concern both families. My people will obey his commands as if given by me, and I will serve him in any manner he requests.

"And, last but by far not least, I would like to apologize to

Wowoka's daughter, Sha'kona. I was cruel to her and she saved my life with courage and marksmanship that shames even me. In the future I will be extremely careful who I call a 'scrawny little girl'." Ohanko beamed at her and the now united families laughed and applauded.

When the noise stopped, it was Wowoka's turn.

"I extend my own and my tribe's friendship to Ohanko and his family and welcome you to your new home. It is my wish that we share our traditions and this land's bounty. We will learn from each other so that together we are stronger than we were apart. May the Great Spirit bless this union.

"To commemorate this day, at the end of our harvest we will hold our first celebration as one tribe. We have much to be thankful for."

The cheers grew louder than ever and random conversations broke out everywhere as strangers got to know each other, taking their first steps down the road to true friendships. Enapay and some of the men brought Ohanko back to his tent. He would need much rest and constant care before he would heal completely and return to normal.

Whatever that was.

*W*owoka turned to Sha'kona and reached out to take her hand.

"Could I have the pleasure of your company? I would love a little father daughter time with you before you are all grown up. We don't seem to get much of that anymore and there is so much I want to talk to you about."

Their moment was interrupted before it began.

"Sha'kona, Sha'kona! Did you really shoot one of Dad's hunting arrows and kill two giant buffalo stone cold dead with one shot from the other side of the valley while riding backwards on Tasunke in the middle of a stampede?" Kewa was still in his war paint and buzzing like a swarm of bees. The story of her exploits had grown with each telling and was fast attaining mythical proportions.

"Kewa, calm down!" Wowoka laughed. "You and your sister can stay up all night going over every detail of the story if you wish, but right now I want a few minutes alone with her, if you don't mind. Besides, I need someone I can depend on to watch out for our warriors returning with the rewards of the hunt. That's an important job, but I think you are just the man to do it." As he made his wishes known, he tousled his son's hair.

"You can depend on me!" Kewa declared with authority. "I'll come and get you as soon as I see them. Sha'kona, Sha'kona did you hear that? He called me a man!" Ecstatic at his new status and responsibility, he skipped off, pretending he was riding his horse, firing deadly hunting arrows at an imaginary buffalo.

"Now, maybe we will get a chance to actually have a conversation. Let's walk. I could use some time to relax and I can't think of a better person to spend it with than you." It was clear that the Great Chief was looking forward to a few moments with his daughter.

"You have brought great pride to me and our whole clan. Your guidance has brought us to a New World and a new life with unlimited possibilities. I thank you for that." Wowoka was speaking from his heart. "All of the extraordinary gifts you have been given are well beyond my comprehension but I do know they are a heavy burden for someone so young. Remember, you do not have to carry it alone. I am always here for you to lean on and confide in. You have my love, my trust and my support."

Sha'kona let go of his hand and started to sob uncontrollably. Her father had never seen her break down like this.

"What is wrong?" he asked.

"You can't trust me." She could no longer hold back the truth she had been hiding. "I disobeyed you and lied to you by not telling you what I did." She could barely speak. "I saw Ohanko's son after you told me not to." Unable to look at her father, her eyes were glued to the ground.

Wowoka was shocked speechless. For what seemed like an eternity to Sha'kona, he remained silent. When he finally spoke, he carefully chose his words.

"I am more disappointed than you could know. I expected more from you. I am not only your father, I am your chief. You have dishonored me with another chief's son, making me seem weak and foolish. Who could respect a leader who cannot control his own family? I will take into consideration the pressure you have been under, and all of the good you have done, but you have betrayed me and our tribe. You must be punished in a way that will ensure you never forget your mistake."

Sha'kona raised her head. The expression on her father's face was one she had not seen before and did not want to see again. No physical act could ever cause that much pain.

"I have seen how you stare at that boy and was about to tell you that you could spend time with him if that is where your heart led you. That will not be. From this day forward, you are never to speak to him or be alone with him. I will make sure Ohanko knows that is my command. Go find your mother and tell her what you have done."

Wowoka's voice was as hard as stone. He walked away without ever looking back.

*W*owoka would not have much time to reflect on his daughter's behavior.

"Dad, Dad, they're back! With two humongous buffaloes. I mean humongous! There must be a thousand horses dragging them. I did my job like a grown-up warrior. I saw them before anybody else. You won't believe it when you see the size of those things!" Kewa was his usual overexcited self.

"I actually got pretty close to both of those humongous things," Wowoka replied. "Come with me and let's go check them out."

Father and son headed to the center of the village where there was already a beehive of activity surrounding the returning hunters and the two carcasses. The men were being given a hero's welcome and brought up-to-date with the news of the united tribes while the women of both families came together to work on the freshly killed game.

They would make sure no part of the animals was wasted, meticulously separating and preparing the meat, skin and bones to be used for food, clothing, shelter and tools. Some of the flesh would be eaten fresh, but most would be cut up and dried in the sun to make buffalo jerky. This preserved meat would feed them throughout the next winter.

Tanning the hides was a laborious process. After a thorough cleaning, they would be soaked in water to soften them. A mixture of some of the animals' organs, fat and soapweed would then be rubbed into the skins. Next would come stretching, drying and finally, smoking over wood chips to keep them soft and give them different colors. It could take weeks to complete the arduous task, but that was a small price to pay for the end result - warm, almost indestructible clothing and rain and wind-proof coverings for their homes.

Nothing was thrown away. The horns and bones were used for tools and eating utensils, the sinew for ropes, sewing thread and strings for their hunting bows, and the coarse hair for brushes and clothing ornamentation. Even the animal's dung, known as buffalo chips, was dried and used for cooking fuel and fertilizer.

As they worked, the women prayed for the buffalo, thanking it for giving its life as part of the circle of life. They honored that gift by using every bit of the sacred animal.

Sha'kona worked hard all summer tending crops and taking care of the animals. The busier she stayed, the better, because it kept her mind occupied. The last thing she wanted was time to think about what she had done and what it had cost her. Seeing Enapay almost every day and not being able to speak to him or even acknowledge his existence reinforced that lesson in the harshest of ways. She had hoped the longer she didn't talk to him the easier it would become and the less she would think about him. That wasn't the case. It got worse and she thought about him more.

Her mother gave her regular talks about how she was changing into a woman and what that meant and about boys and her future. Every time one of those discussions began, Sha'kona would cringe. It was too much for her to deal with. She just wanted to be left alone. For a while her parents never let her out of their sight, but as the season wore on, they became preoccupied with other things and stopped watching her every move.

There was one good thing. Her "other eyes" had stayed closed since the hunt. Every time they opened she was faced with more responsibilities and some catastrophe. She was still trying to figure out what all of the things Wa'kanda told her meant. That alone was enough to give her a headache. People called what she had "gifts," a funny name for something that took so much from her.

*S*uddenly the harvest was upon them. The leaves on the trees glowed with the burgundy and golden hues of fall. Cool breezes from the north brought with them the fresh, crisp scents of the changing season. It was time to reap the rewards of their labors. After weeks of hard work by both families, they were blessed by the incredible riches of Mother Earth. There were beans, squash, potatoes, tomatoes, sweet potatoes, pumpkins, artichokes, sunflowers, wild rice and herbs of every kind. And of course, corn, the amazing new crop that would be a staple of their diet from then on.

After much anticipation, it was time for the First Celebration. There was electricity in the air as the tribes prepared for the festivities. Besides giving thanks for the bounty of the harvest, tonight they would officially become one nation.

"*H*ey, Lady Buffalo Killer, why aren't you getting ready?" Chepi asked as she bounded into Sha'kona's home, her usual bundle of energy. Sha'kona was lying on the floor staring at the ceiling, still in her everyday clothes. Her cousin was wearing her best leggings and top and enough jewelry for half the women in the family.

"I don't think I'm going. And stop calling me that. I'm trying to forget that day." Sha'kona had no desire to go to the celebration. She had spent the whole summer avoiding Enapay. Being at a party that close to him and not even being able to say hello would be torture.

"Oh yes you are!" Chepi commanded. "You spent the whole summer either moping around or with that dumb horse of yours. I know you are upset at yourself and heartbroken, not a good combination, but you have to get over it and move on. You can't be miserable for the rest of your life." She was on a roll, and kept it going.

"Now get up and get ready. You need to have some fun and stop pining away for Mr. Cute Son-of-the-Chief. You made a mistake. So what? It won't be your last. Beating yourself up for it isn't going to make anything better. There will be plenty of boys there tonight fawning all over you. I need you there. If you go, I might just get lucky enough to have one of your castoffs look at me!

"There is one more thing I have to ask. Just between you, me and this tent, have you really not spoken to 'what's his name' at all, not even a quick hello? You know you can tell me; wild buffalo couldn't drag it out of me. My lips are sealed." Chepi sat down on the floor next to her cousin intent on getting an answer.

"I can't believe you asked me that!" Sha'kona bit back. "Absolutely not! And if I had, I wouldn't tell you. You couldn't keep your mouth shut if you were the last person on earth with nothing to talk to but a clump of dirt! And his name is Enapay!" She sat up, clearly annoyed.

"You really are in a bad mood. That was cruel." Chepi was hurt. "You are my best friend and I would never do or say anything that could get you in trouble. Since you came back from the hunt I haven't bothered you or asked you to tell me anything about what went on that day. You know how hard that was for me? I'm the nosiest person in the world. Now I ask you one little thing - don't make me go to this feast alone - and you turn me down. If I go alone, I will stay alone."

Sha'kona realized how mean she had just been to her cousin and felt she had to make up for it. She wouldn't let Chepi go by herself.

"You're right. I'm sorry. I'm all mixed up about a lot of things. I'll go, but I'm not dancing!"

"That's what I wanted to hear," Chepi grinned, "except for the 'not dancing' part, but we can deal with that later. By the way, I think you're pretty amazing. Even if you didn't have all those superpowers, I would love you the same, maybe more. Especially if you can help me get a boy to even notice me." Ever resilient, Chepi laughed and pushed Sha'kona over. The gifted girl smiled for the first time in a long while and got up to get dressed for the big event.

*C*aressing the land with the golden glow of sunset, the sun gently bedded down below the horizon. The village was ablaze with activity as final preparations for the festivities were completed. Everyone was wearing their finest clothes and their best attitudes. Even Kewa was dressed for the occasion in his most ornate regalia and a brand new pair of moccasins his sister had helped him make.

Sha'kona and Chepi arrived early at the area in front of the meeting house where the celebration was being held so they could help the rest of the women lay out the meal. They both looked spectacular. Sha'kona was wearing new butter-soft deerskin leggings with a tunic covered in intricate beadwork painstakingly created by her mother. With feathers in her hair and a polished stone and bone choker around her slim neck, she could not have been more radiant. If she couldn't talk to Enapay, at least she could look her best for him.

In the middle of the open space the men had already built a bonfire. The children gathered around it to watch the dancing flames and enjoy the warmth it provided against the brisk night ahead. Bustling with conversation and good cheer, the adults from both families filtered in eager to enjoy the night.

Once everyone was gathered together, Wowoka asked them to form a circle around the fire. He was joined by Ohanko, who had made a miraculous recovery from the injuries he had sustained in the hunt, and Wa'kanda, carrying a bowl of burning sage for the spiritual renewal and cleansing of the tribes. The medicine woman completed her ritual of purification and Wowoka began the opening prayer.

"Thank you, Great Spirit, for all the blessings you have provided and for this opportunity to express our appreciation to you and to each other for all we have been given. Thank you also for the animals that have given their lives for us and for the magic of the tiny seeds from which the great bounty of our harvest has come. May we always remember to honor the Sacred Gifts of Mother Earth and to live in peace and harmony with every living thing. This is a momentous occasion for us all, our first celebration in the New World. We ask that there be many more to come."

After a brief silence, Ohanko spoke.

"I would like to add one thing to the Great Chief's words of wisdom.

"Let's eat!"

There was food everywhere. Copious amounts of buffalo meat and venison were accompanied by equally large quantities of the wide variety of crops the families had grown. Completing the symphony of appetizing delights was an assortment of wild berries and nuts gathered by the children earlier that day.

Everyone ate until they were ready to burst, all agreeing it was the most spectacular meal they had ever eaten. Conversation that was more laughter than speech echoed throughout the festivities, reflecting the mood of the combined families on this special evening. With two notable exceptions, all the members of both tribes were happier than they had been in a very long time.

The large serving bowls were empty and stomachs were full. It was time for the second part of the celebration to start. The crowd grew quiet as Makawee stood and began to tell a story passed down through untold generations of her family. Though they all had heard the fable of the coyotes who danced with the stars many times, her animated delivery was so engaging they sat spellbound, children and adults alike, listening as if it were the very first time the tale had been told. The oral tradition of storytelling was an important part of their culture and you could understand why when someone as enthralling as Makawee practiced it. When she was finished, the audience applauded enthusiastically and begged for more, but the storytelling was over.

The high point of the night had arrived. A huge drum made of buffalo hide stretched across a circular cedar-wood frame was positioned near the fire. Four of the best drummers took their places around the instrument and pounded out a deceptively simple beat, like rhythmic thunder under the autumn sky. With distinctive vocal stylings featuring unique chant-like melodies and emotional glissandos, they sang a song about the hunt that had brought both tribes together.

As the music played, two men wearing buffalo heads mimicked the moves of the sacred animals on that fateful day before the summer began. They were joined by twenty more men, including Enapay, portraying the hunters of the two clans. In an exquisitely choreographed performance, the hunters followed the hunted in a circle around the fire, depicting in expressionistic detail every emotion and action of the warriors and their prey. Their movements were at once graceful yet powerful, the story clearly conveyed with passion and reverence.

As the tempo became faster, the dancers stomped their feet harder and harder on the earthen floor, raising a dust cloud - and the heartbeats of all who watched. By the climax of the presentation, sweat was pouring off the faces and down the backs of the dancers, their physical power outdone only by the strength of their spirit.

The end of the dance brought a totally unexpected response.

There was only silence as the memories of the events that had just been reenacted were honored. The lives of everyone there had been changed for the better by the unanticipated outcome of the challenge. It had begun with two tribes divided, and ended in a call for unity from the Great Spirit. That call had been delivered by the sacred white buffalo through the mouth of the young girl warrior. Tonight it would be answered.

Suddenly the silence was shattered by a spontaneous outburst of cheers and jubilation. Hugs and handshakes were exchanged as emotions ran high over what was soon to come.

Wowoka was thrilled. He took his responsibilities as a leader very seriously. The reactions he was witnessing showed him he was performing that role better than he had thought possible. He was his own worst critic, so this was deeply satisfying.

Tokanosh was on the ground next to his brother playing with Mingan and the other dogs, seemingly oblivious to everything going on around him. Wowoka looked down at him with an ear-to-ear grin.

"Next time I am going to make it an official command that you have to dance. That would be worth paying for!" the Great Chief teased.

"And I would officially disappear into the mountains for a few years. I would rather fight a black bear barehanded than dance one step," Tokanosh replied gruffly as he fed scraps to his pups. "I have my own tribe right here. We would be quite happy alone in the wilderness."

"I think you love those dogs more than you love yourself. I'm sure they would like to see their master do a little fancy dance. They need a good laugh," Wowoka quipped.

"Ha, ha! Very funny. You're just jealous. Now why don't you leave us alone and go do your chief thing. Don't you have some boring speech to give?" Tokanosh liked it when he and his brother teased each other. It reminded him of when they were young boys and the biggest pressure was getting home before sundown.

"It will probably be boring to you because it's over your head. If you don't understand it, ask your canine friends to explain it to you." Wowoka walked away, a bounce in his step, a smile on his face.

He was about to give the most important address of his life.

"Sha'kona, did you see that boy dancing behind your Enapay?" Chepi was giddy with excitement. "He is cute! I've seen him around but really didn't pay much attention. I thought he was a little roly-poly for a warrior, but seeing him out there was something else. He has got some moves! Oh, and did I mention how cute he is? I'm in love!"

"First of all, he's not 'my Enapay,'" Sha'kona snapped back. "And second, you are boy crazy. Don't you ever think of anything else? I have no idea who was cute or not. I wasn't paying attention to that." All night she had been in a cranky mood.

"How could you? Your eyes were glued on Mr. Perfect Smile. I thought they were going to pop out of your head." It was Chepi's turn to speak her mind. "You have got to stop. You know what your dad said. Unless you have a death wish, you need to get him out of your brain. Though I have to admit, he is a looker."

"You're probably right. I just don't know how to do that."

Sha'kona sounded defeated. "By the way, I did notice the boy next to Enapay. He's not so 'roly-poly' as you called him. Actually, I think he looks pretty good, and he can really dance. What are you going to do about it?"

"Nothing, as usual, except dream. I'm not like you. Boys don't notice me. I know I'm kind of plain and I'm all right with that," Chepi stated matter-of-factly.

"That is such nonsense. You are beautiful with the best personality in our family. You're just a little shy with people you don't know very well. Once somebody gets to know you, they love you.

"I may not be able to talk to Enapay, but that doesn't mean I can't help you meet your Mr. Wonderful, to borrow an expression from you. I've got a plan." For the first time that night, the lights were on in Sha'kona's eyes.

The two girls walked arm in arm toward where Wowoka was getting ready to speak. Sha'kona finally felt she understood the words of the sacred white buffalo. Though Enapay might not ever be able to tell her, he had given his heart to her as she had to him. The price fate demanded was that they would never be together.

She would just have to accept that.

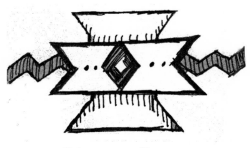

## Chapter Seven

# The Spirit of One

"And while I stood there I saw more than I can tell, and I understood more than I saw; for I was seeing in a sacred manner the shapes of things in the spirit, and the shape of all shapes as they must live together like one being."

~~ Black Elk ~~

*W*owoka and Ohanko stood before both families. They had all traveled a long road to be here. When they left their homes in the old world, they could never have predicted that this would be their destiny. Over the summer a deep respect had grown between the two leaders that flowed down through their tribes. The bond that had developed was about to be made official.

Wowoka began with a prayer as he always did.

"Thank you, Great Spirit, for this time of communion and for guiding us on the arduous journey that brought us all here. We celebrate the joining of our two families into one. Though many in number, from this day forward we will be of one mind, one heart and one spirit. We ask that you bless this union that it may last as long as there are stars in the sky and that forever we may live and prosper as one people, with honor, dignity, wisdom and respect."

Ohanko had brought with him a smoking pipe made from the bones of the buffalo that nearly killed him. The fragile creation was ornately decorated with painted images and colorfully dyed feathers hanging from its stem. With two hands Ohanko carefully presented the beautifully crafted implement to Wowoka and together they held it as the Dark Chief spoke.

"This sacred buffalo pipe will be a symbol of our unity, that from now until the end of time we will be one tribe. It will bind us together, healing our differences and renewing our resolve. We will embrace and defend with all of our being this new nation that we have become. May this pipe represent all the blessings and responsibilities this union brings.

"I say these words and these words are true."

Ohanko concluded by filling the bowl of the pipe with dried leaves from the sacred tobacco plant and passing it to Wowoka. Wowoka lit the tobacco with a burning branch from the fire, placed the stem of the pipe in his mouth and drew in the smoke. He handed it back to Ohanko who did the same. From this day forward tobacco would only be used as a part of this very special ceremony.

The two chiefs exhaled and together raised the pipe high above their heads for all to see. Their eyes were closed in reverence and gratitude and to conceal the tears of joy they had both begun to cry.

Wowoka opened his eyes and spoke once more. "Our first official act as this new nation will be a social dance where we can show our Spirit of One. I want everyone to take part, including my beloved brother Tokanosh."

Everyone laughed except for Tokanosh, who just scowled and went back to playing with his dogs.

---

"*L*isten, girl, here's your big chance," Sha'kona said. "We've got to get you into Mr. Wonderful's dance circle. As good as you move, he will definitely notice you." She grabbed Chepi's hand and dragged her toward where the boy and his friends were engaged in animated conversation.

"Are you insane? What are you doing?" Chepi demanded. "He will never ask me to dance with them. And if he did, I wouldn't know what to say."

"Just leave it to me. All you have to do is be your normal amazing self. I'll take care of the rest." Sha'kona was on a mission.

Her cousin wasn't convinced. "This is so embarrassing. If he ignores me in front of everybody I will just die."

Sha'kona wasn't hearing it. She marched Chepi up to the group of boys and stood right in front of her cousin's heartthrob.

"I am Sha'kona, buffalo slayer and daughter of the Great Chief, Wowoka. This is my cousin, Chepi, a warrior and incredible dancer in her own right. My father thinks she should dance with you. What is your name?"

Chepi was mortified and the boy stunned. He had never met a girl so forward.

"I, um, I am, um, um, Niichaad," he stammered.

"All right, then. I'll leave you two to get to know each other and have a good time. Remember, I will be watching," Sha'kona declared emphatically and walked away. Chepi watched her go with eyes full of hate. Niichaad didn't know what had hit him.

"*W*here are you going, daughter? Come over here. I want to talk to you," Wowoka called out over the noise of the crowds. With him were Ohanko and Enapay.

Sha'kona froze. What had she done now? And why was Enapay with them? Her father wouldn't dare add insult to injury and shame her in front of the Dark Chief and his son, would he? She lowered her head and forced herself to go to them.

"I have something important to tell you," Wowoka began. "Ohanko and I have been talking and have decided we must make an important change concerning our children."

She looked up. Both chiefs were grinning. Enapay looked completely baffled. She was confused. What was this about?

"In the spirit of unity," Wowoka went on, "and new beginnings, we feel you both have paid the price for your mistakes. You deserve a chance to get to know each other. If that is still what you want, we would like to properly introduce you two and give our blessings to your spending time together as the traditions of our people allow. It is a good thing that the children of two chiefs are interested in each other."

Sha'kona couldn't believe what she was hearing.

"Wowoka, with your permission I would like to introduce my only son, Enapay to your daughter," Ohanko added in a most formal manner. He took his befuddled son by the shoulders and moved him face to face with Sha'kona.

"You have my consent," the Great Chief replied, with equal formality. "And may I introduce my only daughter, Sha'kona, whose reputation surely precedes her, to your son."

Neither one of their children said anything. They just stood and stared at each other.

Ohanko spoke again.

"With that done, both of you go enjoy the dance. Wowoka and I have some business to attend to. And don't thank us all at once!" Ohanko put his arm over Wowoka's shoulder and they strolled off, relishing the moment.

*T*ime stopped as Sha'kona and Enapay just stood there, awkwardly looking at each other. It wasn't until their fathers were far away that Enapay broke the uncomfortable silence.

"That was a little weird. I think I may have liked it better when they were enemies," he commented nervously and waited for her to respond. He didn't have to wait long.

"It was weird," Sha'kona agreed and stopped mid-thought.

It was happening again. What was it about being around this boy that made it impossible for her to put two sentences together that made sense? She was either mute or letting crazy things come out of her mouth. While she had not been allowed to speak to him she had thought almost incessantly about what she wanted to say. Now that she was with him, her mind was a complete blank.

Sha'kona turned to look at all of the people laughing and carrying on and wished she could hide away in that crowd right now. This would be a perfect time to hop on Tasunke and ride off into the night. If Enapay didn't think she was an idiot before, he certainly must be convinced now.

She had to say something.

"Um, fun party," she forced, grimacing as soon as she said it.

Great, she thought. She had been waiting all these months

to spill her heart out, and that was the best she could come up with? Pathetic.

Enapay wasn't doing much better. He took a deep breath.

"Yes it is. And, um, you look beautiful," he fumbled, then recovered. "Do you feel as clumsy and bumbling as I do right now? I have waited what feels like forever to talk to you and now that I can, all I'm doing is standing here staring at you like a fool. I guess I'm still shocked by what our fathers just did. My dad is getting stranger every day. Ever since he nearly died he's been a different person, happy all the time. And he never leaves me alone. He wants to spend every free moment with me. Before, he never even noticed me. I'm not sure which I like better."

Now Enapay suddenly stopped speaking.

"What is wrong with me?" he complained, shaking his head. "First I don't know what to say and then I can't shut up. I'm sorry."

They were quiet for a moment and then both of them started to laugh.

"We are some pair!" Sha'kona declared. "I feel as ridiculous as you do. My mouth seems to freeze up, along with my brain. I mean, it went from my dad saying I could never speak to you as long as I lived, to having his blessings to spend time with you – all in a heartbeat without any warning. A bit of a shock, as you said."

The butterflies in Sha'kona's stomach were beginning to land.

"It's really good to be able to talk to you, even if we don't," she said with a grin.

"Maybe we shouldn't try yet. Would you like to join the dance?" Enapay asked and then smiled that smile.

Sha'kona finally knew exactly what to say.

"Yes. Yes I would."

*C*hepi and Niichaad were not off to the best start. Sha'kona had basically shoved her cousin down his throat with that nonsense about how her father had ordered Mr. Wonderful to dance with her. And what was that, "Chepi is a warrior and an incredible dancer" about? The only battle she ever had was putting her knee-high moccasins on when her feet were swollen. Talk about pressure. No wonder he was standing there like a bump on a log. Somebody had to take charge or this was going to be a disaster. Chepi knew who that somebody was going to be.

"Listen, Niichaad," Chepi began, not knowing where she would end up. "Neither one of us wants to be here right now, but, apparently, for some unknown reason, it's the Great Chief's orders that I dance in your circle. Otherwise, he is going to throw you to the wild dogs or something like that. So let's make the best of it and get it over with quick."

Niichaad's jaw dropped. He had heard all of the stories about the Great Chief and didn't doubt for a moment what she said was true. If he didn't want to end up as dog food, he was going to have to do something.

Girls were not his specialty. He didn't understand them at all. The few times he had even tried to start up a conversation he had failed miserably. Just this summer he had run into a girl from the Great Chief's family out under the trees near the cornfields. She was really pretty and there was no one else around, so he thought he should be

189

polite and at least say something. So what did he say?

"Nice weather."

That's right, "Nice weather." Which would have been fine except that it was pouring rain that afternoon! That's why she was under the trees - to keep from getting wet. She laughed and made some comment about how he should go talk to a rock, it would be more his level. That was the way it was for him with girls.

Like it or not, he had to try. Hopefully the results would be better than being torn to bits by that big guy Tokanosh's wolves.

"So, uh, uh, do you, um, uh, l-l-l-live around here?" Niichaad asked and immediately recoiled in horror. He had done it again. Of course, she lived around here. Where else would she live? In the lake? He had already blown it. He could just about feel the wild dogs' jaws clamping on his legs.

Chepi wasn't sure how to answer that. She almost felt sorry for the poor boy. He stuttered and stammered and fidgeted and was shyer than anyone she had known, except maybe her uncle. But he was cute in his own way and he was trying. It wasn't like she was doing much better.

She could sympathize with how he was feeling. This whole situation was as uncomfortable as a wool coat in the summer. Niichaad had practically been threatened with his life if he didn't dance with her. That was certainly a romantic way to meet someone.

Chepi's stomach was doing flip flops. She would like to believe it was because of something she ate, but she knew better. She decided not to address how ludicrous the question was. He meant well.

"Yes, I live right there next to our meeting house. It's the highest place in the village so I have a great view when I wake up,"

Chepi answered, sweeter than honey. "I'm sorry about my cousin being so pushy. You know how it is with girls who go around killing buffalo." She had just topped Niichaad in the stupid conversation category. What was she talking about? Why did boys make her act so crazy? Especially this one.

"Uh, uh, that's, um, alright." Niichaad stumbled. "I-I-I-I don't care too m-m-m-much about hunting. I-I-I prefer, um, uh, fishing and farming. And, of course, um, uh dancing. She s-s-seems awfully thin to be a, um, um uh, warrior. You look m-m-m-more like a warrior. A really pretty warrior. I l-l-like how you look, um, uh, better."

Had she just heard right? Had this cute boy, excuse me, this very cute boy, just called her pretty? Prettier than Sha'kona? Either he was blind or she had found the boy of her dreams.

"That is the sweetest thing anybody has ever said to me. Thank you," Chepi said, suddenly much more interested in him. "I don't like hunting either but I do like fishing. I don't care if I catch anything, I like relaxing by the water and daydreaming. By the way, you are an amazing dancer."

"I l-l-like daydreaming too," Niichaad replied. "And I play the flute and make p-p-paintings on the boulders in the w-w-woods. Maybe one day I c-c-could show you."

Unless Chepi was terribly mistaken, for the first time in her life, a boy had asked her to do something with him, something really special. And not just any boy, Mr. Wonderful, as Sha'kona called him.

How should she answer? She prayed that she wouldn't put her foot in her mouth.

"I would like that. I paint a little. I did the designs on some of the serving bowls we used tonight. I'm not great at it but I enjoy it." Her feet were still in her moccasins. Chepi was actually enjoying being with Niichaad. He was easy to talk to.

"They all looked beautiful. Will you show me which ones you did?" he asked, with real interest. "But before you do, would you like to dance with me? It's alright if you don't want to, but I would be honored if you did."

Niichaad had asked her to dance. And he hadn't stuttered once. Chepi felt something flutter in her chest.

"I-I-I would love to." Now she was stammering.

And she couldn't have been happier about it.

*The* two leaders returned to their place by the fire feeling good about what they had just done. Their joy was multiplied by the happiness surrounding them. There were not many days like this in a chief's life. Usually they were filled with never-ending problems that needed to be resolved. Even now there were issues Wowoka and Ohanko had to discuss.

"We should talk about how we intend to govern this new nation. We must come up with a plan that will make everyone happy," Wowoka began. The concept of unity was simple, the practice a lot more challenging.

"I don't think it is possible to please everyone. The best we can hope for is that more people like what we come up with than do not," Ohanko countered, clearly feeling the weight of his responsibilities. "I meant what I said back at the lodge about you leading all of our people. I will be at your right hand for whatever you need."

"I gratefully accept that position, but I have an idea I would like to put forth that may help keep this union strong," Wowoka replied. "I propose that every adult have a say in the important decisions we will have to make as we move forward. We can meet regularly in the lodge and our people can each cast their vote on those matters. This way, everyone will have a say. It will be our duty to make sure the decisions of the majority are carried out."

Ohanko thought for a minute, letting this proposal sink in. After a while he commented.

"Your idea is brilliant. It may take our people a little time to get used to it, but in the end it will solve many problems and keep us as one strong nation. We should bring this to our people tomorrow. Tonight should be for fun."

Wowoka was quick with his response.

"Let's hope we handle our new government better than we do our own children!" he said, and in a gesture of friendship, embraced Ohanko.

Ohanko always liked to have the last word.

"It is sometimes easier and safer to go into battle than to raise a child."

Wowoka could not disagree.

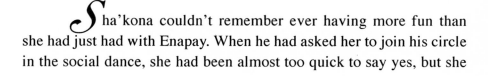

*S*ha'kona couldn't remember ever having more fun than she had just had with Enapay. When he had asked her to join his circle in the social dance, she had been almost too quick to say yes, but she certainly didn't regret it now. He had taken her by the hand to escort her and the same lightning bolt that had hit her the last time she was with him struck again. She had never held hands with a boy before. Her knees got weak, but she wasn't afraid like before.

This was definitely unfamiliar territory. She wasn't sure how to deal with all of these new feelings, but she would take it slow and learn. Running away was not an option.

It looked like things had worked out with Chepi and Niichaad as well. It was hard not to notice - everyone was looking at them. They were by far the two best dancers out there. Sha'kona tried to get Chepi's attention to ask how things were going, but her cousin and Mr. Wonderful only had eyes for each other. They were both beaming from head to toe. That was all the answer Sha'kona needed. She couldn't wait until after the celebration when she would find out everything from Chepi in a late night girls' talk.

With absolutely no help from her "other eyes," Sha'kona had seen a very special kind of magic happen tonight.

Once the dance was over, Sha'kona and Enapay stayed close to each other, talking about everything and nothing. The more time she spent with him, the better it got. The only subject they had avoided was the choices they had made at the beginning of the summer that had nearly ended their relationship before it began and caused such agonizing problems with their families.

Enapay must have been reading her mind. He walked her away from the noisy crowd to the entrance of the meeting house and took her hands in his.

"I want to apologize to you for my behavior when we first met," he stated with deep remorse.

"There is no need to apologize," she asserted.

"Please, let me finish," Enapay continued. "I showed total disrespect to you and my father when I disobeyed his command not to see you or speak to you. I was being selfish.

"From the moment I saw you behind that bush, I wanted to get to know you. All I did was think about you. I put my wants above doing what was right and asked you to join me in my bad judgment. Because of my actions, we both got into serious trouble with our families and might not have been able to see or speak to each other again. I have learned a lot from this experience and will never make those same mistakes. I am truly sorry and ask for your forgiveness."

Enapay's eyes did not leave hers as he spoke and she hung on his every word, the guilt and sorrow painfully obvious. His humble honesty was a beacon to her heart, beckoning her to come closer. She had thought time would have caused her feelings to wane, but, in fact, they had only gotten stronger. He had opened up to her like no one had ever done and what she saw was better than she had thought possible. Why their fathers had finally allowed the two of them to be together was a mystery to her, despite what they had said, but it was a mystery for which she would be eternally grateful.

It was time for Sha'kona to be really truthful. She didn't have to think about what she was going to say.

"It was all my fault, Enapay," she stated in a way that made it clear that for her this was the fact of the matter. "If I had obeyed my father, none of this would've happened. I had never gone against his will before that. I am ashamed of my behavior. I made a choice, a bad choice. No matter how much I wanted to see you I should not have done what I did. I compromised my principles and as a result, I let down my father, myself, and you too. I was responsible and I paid the price." Her eyes began to water so she looked down to conceal the oncoming tears.

"When I confessed to my father, I accepted my punishment as well deserved," Sha'kona said, no longer trying to hide that she was crying. "But when he said he was going to tell your father, I was devastated. I knew that would cause big problems for you and that wasn't what I wanted. I would never do anything to hurt you. I am so sorry."

"We can agree that it was on both our shoulders," Enapay added. "You didn't cause me any problems. As soon as we got my father back to our tent after he was injured, I told him everything. I couldn't live with myself lying to him. He was not happy. Besides not being able to speak to you, he took away Achak. I don't have to tell you how that felt."

"I had no idea. I feel even worse." Sha'kona wiped her eyes, determined to stay strong. "That's all behind us now. We have to look to the future. What has happened with our tribes becoming one nation is pretty amazing. It means we don't have to worry about ever being separated."

As she made the last comment, she realized how forward she was being and quickly added, "I mean if we don't want to be."

"I don't want to be. I owe you a lot. Thank you."

"What do you mean? What do you owe me for?" Sha'kona asked, puzzled.

"First of all for saving my father's life," Enapay answered. He held her hands tighter. "And second, for being you."

The butterflies soared. Sha'kona felt suddenly dizzy, almost like her "other eyes" were taking over, but they weren't. And he hadn't even smiled.

"Enapay, I am really happy. Thank you for that." She was glowing. This had turned into a perfect evening. And to think, she almost hadn't come.

Everyone was starting to leave. Sha'kona didn't want the night to end, but it was that time.

"It's getting late," she said softly and squeezed his hands. "Would you mind walking me home?"

"I would be honored," came his reply. She put her arm in his and they headed toward her house.

Sha'kona had been so afraid that the sacred white buffalo's prediction about the price she would pay for Enapay's heart would come true. For once her "other eyes" had been wrong.

And wrong could not have been more right.

## Chapter Eight

# The Enlightened Time

"It is no longer good enough to cry peace, we must act peace, live peace and live in peace."

-- Shenandoah --

*T*hroughout that autumn the union of the two tribes kept proving itself even more successful than anyone had imagined or hoped for. Friendships were made and bonds formed as they prepared for the first winter in their new home.

Even Tokanosh met someone without four legs and a tail who he didn't mind being around and with whom he actually almost enjoyed having a conversation. One of the elders from the other family was an eccentric character who lived alone except for the twelve canine companions who were always with him. What had impressed Tokanosh was the fact that the old man had taught his dogs all kinds of useless but highly amusing tricks, like dancing on their hind legs or fetching a neighbor's moccasins. The two men and their twenty friends whiled away many hours in pursuit of what seemed like the silliest animal behavior possible.

The rest of the nation had more serious tasks to attend to.

The dwellings for Ohanko's tribe were well on their way to being completed, using new construction techniques developed by the joint workforce. Called tipis, they were cone-shaped tents built from ten to twenty poles, depending on how big they were going to be, covered with buffalo hides and lined with deerskin. An opening in the top allowed those living there to cook and heat the space with an open fire without smoking themselves out.

The Dark Chief had wanted to have homes that could be moved if for some reason he wanted to change locations, like to follow the bison when they migrated. Portable, yet as solid and secure as the permanent structures in the village, these tents satisfied his wish. Led by Niichaad and Chepi, a team of the best artists painted the outsides with their own original designs inspired by each family's unique history and journeys.

Meanwhile, the women busied themselves with work that had to be completed before the snow began. Some of them made new cold weather clothing and boots, also from the hides of the tatanka. These hides were warmer and more durable than anything they had used before. Others, following Makawee's direction, were getting food ready to last throughout the cold season. Most of the fruits and vegetables and all of the different meats were sun-dried to keep them from spoiling in the months to come when fresh food might not be readily available. The root vegetables, like potatoes and carrots, were placed in earthenware containers filled with wool to absorb excess moisture. Everything would have to be stored in a cool dry place to protect it from the elements and keep it safe from the winter-starved animals that prowled incessantly in search of something to eat.

The new government was overwhelmingly approved and supported by all. Wowoka was a wise and compassionate leader and Ohanko, with his down-to-earth, no-nonsense approach to everything, was the perfect counterpart. The right of everyone to have a voice and a vote in all of the major decisions that were made was embraced by everyone and was probably the biggest contributor to the sense of unity the nation enjoyed.

*F*rom decorating the tipis to endless walks at the end of each long day, Chepi and Niichaad were virtually inseparable. She shared with him all she knew about farming and crops. This was a considerable amount of knowledge; her family had tilled the soil for many, many generations. He learned about irrigation, crop rotation and fertilization and most importantly how to care for the land and use it wisely so it would not be damaged or destroyed. Both of them believed, as their people always had, that the land did not belong to them; they were only borrowing it from their children.

Niichaad loved how passionate Chepi was about things. She didn't do anything half-way. When she said she wanted to know how to play the flute, he jumped at the chance to teach her something that was so dear to him. Besides his natural talent as a dancer, something he had in common with Chepi, Niichaad was a gifted musician. She struggled to even make a sound come out at first, but stuck with it and soon, to his absolute delight, showed a real talent for making music.

Not long after Chepi played her first song for him, Niichaad surprised her with a flute he had made especially for her. During one of their nightly walks in the fields beside the lake, he shyly pulled the instrument from inside his coat and handed it to her without saying a word. Along with detailed hand carvings, he had decorated it with an intricate butterfly motif because she reminded him of that elegant creature.

Chepi was flabbergasted. She had never received a gift from a boy and this wasn't just any gift from any boy. It was the most special present she could imagine receiving and it was from her own Mr. Wonderful. Overcome with emotion, she threw her arms around him, nearly knocking him down, and squeezed so hard he knew his ribs were going to crack.

Only one thought popped into Niichaad's head.

As dangerous as it might be, he liked making Chepi happy.

*S*ha'kona could not imagine being happier. The expanded family had become a source of exciting discoveries and positive energy. Every day was filled with new ideas, accomplishments and plans for the future. The two tribes had truly become one, a synergy where the sum was definitely greater than the individual parts.

Enapay had become woven into the fabric of Sha'kona's life, a faithful friend and companion, someone to whom she could reveal her silliest thoughts and most secret dreams. There was nothing she was afraid to confide in him. He in turn had opened up completely to her, confessing his darkest fears and divulging his loftiest hopes. One day he would be a chief. He knew this was his destiny and he wanted to share that future with her.

They spent every free moment together and had even started to think alike. Often they would find themselves completing each other's sentences and then laughing about how ridiculous they sounded. Their joy was contagious. Everyone around them seemed to become infected with their high spirits, peace of mind and sense of purpose. Sha'kona would sometimes lay awake at night, afraid that her life was some kind of bliss-filled dream. But it wasn't. It was a much-needed reality that seemed to provide stability to her "other eyes" experiences.

As the young couple's connection grew stronger, so did Sha'kona's understanding and control of her unique gifts. Little by little their power and depth became evident in her everyday experiences.

Like the morning her mother woke her to let her know Ohanko's niece had gone off to the shore of the lake with her sisters to have her baby. It was hard to believe nine moons had already gone by. Makawee was bubbling over with excitement at the prospect of the first child born into the new nation; it was a special blessing on that union. She was also extremely curious as to the sex of the baby.

"It doesn't really matter if it's a boy or a girl, but it would be wonderful to have a female addition to the population of our tribe," Makawee remarked, making what she wanted quite obvious.

"You will have your wish," Sha'kona responded without any hesitation.

"How do you know that?" her mother asked, somewhat taken aback by her daughter's matter-of-fact manner.

"I'm not exactly sure how. I just know, kind of like how great-grandmother knew these things," Sha'kona replied as calmly as if she were telling what she had for dinner the night before.

Sure enough, two days later, the young mother returned to the village with a beautiful baby girl swaddled in her arms. Makawee never questioned her daughter again about her "other eyes."

Sha'kona also seemed to know what the weather was going to be. Once again, she didn't know exactly how it worked, but somehow animals and plants and trees communicated with her. When she was near them or touched them they would let her know all kinds of things, including if it was going to be sunny or raining or windy or still or any of the variations in between. Even what the coming seasons would be like was clear to her.

If any of their livestock were sick or hurt she could sense that too, and knew exactly what to do about it. Sometimes just her presence could heal an animal. Wild creatures would seek her out and accompany her on walks in the woods, as tame and peaceful as any of Tokanosh's dogs - actually, a lot more so. Young children would follow her just to watch in amazement.

The seven eagles had made it a habit to regularly visit her, finding perches on the lowest branches of the trees near her. They especially liked to be around while she groomed Tasunke because then she would speak to them in the same baby talk she used to address her beloved horse. The magnificent birds would flap their wings and cry their unique squeals when she spoke, responding as if they understood every word she said.

Though Sha'kona really didn't want to, she could predict the winner of any of the games the children or adults played, especially Kewa's favorite, bowl and bones. She didn't let anyone know she had that ability for fear no one would ever let her join in. Even though she knew the outcome, she still had fun playing.

These were only a small part of what she was discovering she could do. No longer did these talents frighten her. Instead, she was fascinated and spent as much time as she could trying to master their use. With every new skill Sha'kona discovered, she learned more and more about herself. Enapay would sit and watch in awe as she took control of her journey toward the warrior she was meant to be. He was eternally thankful for every moment.

*I*t was an unusually mild day considering the frost that had coated the land during the night before. Sha'kona was taking advantage of this last remnant of warm weather, sitting outside her home working on a new coat for Kewa. In appreciation for saving his life, Ohanko had given her a large piece of buffalo hide from the animal she defeated in that first hunt and she was using it for her brother's winter wear. The skin was thick and practically indestructible. As hard as her brother was on clothes, she hoped it would last him until spring.

Sha'kona was ready for a break when her mother approached.

"How is your masterpiece coming? You have been at it for quite a while," Makawee commented, appraising the job her daughter was doing.

"It's going slowly. Bison hide is a lot heavier and much more difficult to work with than deerskin but I wanted something that could survive Kewa for an entire winter." Sha'kona stood up and stretched. She had been sitting in the same position since morning and her muscles ached.

"I don't know why you bother," her mother chuckled. "Before you know it, he is going to outgrow what you're making or destroy it. With him, those are the only two options. You could make him a coat out of rocks and he would find a way to wear it out." She was amusing herself more than Sha'kona.

"You're probably right," her daughter agreed, "but I thought I would give it a try anyway. By the way, how is it going with getting all the food ready? I can't believe how much we need to stockpile now that there are so many more of us."

"That's what I wanted to talk to you about." Makawee had shifted into her mom voice. "There is too much to store in the community house. It's almost full now and we still need a lot more space. Plus, your father says we need to be able to use the house this winter for council meetings and voting."

"How can I help? My 'other eyes' are getting better but I don't think they can make the lodge bigger," Sha'kona teased.

Her daughter's gifts were a constant source of amazement to Makawee. She did not think she would ever get used to them. But, right now, Sha'kona's unique abilities were not what she needed.

"I know, Sweet Pea," her mother responded. "That's not what I want to ask you. I don't expect you to move mountains or make the meeting house grow. I was just wondering if you could show me the cave where you found the corn. That might be the perfect spot to keep our food supplies for the winter. Is it nearby?"

"It's a bit of a walk, but not really that far. It's in the woods at the top of the hill where we first met Ohanko. When would you like to see it?" Sha'kona was ready for a change of scenery.

"How about now? I haven't been back to that forest since we got here. It seems I always have one more chore to do here in the village. Let's just go," Makawee said, as eager to leave as Sha'kona.

"Should I get Kewa?" Sha'kona asked, but didn't really want him to come. She was hoping for some time alone with her mother.

"If you don't mind, he can stay home. You and I haven't spent time together by ourselves in quite a while. Let's make it just us girls." Makawee put her arm around her daughter and they started toward the cave.

They were in no hurry. The balmy fall afternoon was perfect

walking weather. As they strolled, the Great Chief's wife thought about how much had happened since they left their old home. They had been truly blessed, especially Sha'kona.

Makawee's little girl was growing up and finally seemed happy. The responsibilities thrust upon Sha'kona during the long journey and after arriving here in this New World had taken their toll on her. She was much too young for that kind of stress.

It was good to see her smiling and laughing again. Her mother knew that Sha'kona's relationship with Ohanko's son played a large part in the young girl's happiness. Ever since Wowoka had rescinded her punishment, their daughter had blossomed. Even her gifts no longer frightened her. She was learning more about them all the time and becoming more comfortable with them as a part of her life.

Makawee realized that for the first time in a long time, she was happy too. She put her arm around Sha'kona, leaned over, and kissed her on the cheek.

"What was that for?" Sha'kona was surprised by her mother's random display of affection, but quite pleased.

"For nothing. And everything," Makawee said wistfully, then continued more upbeat, "How are things with you and Enapay? Like I really need to ask."

"Mom!" Sha'kona moaned, a little unsettled by the question but excited at the same time for the chance to talk about her relationship with the boy. She really hadn't discussed it with anyone but Chepi.

Her mother had never asked about anything so personal before and Sha'kona was unsure about what to say. To her amazement, as soon as she opened her mouth, the words came easily.

"Fine," the young girl said. "Actually, a lot more than fine. As the whole world knows, we had a pretty rocky beginning, but now he has become my best friend. He accepts me just the way I am and is there for me no matter what. He doesn't even think my 'other eyes' are weird. He says they make me stronger and more unique, two important qualities of a great warrior and leader. One day, I hope that's what I will be. So does Enapay."

"I am thrilled for you." Makawee was beaming with pride and joy. "You deserve the best and it seems you have found it in more than just Enapay. You are on your way to becoming an extraordinary woman.

"I don't think I ever told you about how your father and I got together. Our start wasn't that different from yours and Enapay's. When I met Wowoka it was love at first sight for me but not so with my father. He didn't think any man was good enough for me, especially not the ambitious young warrior I had my heart set on. It took a long time for him to finally earn my father's blessing.

"As you know, our Great Chief is quite persistent, some might even say stubborn. He refused to give up and finally got what he wanted. He made me feel special then and still does today. He is not just a great chief, he is a great husband and father. And I am a lucky woman. I have him and he gave me you and your brother."

Sha'kona had never heard her mother speak this way, straight from her heart. She was normally a quiet woman who kept her feelings to herself. The young girl looked at her mother as if for the first time. Makawee was glowing and tears of joy brightened her eyes. Overcome with love, Sha'kona hugged her in a way she had not done before. At that moment, their already strong bond changed forever, and they both understood how amazing that was.

"What was that for?" Makawee asked, already knowing what the answer was.

"As someone special once said, 'For nothing, and everything.' Now let's go find that cave." Sha'kona took her mother's hand and the two of them headed up the hill to the woods. The smiles on their faces lit up the path ahead.

*T*heir destination was further into the woods than Makawee had expected, but well worth the trip. Hidden behind a growth of green ash trees and little bluestem, the mouth of the cave opened into the perfect storage place for their winter cache of food and extra supplies. It was high and dry, filled with wide ledges and nooks and crannies in the solid granite, ideal for keeping their precious goods safe.

"This is exactly what we need." Makawee was thrilled, her mind already racing with plans for where to put everything. "It's a little far to walk, but with the horses it should be no trouble at all."

"I'm so glad you thought of this place," Sha'kona replied. "The only problem I can see is how to get the horses around that huge boulder blocking the trail at the top of the hill. It was hard enough for us to scramble around. The forest is too thick and filled with rocks for even my nimble-footed Tasunke to get through."

"That's what the men are for," her mother declared with a grin. "We will get them up here tomorrow morning and they can move it out of the way. I'm not giving up this spot for a little obstacle like that oversized pebble."

"I don't know if I would call it a pebble," Sha'kona laughed, "but I agree we should ask them to move it. It will make life a lot simpler not to have to find another place as good as this one."

With that settled, mother and daughter headed back to the village. It was the perfect end to a perfect afternoon.

*W*owoka and Tokanosh brought twenty of the strongest men with them to clear the way to the cave. Sha'kona and Makawee were already there, having arrived earlier on foot to start cleaning up the space. Because Ohanko was still not fully recovered, Enapay came in his place. Over the summer, the young warrior's body had filled out and grown solid from all the hard work he had done. He now looked more like a man than a boy.

In the morning light, the boulder appeared a lot bigger to Sha'kona than it had the day before. Makawee was thinking the same thing.

"If this is what you call a pebble, I would hate to see what you call a rock," Tokanosh grumbled to his brother's wife.

The immense chunk of stone stood taller than a man on horseback and was tightly wedged between two massive redwood trees. This was going to be a lot more difficult than any of the men had expected, if they could move it at all.

"Let's all get on the high side and try to push it down the hill. If we can free it from the hold of those trees, it just might roll there on its own," Wowoka suggested. He had grave doubts that his plan would succeed, but it was worth a try.

The braves positioned themselves like an army of ants

attempting to move a mountain. Tokanosh had his back pressed firmly against the enormous piece of granite so he could use his powerful legs to his advantage. Next to him Wowoka leaned his weight on his right shoulder, ready to bear down.

"All right, on three, give it everything you've got!" the Great Chief ordered. "One, two, three! Now!"

Muscles strained and faces contorted as the men exerted every bit of strength in their bodies to try and force the boulder to move. Animal-like grunts and groans accompanied their tremendous effort, but despite how much power they put forth and how hard they tried, the huge rock would not budge.

"This is not going to work. It is much too heavy," Wowoka said. He was covered in sweat. "I have another idea. We will tie ropes to the top of the boulder and attach them to the horses. While they pull, we will use long, thick branches shoved underneath it to lift it up so it can roll freely."

His instructions were rapidly heeded. The horses pulled with all their might as the braves put their weight and more on the ends of the branches, but the giant stone remained immobile. Wowoka signaled for them to stop. It was hopeless.

"I'm afraid this is one battle we are not going to win," Wowoka reported with an air of resignation. "This 'pebble' and the earth are not going to part ways. Makawee, either you figure out another way to bring the horses or find a new storage place. I'm sorry we could not help."

His wife's disappointment was etched into her face.

"Thank you all for your hard work, attempting what appears to be the impossible. I truly appreciate it. It looks like I am running out of options, but I will have to think of something," Makawee stated, clearly concerned.

While she was speaking, Enapay walked over to Sha'kona, wiping the sweat from his brow with the sleeve of his shirt.

"Maybe you can help," the boy whispered in Sha'kona's ear.

"What can I do that twenty of you strong men can't do? My father is right, we have to come up with another solution," she responded.

"Do you remember a few days ago when we were playing bowl and bones and you moved one of the bones without touching it?" he asked, still speaking very quietly.

"Yes, but what has that got to do with this situation?" Sha'kona demanded. "If you think because I was able to make a tiny bone jump out of a bowl I could move that mountain, you are crazy. I'm not even sure how I did it. It just happened, I didn't plan it. I don't believe I could do it again."

"Well, I believe you can do whatever you set your mind to. I believe in you. What's the harm in trying?" As he was talking to her, Enapay reached over and took her hands in his.

Again she had the feeling of being struck by lightning. A surge of power rushed through her body, electrifying her senses. Her skin tingled and she felt her "other eyes" open wide. She looked over at her mother and saw the expression on her face. Suddenly the impossible seemed possible.

Sha'kona let go of Enapay's hands and approached her father. An almost visible aura of intense calm surrounded her.

"Can you please ask everyone to step far away from the

boulder? And back the horses off as well." She addressed her father in a voice that commanded his attention.

"Why do we need to do that? Is something wrong?" the Great Chief asked. He could not help but notice the change in his daughter's countenance.

Sha'kona did not answer. Though he did not understand the reason for her request, Wowoka did as she asked. Once the men and animals had moved away, she closed her eyes and stretched her hands out, palms up, toward the gigantic stone. No one was quite sure what was happening. They all stared in astonishment as a blue glow began to emanate from the young girl's body. The color grew brighter and more profound and started to pulse as though driven by her heartbeat. Without warning, waves of indigo light leapt from her hands and careened toward the huge hunk of granite, crashing into it with incredible force. A sound like summer thunder accompanied each impact. The noise was deafening.

Almost imperceptibly at first, the boulder began to rock back and forth as each swell of iridescent energy struck it. Slowly, the movement increased until the giant stone uprooted itself from the earth and rolled end over end down the hill, finally settling at the bottom in a cloud of dust and debris. The path to the cave was clear.

Silence seized the moment. The blue light vanished and Sha'kona's arms dropped to her sides. She opened her eyes and for a moment was uncertain of what had just transpired. Her confusion was quickly replaced by feelings of satisfaction and accomplishment. Though exhausted by the ordeal, she was not frightened. This time her gifts left her confident and content. She had been in control, not the other way around.

Makawee ran to her daughter's side and took hold of her. Her strength sapped, Sha'kona leaned on her mother for support.

"That was for you, Mom," she said softly. Makawee looked in her daughter's eyes. A beautiful young woman was looking back.

The men recovered from being dumbstruck with awe at what they had just witnessed by erupting in spontaneous cheers and laughter. Though everyone knew of Sha'kona's talents, no one could have ever expected anything like what they had seen take place. This was what legends were made of.

"I want some of whatever you have been eating," Tokanosh announced loudly as he threw his arms around his niece and her mother.

His brother hurried over and embraced all of them.

"I don't know what to say," the Great Chief revealed to his daughter. "In my life I have known many powerful medicine men and women, but I have never seen anything like what you just did. The spirit of your great-grandmother and your great-aunt live on in you. We are all blessed by your gifts and thank you. With that cave as the place we store our supplies, the winter will be much easier. But even more important, you have made your mother a very happy woman and saved her a lot of work." He grinned a big bear grin.

When Wowoka finished speaking, Enapay found his way to Sha'kona and joined the group hug.

"I knew you could do it," he said proudly, finishing his thought with a look Sha'kona understood.

The five of them reluctantly separated and Wowoka helped Makawee onto his horse. He climbed on behind his wife, wrapping one arm affectionately around her.

"Enapay, would you mind giving Sha'kona a ride back to the village?" the Great Chief asked and then took off without waiting for a response. He already knew the answer.

*S*ha'kona and Enapay took their time on the trip home. Achak moved at a very relaxed pace, enjoying the crisp, late morning air and the company of his passengers. The absence of conversation was not at all awkward to Sha'kona, but, instead, rather comforting. With Enapay she did not always have to speak to be heard.

Her fatigue had subsided and in its place an almost euphoric tranquility had set in, complemented by the steady rhythm of the horse's gait. Over the past two days Sha'kona had felt a major change come over her, brought on by the discovery of the miraculous connection between herself and those she cared for. She understood how she was able to move the gigantic boulder and where her gifts came from. The answer had always been right there in front of her eyes.

Sha'kona had found her fourth power.

*Chapter Nine*

## The Medicine Woman's Vision

"Seek wisdom, not knowledge. Knowledge is of the past, wisdom is of the future."

-- Lumbee --

*S*ha'kona heard Migisi calling out to her, repeating over and over again, "Your journey is not over yet, your journey is not over yet. Remember what I have said. You must come with me." The spirit voice was strong and pure, nothing like the frail whisper that had first delivered those words.

Without truly waking, Sha'kona floated from her bed and drifted toward the plaintive cries. Caught in that moment between a dream and waking, she was carried to another place far away where the night sky was filled with majestic stars and electrifying colors swirling in clusters of exaggerated beauty.

She glided deeper and deeper into this surreal space of supernatural vistas endlessly dissolving inside each other. It was like a kaleidoscope of magical possibilities. As one skyscape began its transformation, a cloud as delicate as a snowflake was dragged in front of her on the tail of a turquoise shooting star. From within the diaphanous mist, Migisi appeared.

It was not the Migisi that Sha'kona remembered. This was a stunning young woman with long black hair and deep green eyes filled with life. When she spoke, it was with a calm confidence that Sha'kona had not heard before.

"Come with me child," Migisi implored. "We must go

*eastward again, to where all things are new. It is there you will finally understand your destiny and discover the purpose of your gifts." She took hold of her great-great-niece's hand to lead the way.*

*Sha'kona trusted in Migisi and was eager to follow, but, before their journey could even begin, a ferocious blast of icy wind drove them apart, pushing them in opposite directions with devastating force. Migisi was terrified. In vain she tried to grab hold of the young girl, but Sha'kona slipped away, tumbling head over heels as she flew off into the west.*

*As she sped away, Migisi suddenly morphed into a decrepit, cadaver-like version of Sha'kona. The real Sha'kona recoiled and screamed in horror at this grotesque caricature of herself.*

*"Sha'kona! Come back, please. You must go with me. For all of us!" The apparition pleaded as it crumbled into dust and fell into the void below.*

———

*S*ha'kona snapped out of the dreadful dream drenched in sweat, her heart racing. She had had frighteningly real nightmares before, but nothing like this. To make sure it had only been in her mind, she touched her face. She felt warm smooth skin and breathed a sigh of relief. The ancient, wrinkled Sha'kona and the desperately beautiful Migisi had only been figments of her imagination.

Or had they?

The boundaries of Sha'kona's reality had been shattered so often she no longer was certain of what was real and what was not. Something about Migisi's message rang true, but Sha'kona wanted to forget she had heard it. She was afraid of what it meant. There had been enough challenge and change in her life. All she wanted to do was have the chance to enjoy what she had.

*S*even days had passed since the miraculous turn of events at the cave and the unsettling dream she had experienced that night. She had put the bizarre vision out of her mind. It was too much to think about.

The moving of the boulder was another matter. With that one act, she had come to understand her gifts and have confidence in her powers. She had never felt so alive and she knew why. It had all become clear to her. As of yet she had not told anyone of her discovery, not even Enapay. In the back of her head was the nagging suspicion that if she talked about it there would be consequences she did not want to face.

*A*ll week Sha'kona had been buzzing around like a hummingbird. Nearly every person in the village was begging her to do her "magic" for them. She barely had time to breathe. Women came to her to feel their bellies to find out if they were pregnant. If they were, they wanted to know if it was a boy or a girl. The men wanted her to tell them where the best hunting and fishing would be. Some of them even asked if she could control the animals with her mind to make the conquests easier. That she would not do. And the children asked her to predict the winners of their games. She wouldn't do that either.

Healing was a new talent she had discovered. Most of her time was spent treating the minor illnesses and injuries that seemed to crop up everyday. The more she used her gifts, the better she became at achieving the results she wanted. There were some things she could do more easily than others, but some things she could not do at all. Yesterday her mother had asked her to use her powers to help move the supplies from the meeting house to the cave. Despite having been able to move the giant boulder, Sha'kona had only managed to bounce some squash aimlessly around the village. The children were delighted in the spectacle, but some of the elders who had to seek shelter from the flying vegetables were not so pleased. She would have to work on that particular gift.

The one person she had not seen was Wa'kanda. It wasn't that Sha'kona was exactly avoiding the medicine woman, but there was a huge element of procrastination involved. In fact, the gifted girl was secretly glad they had not yet met up.

Wa'kanda had been emphatic about the need to see Sha'kona when she discovered what her fourth power was. Sha'kona was not ready to do that. She was afraid of what the healer would tell her. Every time she even considered meeting Wa'kanda, a gnawing feeling in the pit of her stomach warned against it.

Today Sha'kona had managed to block out all thoughts of her terrifying nightmare and the impending visit with the medicine woman. Instead, she busied herself with her rounds and the positive spirit of the people that surrounded her.

After a hectic morning, she had gone by herself to the lake for a much-needed break. She was delighted by the peace and quiet of the tranquil setting. She could not have been happier.

Until she heard Chepi scream.

*It* was a blood-curdling cry of terror and despair. Sha'kona recognized its urgency and bolted in the direction of the wailing. All of her senses were on alert. As she got to the village she saw her cousin on her knees in the dirt in the middle of one of the pens where the animals were kept. Cautiously, Sha'kona approached the entrance to the enclosure. Chepi was rocking back and forth as though possessed, frantically shrieking. In her hands were clumps of white fur. Sha'kona rushed to her side.

"Chepi, what's wrong?" Sha'kona implored, wrapping her arms around her cousin to try to console her. The panicked girl was in a state of shock.

"My baby, Weeko is gone! I know something terrible has happened to him," she bawled, almost incomprehensible. "You have to help me find him!"

Weeko was Chepi's most beloved animal, a tiny lamb born on the girl's birthday. He was so small and sick at birth no one thought he would survive. Because he shared her birthday, Chepi felt the baby sheep was special, so she hand fed him and nursed him back to health. An unusually strong bond formed between them. Weeko acted as if Chepi were his surrogate mother, following her anywhere she went. Every morning when she took care of the sheep, she tended to the little lamb first, and every night made sure to check up on him before she went to sleep. They were practically inseparable.

"Tell me what happened!" Sha'kona demanded.

225

"I don't know, I don't know," Chepi sobbed. "When I got here the sheep were all huddled in the corner of the pen where they are right now, scared to death. Baby Weeko wasn't with them. I looked everywhere and couldn't find him. Then I saw this." She held up the balls of fleece she was holding in her hands. "These are his. They're everywhere. And look over there." She pointed at the gate.

Sha'kona saw the blood on the ground at the opening of the enclosure. She had a bad feeling about this.

"You have to pull yourself together and come with me," Sha'kona urged her. "We need to find Liwanu. The animals are his responsibility. He'll know what to do.

"There has got to be some explanation. The dogs would have warned us if a wolf or a mountain lion had even come near the pen. Nothing else could have taken Weeko. He might have just wandered off. And we don't know for sure where that blood came from. Maybe some of the women were skinning a buffalo or a deer nearby."

Even as she spoke, Sha'kona didn't believe her own words. Something was very wrong and her "other eyes" were not picking up on what it might be. It was as if they were being blocked. When she really needed her gifts they were failing her - and Chepi. This deeply troubled her.

She helped her trembling cousin to her feet and they hurried to tell Liwanu.

*L*iwanu was just walking out of his home when he was startled by the sight of Sha'kona and Chepi running full-speed straight at him. Chepi was nearly hysterical, tears streaming down her cheeks.

"Slow down, girls! What's your hurry?" he said in his easy-going way. He was an even-tempered person who took life as it came and believed there was a calm solution to everything. Nothing seemed to bother him too much. But when he saw Chepi's state and Sha'kona's distress, his manner changed dramatically.

"What's the matter with your cousin?" he asked, worry creasing his face. "She looks as if she's just lost her best friend."

"She did!" Sha'kona answered impatiently. "Baby Weeko is gone. She searched all over for him without any luck. We were just at the pen and there is fur everywhere and blood as well. The rest of the animals are acting really weird too. You have to do something!"

Liwanu didn't like what he was hearing. If any of the animals were in danger, he needed to know about it. Any threat to the livestock was a threat to him and the whole tribe. He wanted answers.

"Take Chepi home and make sure Hakan is there to take care of her," he instructed Sha'kona. "I will let your father know what's going on and get Tokanosh. Your uncle is the best tracker in the tribe. If anybody can figure out what happened to Weeko, he can.

"Let's meet back here as soon as you can. I don't want you going near the animals alone. It could be dangerous or it could be nothing. Until we know, I don't want to take any chances. We will all go together. Your special talents might prove to be very helpful."

Liwanu dashed off to alert his cousins and Sha'kona took Chepi by the hand and led her home.

Sha'kona felt helpless. Recently she had been in such control of her powers and suddenly they weren't working at all. She had absolutely no sense of what had happened. Her mind was a complete blank. Had she lost her gifts because she did not go to Wa'kanda?

She explained everything she could to Hakan and left Chepi with him. He promised to send someone to get Niichaad. As quickly as she could, she returned to meet Liwanu, Tokanosh and her father. The three men were already waiting for her. Sha'kona did not like the looks on their faces.

Before she could say a word, Wowoka asked, "How is Chepi doing?"

"She's still very upset. She can't stop crying, but she's a strong girl. She will be fine," his daughter assured him.

"And you?" Her father knew something serious was bothering her.

"I'll be all right. I just want to know what happened," she said anxiously.

"We all do. Is there anything else you can tell us about what you saw?" The Great Chief spoke softly but his intensity made it clear that he was searching for answers. He hoped Sha'kona could shed some more light on the disturbing event that had occurred so unexpectedly.

"No, father, I can't, but I don't think it's over. I believe something awful is just beginning." She realized how ominous what she had said sounded.

"Let's not make more out of this than it is," Tokanosh interjected. "I'll get Mingan and we'll see where the trail leads us. With your 'magic eyes' and my pup's nose, we'll catch whoever did this. When we do, they will have to answer to Uncle Tokanosh. Trust me, you wouldn't want to be in their moccasins when that happens!"

He grinned a sly grin. He was ready for action. As always.

"'Other eyes,' uncle, 'other eyes,'" Sha'kona corrected, feeling a little better because he wanted her help. She wasn't about to tell him she didn't know if her "other eyes" would be of any use at all.

"That's what I said, 'magic eyes.' Now, enough talking. We've got a baby Weeko to find!" Tokanosh growled.

Wowoka touched his daughter's shoulder and squeezed it.

"You two take care of my little girl," he ordered. "And don't come back empty-handed. I will inform the rest of the tribe of what has happened and make sure no one wanders too far from the village until we know the whole story. We have to keep everyone as safe as possible. Good luck!"

When Sha'kona, Tokanosh, Liwanu, and Mingan arrived at the animals' pen, the crisp autumn air was almost suffocating in its eerie silence. The sheep were still huddled together for safety at the far end of the enclosure, motionless and not making a sound. They seemed frozen in fear.

The rest of the animals were agitated, their nervousness apparent in their peculiar behavior as the three members of the search party approached. The goats lay on their sides playing dead, their legs twitching in the air and the horses skittishly cowered by the watering trough.

Sha'kona rushed over to Tasunke and reassuringly stroked the frightened horse's soft mane. She felt guilty she had not checked on him before. He neighed softly as he began to calm down. She gave him a kiss and a big hug, promising never to forget about him like that again.

"Liwanu! Sha'kona! Come here!" Tokanosh shouted as he waved them over. Liwanu had been checking on the other animals while she was comforting Tasunke.

"I don't understand this," he added. "There is fur and blood everywhere but Mingan can't pick up a scent. He's completely confused, going around in circles, whining and barking anxiously. I've never seen him act this way. It's as if the trail has gone completely cold. I don't see how that's possible. The lamb has only been missing a short while. I saw him early this morning when I was out walking my dogs.

"To make matters even stranger, there are odd-looking tracks here at the gate alongside the blood. I have never seen anything like them and I thought I had seen just about every type of impression made by man or animal. These don't even match!" As he spoke, Mingan was wildly sniffing all over, his nose glued to the ground, searching for the lost scent.

"What do you mean, they don't match?" Sha'kona hadn't even noticed the unusual markings on the ground below her.

"Take a look," her uncle answered. "These footprints are obviously from a four-legged animal, but the next set of prints is from a two-legged creature - and I only know of one of those: humans. The tracks alternate like that up until they stop right here, in the middle of this wide open space." He pointed to the spot where the trail ended just past the gate to the pen.

"It doesn't make any sense. What kind of animal walks on its hind legs and on all fours at the same time? Bears will stand up, but they travel on four legs, not two." Tokanosh couldn't stop staring at the tracks, trying his best to decipher what they meant and to whom or what they belonged.

"Maybe it's not an animal. Maybe it's a man with a misshaped foot," Liwanu commented, as puzzled as his cousin.

"Do you really think a man could have done this?" Tokanosh responded. "What man walks and then crawls every other step? And, look at all the blood and fur. No man would have done that. This was done by some kind of animal I don't know about. But what animal or man vanishes into thin air and leaves no scent?"

No one said a word. A chill ran up Sha'kona's spine. She had been listening to every word and trying to open her "other eyes" so she could help. Inexplicably, she couldn't. The fact that her uncle was baffled only added to her concern.

Tokanosh noticed her worry.

"We don't know anything yet, so let's not start creating monsters," Tokanosh said, trying to alleviate some of the tension. "All we can do at this point is wait and see what happens next, if anything. We should stay here tonight to watch over the livestock and see if our mysterious visitor pays us another visit. If it does, it will be its last."

Sha'kona and Liwanu looked at each other and nodded an uncomfortable endorsement of the plan.

She feared it would be a very long night.

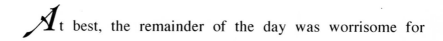

*A*t best, the remainder of the day was worrisome for

Liwanu, Tokanosh and Sha'kona. The animals remained restless and unruly. Most of them were anxiously pacing, moving in groups, not wanting to be alone. Sha'kona stayed with Tasunke most of the time and Liwanu tried his best to keep the rest of the livestock calm. Tokanosh kept Mingan on his toes by routinely leading him around the perimeter of the pens, trying without success to pick up on anything they might have missed. Though they tried to stay occupied, nightfall came upon them more quickly than they had hoped for.

As it began to get dark, Tokanosh had the three of them and Mingan hide behind a large pile of cedar logs stacked high enough to keep them from being seen by the possible intruder. The two men were ready with spears and hand axes.

After what seemed like an eternity of sitting quietly under the clear night sky, Sha'kona's senses suddenly and unexpectedly fired an alarm that something was terribly wrong. Her "other eyes" were still blinded but an even deeper and more primal part of her had sent out a disturbing warning of an encroaching threat. Mingan's fur stood on end as he started to growl. The other animals were frenzied with fear.

Out of the corner of her eye, Sha'kona noticed a shadowy figure stealthily creeping toward the pen. Goosebumps broke out all over her body. Instinct, rather than her gifts, alerted her to the impending danger. As though it knew it had been spotted, the menacing shape abruptly stopped in the exact place where the trail of unnatural tracks ended.

Sha'kona reacted.

"There it is!" She screamed, catapulting Tokanosh and Mingan into action. Liwanu followed suit and they tore in the direction she was pointing, desperately trying to catch whatever it was before it could get away. Their efforts were for nothing. As soon as they started to move, the sinister figure disappeared.

Tokanosh and Liwanu came to a dead stop and just stood there, staring at where the figure had been, totally perplexed. Mingan howled in frustration, echoing their feelings.

"Did you see that?" Tokanosh asked Liwanu incredulously. Liwanu shared his trepidation.

"I think so, but I definitely don't now. What was it?" the normally stoic Liwanu responded, noticeably on edge. There was little that could upset him, but what had just happened had gotten to him.

"At first it looked like some kind of rabid wolf," he continued, "but then it seemed almost human, or, more accurately, inhuman. And it smelled like putrid flesh. I don't know what it was and I'm not sure I want to find out."

Sha'kona had stayed behind the stacked logs, scared, unable to move. It was not normal for her to be afraid of any animal. She thought she had a special connection with all of Mother Earth's creatures, even the ones that most people feared such as the buffalo and bears. But this thing was different. Whatever it was knew about her and her gifts and was intentionally shutting them down. With or without her "other eyes," she wasn't going to let this creature get away. Tokanosh had brought her along to help and that was what she was going to do. She stepped away from the safety of her hiding place and headed toward the men.

That's when she heard Chepi's cry.

"Sha'kona. Help me. Help me please."

Her cousin's voice came from everywhere and nowhere. It

seemed right next to Sha'kona and far away at the same time.

"Chepi, Where are you?" Sha'kona demanded, unnerved. Though the night was clear, she couldn't see see her cousin anywhere and had not heard her approaching. What was she doing out here in the middle of the night? She knew how dangerous it could be.

"Come here, Sha'kona. Please hurry." Chepi's voice was a feeble monotone as if she were in some kind of stupor. Sha'kona started to follow the unearthly calls. From out of nowhere a dauntingly tall, not-quite human creature, covered with random patches of matted dark hair, suddenly appeared, leering at her with vicious yellow eyes.

"Sha'kona, it is me, Chepi. I am right here." To Sha'kona's horror, her cousin's cries were coming out of the thing's mouth. The creature distorted its mouth into a macabre grin, revealing rows of deadly, sharp-pointed fangs. Sha'kona was terrified, but she held her ground.

Tokanosh and Liwanu saw the towering figure peering down at her and rushed to defend the threatened girl. Before they could reach her, the creature turned toward them, smiled a wretched smile and vanished right before their eyes. Nothing but empty space and a foul stench remained.

Tokanosh grabbed Sha'kona, who was visibly shaking with tremors of fear.

"What was that?" he demanded, trying to get some grasp on what was happening. "What did it say? I thought I heard a girl crying out, but I couldn't understand what she was saying."

"I don't know what it was, but it called me by my name using Chepi's voice. It didn't just sound like her, it was her voice. It isn't human. It's pure evil!" she yelled back. Bad feelings were something she had become expert at recognizing and this thing gave her the worst feelings she had ever known.

Tokanosh started to say something but was cut short as Mingan began to bark savagely. Baring his teeth, the dog raced toward the sheep. The creature had reappeared on the other side of the pen near the livestock, but now it looked more like a wolf than a man. It was on four legs with its head down as it moved in on the helpless flock, ready to attack.

The animals were in a wild frenzy, desperately trying to find a way to escape. The stalking man-wolf had singled out its prey - another baby lamb, too small to even try to defend itself. As it crept toward its target, the creature's cruel yellow eyes unmistakably identified it as the same hideous thing that had threatened Sha'kona moments before. It howled barbarically, its thirst for blood too intense to care about the two armed men charging toward it.

As they ran, Tokanosh and Liwanu had their spears in hand, aimed directly at the creature. It did not move, but locked eyes with Sha'kona, completely unfazed by the peril crashing its way. She felt a loathsome force trying to take control of her, almost paralyzing her.

She could no longer be a victim of her fear. This horrible thing had to be stopped from killing any more of the animals. Whether she succeeded or not, she wasn't going to give up without trying.

Closing her eyes, she focused on her great-grandmother and Migisi, erasing all images and thoughts from her mind except for their spirits and the powers they had left her. She prayed for her "other eyes" to open and take command of the situation.

Nothing happened. A force emanating from the man-wolf overpowered her ability to call upon her gifts. Instead of being frightened, she started to burn with anger. Though she wasn't sure of exactly what she was going to do, she had to do something. Without regard to her own safety, she marched toward the beast. It might control her powers, but it could not control her spirit.

At that moment the creature lifted itself up on its hind legs, towering like a giant over its adversaries. Its wolf-like body began to shift itself into the shape of a man, but stopped halfway through the process. The end result was a monstrous combination of man and wolf. Hissing and howling, it turned its fury toward Tokanosh, Liwanu and Sha'kona.

Mingan lunged at the man-wolf thing and ferociously bit into its hindquarters. As valiant as his attack was, the dog was no match for the beast. It picked Mingan up with one taloned hand and, in a display of superhuman strength, effortlesly hurled him over the fence that surrounded the enclosure.

"Mingan!" all three shrieked.

Tokanosh reacted instantly. With a fury and force few men have ever witnessed, he hurled his spear at the creature. The lethal weapon struck the thing directly above its heart, but instead of ripping through flesh and blood, the spear sailed unimpeded through its body as if it were made of nothing more substantial than hot air. Liwanu threw his axe with the same result. The man-wolf didn't even flinch.

They were stunned. How do you fight something against which your weapons have no effect? Tokanosh and Liwanu looked at Sha'kona. She was their only hope.

The enraged beast spit forth a violent roar and stormed toward the three warriors. Sha'kona stepped in front of Tokanosh and Liwanu, straight in the path of certain destruction. No matter the price, she would try to protect her family.

Before Tokanosh could push his niece aside, blue and green flames lit up the night behind the creature. The thing froze in its tracks and spun around to defend itself from this new assault.

Out of the darkness Wa'kanda hobbled forth, chanting in her secret language. In one hand she held fiery branches that burned in magic colors. In the other hand was an ancient totem carved in the shape of the man-wolf facing her.

The beast's eyes were locked on the medicine woman as she shuffled slowly around him, waving the branches and jabbing the totem at the sky. The creature could not look away. It was hypnotized by her movements and her mystic incantations. Unable to resist the spell Wa'kanda was casting, it wandered ever closer to her, swaying in rhythm to her conjuring, a gruesome dance from which it could not flee. When at last the thing was close enough, she reached out and touched it with the colored flames. The man-wolf exploded in a scorching fireball that blazed for one brief instant and then died. All that was left were a few ashes that floated harmlessly away with the late autumn breezes.

Wa'kanda stood still and quiet, letting those same breezes carry away the stench and the memory of the vile creature she had just brought to a fiery end.

---

*A*s soon as they knew everyone was safe, Tokanosh and Liwanu wasted no time in finding Mingan. The courageous dog was lying on the damp grass just outside the pen where he had landed.

"Mingipoo, my brave puppy! My sweetums. You're going to be fine. Daddykins is here now." Tokanosh comforted his best friend.

"Mingipoo? Sweetums? Daddykins?" Liwanu laughed. "I think we should get all of the men to use that as their battle cry!" He found it hysterical that the huge hulk of fearsome warrior that was his cousin used baby talk with his animals.

"If you ever tell anyone, I will beat the color right out of your skin," Tokanosh roared, "and then announce to the whole nation how you sing your precious little sheep to sleep. You didn't think I knew about that, did you? I heard you one night while I was walking with my dogs. The only reason the poor animals go to sleep is so they don't have to hear your horrible voice anymore!" Now Tokanosh was laughing.

"I only did that once, or maybe twice. The sheep get stressed out sometimes," Liwanu confessed.

"Whatever you say," Tokanosh said, finished with the discussion. "Now help me take care of Mingipoo, I mean Mingan."

The two men thoroughly examined the dog. Liwanu was an expert at dealing with animal injuries and illnesses. Mingan was shaken but not seriously hurt. Tokanosh gently held his puppy as Liwanu cleaned a small wound on his paw and wrapped it in a piece of deerskin he had torn from his own leggings. When Liwanu was finished, Mingan stood on his own with only a slight limp to show for his battle with the man-wolf. All three of them headed back to make sure the rest of the animals were all right.

*W*hen they arrived, Wa'kanda was standing in the middle of the enclosure with her eyes closed, the totem held loosely in one hand and the remains of the branches still in the other. An air of serenity surrounded her.

"Old woman, what was that?" Tokanosh asked. He had never thought he was afraid of anything, except water, of course, but tonight had changed that. "And don't hand me some story about it being a big, bad wolf. Tell me the truth. Oh, and thank you for saving our lives. I owe you one." He wasn't great at expressing his gratitude. He was also a little embarrassed that a feeble blind woman had done what he could not.

Liwanu was much better at showing his appreciation. "Thank you, Wa'kanda. If you hadn't shown up, the sheep wouldn't have been the only thing that creature had for dinner. I am forever grateful."

Wa'kanda opened her sightless eyes. Even though she knew the medicine woman was blind, Sha'kona could have sworn the healer was staring straight at her. Maybe she was just feeling uncomfortable about avoiding the ancient woman for so long. Sha'kona knew she should say something, but before she could, the medicine woman began speaking in a hushed, even tone.

"What came here today is called a skinwalker or shape-shifter," Wa'kanda told them. "It is an evil spirit that can take the form of any animal it wants for the purpose of doing harm to others. These spirits have the ability to possess your body, steal your soul, and leave you empty, just the shell of a person. They are cursed and have only malicious intent. They will make you aware of their presence when they feel threatened that good is prevailing and thriving. This skinwalker was testing the spirit of the new nation."

"But why did it take Chepi's lamb?" Sha'kona needed an answer for herself and her cousin.

"Because Weeko was the most vulnerable creature in our village. That is how they always start, with the weakest," the healer explained.

"I thought skinwalkers were made up by parents to keep their children from misbehaving," Tokanosh said. "I know my father used to tell us if we were bad, the shape-shifting monster would come get us. I thought the stories he told were scary, but they don't even compare to the real thing. What do we do if another one comes?" Tokanosh did not like this at all. He was getting used to the easy way of life here with the two tribes living together and now he had to deal with evil supernatural beings.

"I will be prepared." Wa'kanda answered matter-of-factly. She turned to Sha'kona.

"I know you tried to use your powers, but they didn't work, did they?" the old woman asked. Sha'kona shook her head and said nothing.

"The skinwalkers know you are special, but they also know you have not mastered the use of your gifts," Wa'kanda disclosed. "They lured you here to destroy you. Don't worry, I would never let them do that. I just want you to understand that with your blessings come certain dangers and responsibilities that you must be aware of. I can teach you these things, but you have to trust in me."

She smiled and stroked Sha'kona's face tenderly with her fingertips. The young girl nodded in response.

"It's time for us to talk," Wa'kanda told her and took her hand.

They walked together toward the old woman's tipi and Sha'kona's destiny.

*I*t was a quiet walk back to the village. Sha'kona's mind was reeling from what she had just been through and from what was about to come. There was so much she needed to know, so many unanswered questions, but she was completely exhausted. Trying to open her "other eyes" had taken its toll on her. She was more fatigued than she had ever been in her life. Wa'kanda sensed her weariness.

"Struggling against the skinwalker for control of your powers must have worn you out," the medicine woman acknowledged. It seemed as if she knew what Sha'kona was thinking. "Under the best of circumstances your gifts require a great deal of energy and this was definitely not the best of circumstances. I'm amazed you didn't faint."

Wa'kanda led the tired girl into her tent. It was dimly lit by a tiny flame burning delicately in a small clay bowl. Sha'kona noticed the cane lying on the floor and wondered how the old woman was able to walk without it.

"When I use my good medicines to fight bad things I have a special strength that allows me not to use that old walking stick," Wa'kanda responded to what Sha'kona had been thinking. Now she knew the healer could read her mind.

The medicine woman pulled a braided sweetgrass bundle from one of the many pouches strewn about the floor of her tipi and lit it on fire. The smoke gently wafted through the air and the sweet aroma of the sacred plant filled the space, leaving Sha'kona feeling relaxed and rejuvenated. The old woman held the burning herbs in her left hand and began her ritual chant, sung in an ancient tongue. She closed her eyes, allowing the soothing spell to completely engulf her. As her body shook ever so slightly, her shoulders slumped and she opened her eyes.

"This is to invite the good spirits and let the positive energy flow within us and around us," Wa'kanda whispered as she fanned the smoke, completely enveloping both of them in a light, scented haze. Sha'kona's eyes felt heavy and she struggled to keep them open. Just as she thought she was going to fall asleep, the frail woman sat on the ground in front of her, staring blindly into space.

"I know you have found your fourth power," the old healer quietly affirmed.

"Yes," was all Sha'kona could say.

"But you were afraid to tell me."

"Kind of. I don't really know. I was more afraid that if I told anyone about it I would lose it or it would be taken from me. I just wanted to enjoy it on my own for a while." Sha'kona suddenly felt very selfish.

"That power can only survive and grow if it is out in the open," Wa'kanda said, with great respect for this important truth. "It has always been with you, all you had to do was recognize it. Until the end of your days, it will be the source of your strength. Nothing can take it from you. It will forever bind our people together and be our guiding force. It is at once the most basic and complex of all powers, and certainly the greatest - love."

Every word struck to the core of Sha'kona's being.

"With your gifts come responsibilities," the medicine woman continued. "If you fulfill them all, great happiness awaits you and our people. If you don't, there will be a price to pay. Your great-aunt Migisi and I both failed to make the right choices when we were young and for that our sight was taken away. We were left with only our "other eyes" to guide us so we would never again be distracted from our calling.

"This does not have to happen to you. A path has been laid out for you that will determine your future and the future of our people. It requires you to make one more journey. You must go east again to your new home."

For a moment, Sha'kona didn't think she had heard the old woman correctly. The dream of Migisi's desperate pleas came crashing into the young girl's mind and jolted her insides. Her nightmare was becoming reality.

"What do you mean? This is our home!" she shouted. "We can't leave here. It is our sacred land and we must be its caretakers. My father said it would always be our home. I can't ask my family to move again."

"It is not your family's journey, it is yours. They will stay," Wa'kanda replied. "Your father and the council will decide who will go with you." Her words were devastatingly final.

"I can't leave here," Sha'kona argued. "Everyone and everything I know and love are here. I need to be with my family. I don't want these gifts anymore or the responsibilities that come with them. I just want to be what I really am, a young girl trying to be the best person I can be. I have been so happy and now you want to ruin that!"

She tried to fight back the tears but they gushed out of her in a downpour. She could never move away from her family. And what about Enapay? After all that had happened between the two of them, she couldn't bear the thought of not being with him. Everything had been going so perfectly and now her entire world was about to be turned upside down.

"I know how hard this is for you," Wa'kanda said, with great compassion. "If you follow your destiny, you will have all you want and more. Anything you give up will be returned to you a hundred times over and the sacrifices you make will be rewarded with untold blessings for you and our nation.

"Whatever is in your heart will never go away. You will use it every day of your journey. All of the broken branches of your life will be healed by your fourth power and you will emerge from this experience a happier and stronger person.

"When I first received my gifts I was told that one day I would meet a young girl who would be called Sha'kona. It would be my responsibility to share with her a vision that was given to me. I have waited my entire life for the moment I would tell you about all the great things that will come to you and all the great things you will do for others. That time is now. You must go and plant the seeds for the future of us all and allow them to grow fruitfully forever."

Sha'kona didn't know how to feel, but she knew she had no choice. She would do anything for the safety and happiness of her family. Again, her people would be depending on her. She would accept her fate, trusting that all of the medicine woman's words were true.

"Do you understand what I have told you and what you must do?" Wa'kanda asked. She had said what she needed to say.

Sha'kona dried her tears with her hands and made peace with her decision.

"Yes, I do."

## Chapter Ten

## The Visitors

*"We are friends; we must assist each other to bear our burdens."*

*~~ Osage ~~*

*W*owoka was neither shocked nor surprised when Sha'kona told him about her meeting with Wa'kanda. His expression remained impassive as his daughter recounted all the medicine woman had said. Sha'kona had half-hoped he would be outraged at the old woman's demand that his little girl had to move to some unknown place very far away. Instead, he listened quietly, nodding his head from time to time. He asked no questions and made no comments until she was finished speaking.

"I have been expecting and fearing the coming of this day since you were born," the Great Chief began solemnly.

Now Sha'kona was really confused. Why was it that everyone except her knew everything about her life?

"Right after your birth, your great-grandmother told me that you would be a very special child. You had been chosen to lead our family to a New World where we would become strong and grow into a great nation. She was always having crazy visions I didn't under-stand, so I didn't pay much attention to what she said at the time. Now I know what she was talking about.

"After we left our old land I began to recognize some of the predictions she had made. She said she would leave you her gifts and, on your own, you would find four powers you would need to complete

247

your life's journey. And you did. From the bear you discovered your strength, from the eagles your direction, from the white buffalo your wisdom and from yourself your love for all things. You have been well-armed.

"Now you must use your gifts and your powers. I have come to know that our sacred land is not just what is under our feet but all of this New World. We will grow in each of the four directions and fill this land, but first you must go east as Wa'kanda has said. It is the direction of birth, of new beginnings. From there will come the greatest blessings and the greatest challenges to our people.

"Besides Ohanko's family, many others will come. It will be up to you to welcome them and teach them our ways so that they can become part of our great nation. The Spirit of One must include all people.

"You will be our ambassador as well as our front-line warrior, if the need arises. There may be some who do not respect our land or our ways. We must protect both. It is our most important responsibility.

"Tomorrow I will meet with the council to decide who will go with you. Unfortunately, Ohanko won't be there. He is not well. His health has suddenly taken a turn for the worse. Wa'kanda thinks it may be connected to the injuries he suffered. I will speak with him alone before I see the others. I would like to know what he thinks. Though he can be set in his ways, I value his opinions and suggestions."

Wowoka suddenly stopped himself. He realized that for quite a while he had been talking with Sha'kona just staring blank-faced at him. She was on overload. One more word and she would burst.

"Please forgive me for being so chiefly," her father apologized. "I wanted to have a father-daughter chat and I ended up giving you a long-winded speech. I'm so sorry.

"First, my little girl grows up, and the next thing I know she's going away. I don't think I'm ready for either one of those things. It's hard to believe your sixteenth birthday is next week. It seems like only yesterday I put you in your cradleboard for the first time and now you're off to follow your own destiny. Where did the time go? I know this will be a great experience for you, but I will miss you more than you could ever imagine. My love will be with you every day.

"It's time to get some sleep. You've had a very tough night and you need to get as much rest as you can. There's a lot to do before you leave, and you have what will be an amazing but demanding journey ahead."

The Great Chief embraced his daughter, holding her for a long, long time.

$Sha'kona$ slept soundly and woke up feeling fresh and energized, exactly the opposite of how she thought she would feel. In the light of day, her whole perspective seemed to have changed dramatically. Of course, she would miss her family and friends, but surprisingly enough, she was looking forward to her new adventure.

Before she had gone to bed, she had told her mother. They both hugged and cried a lot, but Makawee was happy for Sha'kona and proud as can be. She was always supportive of her daughter, but especially about this. Women of the tribe rarely got opportunities like this one. Sha'kona would be a great example for all the females of the nation.

When Kewa overheard their conversation, his reaction was as annoying as expected. He wanted to know what she was going to leave behind so he could scavenge it. In one breath, he said he might miss her once in a while and in the next laid claim to her sleeping space. Sha'kona made it clear, in no uncertain terms, that if he so much as came near her space, she would lead the skinwalker directly to his skinny, obnoxious self. She figured if that threat had worked on Tokanosh when he was a boy, it would work on her brother. Kewa quickly decided he liked where he slept better anyway.

Chepi and Niichaad rushed to see Sha'kona first thing that morning. The family's gossip lines had been on fire since sunrise. When Sha'kona filled her cousin in on everything that had happened, Chepi's reaction to the news was typical Chepi. She was horrified by the account of the skinwalker, but glad no more sheep would be endangered by it. Though saddened by the loss of baby Weeko, she had already made plans to adopt the next newborn lamb and call it Weeko the Second. It was Chepi's nature to learn from the past, but always look ahead.

She thought it was incredible that her cousin was getting the chance to go out on her own with everyone's blessing, but she was also somewhat jealous. Now that she and Niichaad were quite the couple, Chepi was in a hurry to grow up and spread her wings. She wanted to go with Sha'kona. Hakan, however, had a significantly different point of view on that subject. Nevertheless, the two girls made plans for Chepi to come visit as soon as Sha'kona was settled and had figured out exactly what her big mission was.

Niichaad agreed with everything Chepi said, as usual. Things worked better that way.

As Sha'kona and her cousin were finishing the last of the first of their goodbyes, Wowoka arrived from the council meeting. He explained to Sha'kona that her journey had the full support of the nation. Fifty people would go with her, led by Tokanosh and including Liwanu. It would be Liwanu's job to care for the animals they would be bringing. To help them get started in their new home, they needed to take as much livestock as possible. And, thanks to the substantial harvest now stored in the cave, there were plenty of extra supplies they could have. They would be well-provisioned for the trip. Preparations had to begin right away so they could leave before the first snowfall.

Sha'kona had to admit she was getting excited about the upcoming adventure. She still couldn't explain why, she just knew it was going to be a good thing for her and all of her people.

But there was still one burning question she needed answered.

"Did you meet with Ohanko?" she asked her father. He understood what she really wanted to know.

"Enapay has his father's and my permission to go with you, but it is the boy's decision to make," Wowoka told her, then added, "I mean, it is the young man's decision to make. I can ask him, but I think you might want to."

Sha'kona wasted no time in her response. "You're right about that. Can I go now?"

She was out the door before Wowoka had finished nodding his approval. Since the bizarre events of the night before and her meeting with Wa'kanda, she had not had a chance to even see Enapay. She had a lot to tell him. And one question to ask him.

*A* crowd of people were milling around outside Enapay's tent when Sha'kona arrived. From the universal seriousness of their expressions she suspected something was very wrong. She pushed through to enter the tipi, but before she could, Enapay appeared at the doorway. The anguish on his face confirmed her suspicions. He looked much older than his years.

"My father is not doing well," he told her, struggling to contain his emotions. "His wounds have opened again and last night he began to burn with fever. Our medicine woman has been with him since she left you, but so far nothing she has done has made a difference."

"Is there any way I can help?" She wanted to do something to take away his pain and make Ohanko better.

"Wa'kanda thinks it's best if you don't come in," Enapay informed her. "She told me everything that happened and all about your calling. She feels you need to conserve your powers for your journey. There is nothing more you could do here.

"My father's destiny is in the hands of the Great Spirit. Yours is within your own grasp. It's time for you to seize it - for yourself, for the tribe and for the generations to come."

"I can't leave now. I belong here with you. I can't let you go through this alone. There must be something I can do." Sha'kona's voice was wracked with frustration. What good were her powers if they couldn't help the ones she loved?

"What you can do is follow your path. That will be good for everyone. I know our fathers said I could go with you but I must stay here. I'm sure you understand that." Enapay could not hide his sadness.

"Of course, I do," Sha'kona replied. It was all she could do to restrain herself from taking him in her arms and trying to will away his unhappiness. This was not the time. "When your father has recovered, I will know. I will find a way to send for you. Maybe you and Chepi can come together."

"We'll see," was all he could say. She noticed the tears welling up in his eyes as he reached out and held her. He kissed her softly on her cheek and returned to his father's side.

*T*he day of departure was finally upon them. It also happened to be Sha'kona's sixteenth birthday. This was an important day for her. Among her people it marked her becoming a woman. It seemed everyone had to give her their best wishes and a special gift. Enapay gave her a beautiful piece of turquoise he had found and fashioned into a necklace. She put it on as soon as she got it and vowed never to take it off. Most of the presents she would have to leave with her mother; there were just too many to carry. Enapay's would, of course, go with her.

Though they had been exchanging goodbyes for quite a few days already, the final goodbyes took forever. This was a tradition of the families. They didn't actually have a word for "goodbye," but would say "yanire' kida ya," which literally meant "see you down the road." With each exchange of that sentiment, plans would be discussed for the next time those separating would be together.

At last everything that could be said had been said. It was time to go. Tokanosh gave the signal to mount up and Liwanu and his helpers gathered the animals. Wowoka approached his daughter and his brother.

"Travel safely," the Great Chief proclaimed. "May the spirits guide you and keep you. We will wait for a sign that all is well. Sha'kona, I am sure you will find a way to send us that message. Yanire' kida ya! Remember, our love will be your guardian."

With that, the band of fifty-one brave souls moved out and headed east into the unknown once again.

*T*he first few days had been a blur for Sha'kona. Memories of the last journey had repeatedly flashed through her mind. This trip, however, the weather had been kind and for that they were all grateful. Ever since their torturous trek through the Great Storm into the new world, Sha'kona had hoped never to travel in such extreme conditions again. It was too dangerous and uncomfortable. She would not allow that to happen this time. Her "other eyes" were a lot more powerful now and she felt there were still many undiscovered uses for them. Maybe changing the weather was one of them, she thought playfully, only half-joking with herself.

Enapay constantly occupied her thoughts. She worried about his father and how her best friend was holding up under the stress of the situation. Enapay had become such a fixture in her life that she missed even the littlest things about him, like how he would bring her a wildflower he had found every time they would see each other. Or the look of admiration on his face as he would watch her for hours while she practiced new uses for her gifts, sometimes with comical results.

Once she tried to see if she could speed up the process of sun drying the meat. After more attempts than she could count, the end results were always the same - burnt, shriveled-up pieces of an inedible substance that had once been food. Though it was hard as rock, Enapay would dutifully put it in his mouth to sample her work. Always positive, he commented that if they couldn't eat it, they could always use it as a weapon.

These thoughts kept her focused as they fueled and energized her. She needed that on this mystical sojourn toward the sunrise. The sooner they got where they were going, the sooner she would know why she had to go there and when she would see Enapay and the rest of her family again. The only problem was she didn't have any idea where they were going, except east, or how long it would take to get there. Wa'kanda had not given her any clues about those things. She had to trust she would know when they arrived there - wherever "there" was.

Sha'kona wasn't the only one finding the separation difficult. She knew how much her uncle missed her father. They had never been apart since Tokanosh was born. She had witnessed the bittersweet moment when the two brothers said their goodbyes and Wowoka told Tokanosh he would be chief of this new hand-picked tribe. The big man humbly accepted the responsibility. He had always followed the Great Chief's direction without question, but from now on he would have to rely on his own decisions.

Tokanash was proving himself to be exceptional in his role as leader of the group, making wise choices, planning ahead, delegating tasks and keeping morale high. He led by example with common sense and a listening ear, using his brain, not his brawn. He was a natural, just like her father. It must run in the family, she thought to herself with a smile.

# Chapter Ten

*E*verywhere they looked, new and beautiful images captured the eyes of the small band of travelers. Sha'kona was glad their spirits were high as they witnessed the amazing landscapes unfolding before them. Wide open plains gave way to impressive deciduous forests painted with late autumn's lustrous golden hues.

Everything grew denser and closer together than it had back west from where they had come. At times, the woods were almost impenetrable and the little tribe would have to find new pathways to keep moving forward. The going was slow and frustrating, but Tokanosh kept a clear, calm head and a steady pace. He urged his people to relax and enjoy the spectacle Mother Earth was providing them.

Mingan and the rest of the pack stayed near their master and Sha'kona. The dogs seemed to anticipate each change in direction the young woman would make, constantly inspecting the uncharted trail to make sure it was safe for the rest of the group. The myriad of new scents kept Tokanosh's canine companions alert and excited. They sniffed every tree, branch, leaf, rock, stick, and piece of dirt along the way. The Big Chief would sometimes get annoyed by their obsessive behavior, but Sha'kona found it funny. Dogs will be dogs, she laughed to herself, except to her uncle.

By mid-morning on the eighth day, the little tribe was deep within a section of the forest that was so dense and overgrown the sun could barely cast a shadow on the leaf-covered ground. Sounds were muted and silence ruled. It was so quiet you could hear your own thoughts, or, in Sha'kona's case, a loud buzzing in her head accompanied by a peculiar lightheadedness. The noise grew in volume until it was overpowering her ability to even think. She recognized the sensations as alerts her "other eyes" were opening. She rubbed the sides of her head to try to escape the internal pandemonium.

Tokanosh noticed her distress.

"You don't look well," he said. "Are you all right?"

"I'm feeling a little weird," she answered.

"Weird how? Weird sick or weird like your 'magic eyes' are coming to life?" The last thing he needed was for her to get sick. Without her guidance they would be stuck in the middle of nowhere with no idea as to which way they should go.

She didn't bother to correct him. "I'm hearing some strange noises in my head and feeling a little dizzy. It's as if I'm being sent a message but I can't quite make out what it is. It's hard to explain."

"Could it have anything to do with where we are going or how long it's going to take to get there?" Tokanosh asked. "I could certainly use a sign with some answers to those questions. I feel like we've been wandering in circles all morning."

"I'm sorry, but I don't have those answers," Sha'kona responded. "I only know what Wa'kanda told me - head east." She paused for a moment to massage her temples. "I think we have been kind of going in circles. Something nearby seems to be calling to me. That's what my weird feelings are about and why I keep coming back to this area. I just can't seem to find whatever it is.

"I don't understand why my gifts can't be a little more specific and definite. They're always cloaked in some obscure vision or sign that I have to figure out. I would just once like to see an arrow pointing in one direction telling me, 'Go this way'."

"I'm no expert," Tokanosh commented, "but I don't think it works that way. The mumbo jumbo is a big part of the process so you keep people amazed or scratching their confused heads. It makes the whole experience more epic."

As he spoke, Sha'kona's body stiffened and her eyes bulged from their sockets. Tokanosh rushed to grab her, fearful she would fall from her horse. Before he could reach her, all of her muscles relaxed again. As suddenly as the spell had come over her it had gone away, and so did the buzzing in her head.

Tokanosh was alarmed. "What was that?"

"I believe I have found what I wasn't looking for," she stated enigmatically as she slid off Tasunke and began walking away. The other members of the tribe watched, speaking in hushed tones, wondering what the girl with the gifts was up to now.

Just steps from where she had dismounted, Sha'kona came upon a perfectly clear path that led her to between two enormous oak trees. Beyond them, the forest abruptly ended in a narrow open space. On the other side of the clearing, the woods began again but seemed fuzzy and distorted as if they were behind a curtain of mist. Intrigued, she stretched out her hand. Instead of air, she felt something almost liquid that rippled like water with the slightest touch. She jerked her hand back instinctively and, to her surprise, found it completely dry.

Curious about this remarkable phenomenon, she reached out again and slowly put her whole arm through the curtain. She felt a tingling from her fingertips to her shoulder as her arm disappeared, reappearing as soon as she withdrew it. She struggled for an explanation. It was as though there were a crease in reality she could slip through. What was on the other side was not the forest she saw in front of her.

Sha'kona looked back to find her new family staring at her. From where they stood they could only see her standing in the middle of the forest with her hand in the air.

"What are you doing over there?" Tokanosh called out. "Do you see anything?" He was not one to stand idly by and do nothing, but he knew she was having one of her visions and there was not much he could do to help. When she didn't respond, he began walking toward her. Before he could take two steps she suddenly vanished.

"Sha'kona!"

Sha'kona heard her uncle's voice, but couldn't make out what he was saying. She had already stepped through the peculiar mist into the crease she had just discovered and found herself immersed in a liquid that was not actually wet. To her relief, she was able to breathe as though it were the purest air. A sense of safety and belonging washed over her. Swirling points of light flashed all around, and soft, warm currents of energy caressed her skin. She was floating through layers of time and space she never could have imagined existed. As quickly as her ride had begun it ended. A tear appeared in the liquid and she was poured through it onto the ground below. She landed as gently as a feather next to a small oak tree with seven branches extending in every direction. Just ahead of her was the widest river she had ever seen. There was no other side to it.

Tokanosh raced to the spot where he had last seen Sha'kona, frantic to find her. His search was over quickly. There was no place to hide. She was gone. Even Mingan was confused. Her scent stopped cold right there between the two oaks.

"Oh, Great Spirit, what have I done? I have lost my brother's child!" he screamed in anger at himself. "How could I have let this happen?" Tokanosh was beside himself. He was the chief and protector and he had failed.

"Uncle, calm down. I'm right behind you," Sha'kona said with a huge smile on her face.

Tokanosh turned around and looked at his niece as though he were seeing a spirit. A grin started to light his face but he immediately forced a scowl.

"Where were you?" he shouted. "Don't you ever go off on your own again without asking me first! You nearly scared me to death. I could have sworn you just disappeared like one of those skinwalkers."

"I did disappear, at least from here," she told him. "This is going to sound really crazy even coming from me, but I found our home." Sha'kona was vibrating with excitement. The dogs surrounded her, greeting her as if she had been gone for days. They picked up on her energy and barked their approval.

"Will you puppies settle down?!" the Big Chief ordered. "I can't think with all that racket!

"What do you mean you found our home?" he said to her. "We just started the trip. How could we be there already? You've had one too many 'magic eye' spells, if you ask me."

"I can't explain it, I have to show you. Come with me." Sha'kona took her uncle's hand and led him into the crease in the curtain of mist.

By that time all of the small band had gathered close and watched as the two stepped through the crease. The air rippled like a pond when a stone has been thrown into it and Sha'kona and Tokanosh vanished. The tribe looked on in shock. Where their chief and his niece had been was now an empty space.

In an instant, the two of them arrived at the exact same place Sha'kona had the first time she had gone through.

"I don't know what just happened, but that's the way to travel!" Tokanosh exclaimed. "And look at that water! That is one great river. In fact, that is what we will call it, the Great River. There has to be enough fish in there to last an eternity!"

Ignoring the seven-branched tree, he pulled off his moccasins and ran toward the sandy beach. He dashed straight through the waves that crashed rhythmically on the shore and into the icy water. Sha'kona laughed at the big man splashing around like a child.

"It's cold, but not frozen yet! Come get your feet wet," Tokanosh invited. He scooped up a handful of the Great River, tasted it and immediately spit it out.

"It tastes salty! Not much good for drinking, but I'll bet there are some gigantic fish in here."

"We have to get the others, Uncle." Sha'kona wasn't sure how long the crease would allow them to travel back and forth.

Tokanosh reluctantly left the water and joined her by the small tree. Together, they stepped into the fluid curtain on that side and were gone.

Liwanu was waiting with a perplexed look when Tokanosh and Sha'kona appeared, walking nonchalantly out of thin air.

"You're not going to believe where we just were and where we're all going," Tokanosh announced and proceeded to try to explain what had happened. Everyone listened in awe and anticipation. The gifted girl had done it again.

After her second trip, Sha'kona had come to understand that the crease was simply a bend in the reality of one place that joined with a similar bend in another place. It allowed anyone who could find it to travel long distances almost instantly, powered by concentrations of Mother Earth's energy that pooled by the entrances to the miraculous passageway. The trick was to find it.

Oh yes, there was one more thing she had learned about the crease. It was a lot of fun.

In no time at all, the entire expedition had experienced that fun and arrived safely at their new home.

*B*y nightfall, the new tribe had set up their tents on top of a large hill overlooking the now smooth water. Sha'kona lay in bed, reliving the day in her mind. Some members of the group had to be persuaded to go through the crease, and the animals had to be forced into it, but in the end, they all arrived safely and thoroughly enjoyed it. Everyone loved their new home and was incredibly grateful to Sha'kona for guiding them there.

Sha'kona sensed no one could use the passageway without her help. A few of the younger members of the group had wanted to take the ride again just for their amusement, but without her there they couldn't find the crease. It reassured her to know this was all a part of the plan for her and that her gifts were becoming a powerful part of making that plan work. Wa'kanda had told her that great things would be possible for her, but she never expected anything like what had happened today. The happiness of her new family was extremely satisfying to her and all the reward she wanted.

Unable to sleep that night, Sha'kona got up and wandered outside, taking with her the eagle feather she had been given after Migisi's passing. Looking out at the peaceful river, her thoughts turned to Enapay. Though she knew it was not possible, she wished he was there with her to share this wonderful adventure. As a sign for him and a symbol of her feelings, she decided to place the feather in the crook of one of the seven branches of the tree that marked the spot where the new tribe had arrived. Everyday she could look at that tree and be reminded of what Enapay had given to her. As the tree grew, so would her love. One day she hoped to be with him again, but she knew any life they might have together would have to be here. She would never leave her new home. This was where she belonged.

*I*n the days that followed, the tribe explored and learned all they could about where they would be living. Everything seemed closer together here, nothing like the open plains that surrounded their old village. Tokanosh and several of the men went hunting right away and found generous amounts of small game. Wild turkeys were everywhere. Though not as exhilarating a prey as the buffalo, they were a lot easier and safer to catch. Deer and rabbits were also plentiful and would provide them with skins for clothing and shelter as well as fresh meat.

The Great River was a prodigious source of countless varieties of fish, some as big as a man. The same techniques they had always used were even more successful here because there were so many fish. Not a day went by that the men did not catch as much as they needed and then some.

Liwanu discovered a tree he called the birch whose white bark proved to be very flexible and waterproof. By using the bark to cover a wooden frame he created an extremely light canoe that maneuvered well and could easily be carried by two men. This gave them easy access to the many lakes and streams nearby and the fresh water they needed.

Because they had arrived so long before the first snow, the women were able to gather nuts and berries they had not known in their old home and discover all sorts of edible and medicinal plants. They could see the soil was rich and fertile and looked forward to planting in the following spring.

One thing was certain. They would not go hungry.

The lack of buffalo, and thus the hides needed to make tipis, forced them to create new designs and building techniques for their permanent homes. Sha'kona had predicted that winters would be cold and snowy so they needed strong, warm housing. They used the endless supply of trees around them to build what they called a longhouse. Rectangular in shape, they were made from wood, tree bark and rope-like grass, strengthened in some areas with animal skins. The roofs were rounded and the structure was supported with wooden stakes buried deep in the ground. They decided to make their homes communal, with more than one family occupying the space and sharing the workload. Everyone preferred living this way and it brought them closer together as a tribe.

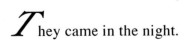

*T*hey came in the night.

Sha'kona had been getting ready for bed when she heard their unique calls. As quickly as she could, she left her longhouse to find them. Perched on the branches of her favorite tree were the seven eagles. Since Migisi's journey into the spirit world, they had come to visit Sha'kona a few times, but always during the day. Their arrival in the darkness was not a good sign. The cold, late fall breezes only amplified the feeling that something was terribly wrong.

She approached them, fearing the worst.

"Why have you come now?" she whispered so as not to alert anyone else of the birds' presence.

They made no sounds in response. They just stared at her and buried their heads beneath their wings. She felt the strength drain from her body as their message became clear in her mind. One by one the seven eagles lifted their heads and flew down next to her. Once beside her, they did what no bird could do. They cried.

Ohanko had just died.

*T*he news of Ohanko's death was a heartbreaking shock for all the members of the tribe. They had grown to care deeply for this great leader. Though he was a complex man, he cared about each one of them as part of his family and was dedicated to the growth and prosperity of their young nation. Everyone had a story to tell about the ever-colorful Dark Chief. Though tears were shed, laughter was also shared, especially over the tales of his eccentric dress and stubborn ways. He would be missed, but he would always be remembered.

Sha'kona was profoundly upset by Ohanko's passing and her

heart went out to Enapay. She couldn't imagine how he was feeling. If it had been her father, she didn't know how she could go on. She wanted to take Enapay into her arms and comfort him, but he wasn't there. Now more than ever she realized how important it was that she be near him. He was her best friend and she could not be with him in his time of need. That had to change.

It was time to send word back to her family that they had found their new home and were doing well. She would also let Enapay know she was thinking about him and her love was with him. She headed to her tree to summon the eagles. By the time she got there, they were already settled on the seven branches waiting for her. They knew what she wanted.

"I need you to do this for me. Please go quickly."

The sacred birds took flight, headed into the west.

*T*he next few weeks passed uneventfully as they went about the work of building the village and preparing for winter. The weather was turning cold, but the longhouses kept them safe from the elements. Sha'kona had moved in with Tokanosh. She was the only one willing to live with the Big Chief and his canine companions so they had the whole place to themselves.

Everyday she made her pilgrimage to the tree. It made her feel more connected to Enapay and the family she had left behind. She found herself spending most of her free time there. It gave her a chance to be alone and think. Since the eagles had left, she had not had any tinglings or other signals from her "other eyes." It concerned her that she did not know and could not sense whether the birds had delivered her message. And if they had tried to, would her family or Enapay be able to understand them?

Her musings were suddenly interrupted by peculiar cries from above she instantly recognized. Looking up, she saw the seven eagles in a V formation flying due east. They continued past her out over the Great River without stopping. Her "other eyes" went on full alert. Something was coming through the crease, led by the sacred birds.

A familiar neighing spun Sha'kona around. Riding toward her was Achak with Enapay on his back. As soon as Enapay saw her, that smile lit up his face. Sha'kona felt like she was literally going to fall apart. She had never run so fast in her life as she did racing to greet him. Even before Achak had stopped, Enapay jumped off and embraced her with his arms, his heart and his soul. She held onto him as tightly as she could and, though she tried not to, burst into tears of pure joy.

He whispered in her ear so delicately the words almost floated away.

"I told you I believed in you."

*S*ha'kona and Enapay had a lot to share with each other that day. They caught up on everything that had happened since she had left the old village. He let her know her family was well and sent their love. They had all understood the eagles' messages. That was why he was here. When they discussed his father, Enapay spoke proudly of him, explaining that though he missed him, he was not sad because the Dark Chief lived on in his heart.

Sha'kona explained how the seven-branched tree had become her connection to Enapay. They both promised never to remove the feather she had placed there. It would be the symbol of the power they had together.

Enapay also informed her of a new tribe that had come to the old village. There were about a hundred people in that family and they too had come from the west. Wowoka had greeted them and welcomed them into the nation.

Others from the tribe had wanted to join Enapay on his journey here, but there was a shortage of horses. A sickness had spread through the herd and many had died, including Ohanko's beloved black stallion. No one seemed to know what to do about it. Even Wa'kanda had been unable to find a cure.

This was an extremely serious problem. The tribe back west depended on their horses for survival. Without them, their way of life would have to change, and not for the better. Sha'kona was extremely concerned about this tragic news. With her gifts, there had to be some solution she could come up with. She would think long and hard on the matter. She would not let her family suffer if she could help it. And she was convinced she could.

*S*ha'kona had a plan. She went to see Tokanosh to tell him about the disease that had killed the horses in the old village and what she thought they could do. They both agreed that horses were not as essential here as they were in the west. Almost everything they needed here was accessible on foot or could be reached by taking one of the birch bark canoes. It was her idea to send the horses to where they were needed most.

Tokanosh agreed wholeheartedly and gathered the tribe together to present Sha'kona's proposal. He had decided to continue the type of government his brother and Ohanko had established. Everyone would have a voice and a vote in the matter. After much discussion, there was a unanimous consent to send the horses back.

Saying goodbye to Tasunke was not easy. Stroking his soft mane, Sha'kona whispered sweet words of affection and love and explained the reason he had to go. Tears streamed down her cheeks as she promised they would see each other again soon. He might even be able to bring Chepi back one day. Tasunke knew what she wanted, as he always did. Whinnying enthusiastically, he nudged her face and strutted to her tree, ready to do as she wished. He would wait for his time to go.

All of the horses were assembled where Tasunke waited. Achak found his way next to his best friend at the head of the herd. The entire village had gathered to watch their cherished animals go and to wish them well. Besides working partners, the family was losing friends and companions.

Sha'kona approached the seven-branched tree with her hands held high in the air. Almost as if rehearsed, everyone mimicked her actions and in an instant the sacred eagles appeared out of nowhere high above. They circled but for a moment then swooped down to land, each on a separate branch of the tree. As Sha'kona moved closer to them, she effortlessly opened her "other eyes" to communicate what she wanted them to do. The birds raised their wings and in unison cried their understanding. With their usual grace and power, they took off and began to fly around the horses and the tree. The herd grew excited with anticipation, neighing and snorting and shaking their heads and tails.

Her hands still held high, Sha'kona backed away. The animals were eager to go where they were needed, to serve their partners and fulfill their purpose for their families.

"I love you all. Yanire' kida ya!" Her voice was choked with emotion.

Sha'kona dramatically dropped her arms and immediately raised them again even higher. As she did, a giant tear appeared in the crease. The eagles soared through the opening leading the horses back to the other side, to the place where their destiny would cross paths with the destiny of the entire nation.

In an instant they were gone, the crease closed. Slowly, the gifted girl and the small band lowered their arms. There was no question now.

This was home.

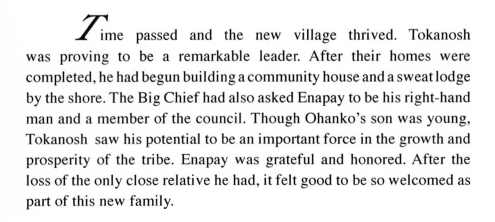

*T*ime passed and the new village thrived. Tokanosh was proving to be a remarkable leader. After their homes were completed, he had begun building a community house and a sweat lodge by the shore. The Big Chief had also asked Enapay to be his right-hand man and a member of the council. Though Ohanko's son was young, Tokanosh saw his potential to be an important force in the growth and prosperity of the tribe. Enapay was grateful and honored. After the loss of the only close relative he had, it felt good to be so welcomed as part of this new family.

Sha'kona continued to develop her gifts. She became the spiritual leader and medicine woman of her people. Her guidance was sought after and followed by old and young alike. Much to the simultaneous chagrin and admiration of the men of the small band, she had also become one of the best hunters.

Her relationship with Enapay could not have been better. Every day, like their tree, it grew stronger. Sha'kona was not only happy, she was content.

But she was restless. Constant stirrings within kept her a little on edge. She recognized her uneasiness as a premonition something was going to happen.

And it did.

*L*ate one afternoon Sha'kona noticed moving objects in the distance, far out into the deep waters of the Great River. She watched for a long time as, ever so slowly, they moved closer. Finally she could make out the shapes. They looked like enormous oddly-formed canoes with giant wings on top catching the wind. She had always wondered how wide the Great River was and where it flowed. Sometimes she thought there was no other side to it. The appearance of these strange-looking boats proved that wasn't true.

She hurried to tell Tokanosh and Enapay of the approaching visitors. Everyone was excited at the prospect of meeting them. Preparations began immediately to greet them with food and gifts as symbols of their friendship. When all was ready, the tribe gathered at the shore to await their arrival.

# Chapter Ten

Sha'kona remembered her father's words; she was to welcome newcomers and teach them the ways of her people. She stood proudly in front of her family as their ambassador, ready to invite the visitors to become part of that family as members of the nation of tribes that called this New World home. Though eager, she was apprehensive, realizing that once the strangers came ashore, there would again be great changes. Because she had already been through so much in such a short time, she felt prepared to face whatever might happen. She would soon find out if that were true. This was her destiny and she embraced it.

As the giant canoes with wings drew closer, there was one thing of which Sha'kona was absolutely certain.

Nothing would ever be the same.

*Epilogue*

*V*ery slowly, Taylor closed the book.

Nana was watching, waiting for her reaction. Her granddaughter sat motionless in the old rocking chair, her hands and eyes still glued to the ancient black book, a look of astonishment on her face.

"That was amazing," Taylor whispered.

She looked up to see her Nana staring at her with her "I've got a secret but I'm not going to tell" look. Taylor had no idea what to think. She tried to open the book again, but the cover wouldn't budge.

"What happened?" Taylor asked.

Nana maintained her unblinking gaze but her lips turned slightly upward toward a smile. Taylor was growing more confused. She didn't know whether to laugh, cry, or declare herself officially nuts. This was all so unreal. She had just lived through her great-grandmother's passing, the second Ice Age and a book coming to life like some high-tech virtual reality fantasy game and she couldn't get her grandmother to answer a simple question.

"I don't understand, Nana. Why did you give me this book? Why does she look like me? And what happened to her?" There was a great deal Taylor wanted to know.

"I am only the messenger, child," Nana finally responded. "Your Nonie only wanted you to see the book. All I did was give it to you at the right time. After that I sat back and watched you close your eyes and be transported to a place I could only dream of going. I have no idea what you saw or heard, but that doesn't really matter, does it? It was meant for you so it's up to you to take from it what you can. Spend some time thinking on it. Nonie left you her gifts as well and you can use them to help you understand. In time those same gifts will serve you in many ways."

"You mean like Sha'kona?" her granddaughter asked impatiently.

"I can't answer that, but I do know one thing," Nana told her. "The young girl in that book was a great leader of our people many generations ago. I've heard of her and her adventures since I was a little girl. Some of the stories that were told to me sounded so extraordinary, I can't imagine how they could be real." Nana sighed and looked through her bedroom window into the night sky.

Taylor was even more perplexed. Maybe her Nana was losing it too. Maybe the whole world was.

"First you tell me Sha'kona was real, then you tell me she's not," Taylor complained. "Which is it? Was the story true or did I just dream it? Please, you have to tell me."

Her grandmother's expression gave nothing away.

"You will come to know soon enough," Nana said quietly. She suddenly looked very tired. "With that knowledge you will begin your own journey, the great adventure of your life. It will be your quest to find the true meaning of who you are and who you are to become. That will come in time.

"There is much we could discuss but it's late. It's time for us to get some rest. Our next conversation should be over some of my seven-layer chocolate cake. Now we both need to go to bed."

Nana gave Taylor a kiss on the forehead, leaving her sitting in the rocking chair, still trying to figure out how and why her life had just been turned sideways. Reluctantly the puzzled girl headed upstairs to her room.

"Goodnight, Nana. And thank you, I think."

Although she was not at all tired, Taylor crawled into bed. She was trying to figure out everything all at once and it was beginning to give her a massive headache. Her mother hadn't asked anything about what she and Nana were doing except whether they had had a good talk. It was a mother question that actually meant "I know what you've been up to, but I want to hear it directly from you." Taylor had just shrugged and said, "Yeah, sure, Mom."

Under her pinecone patchwork quilt, Taylor stared at the glow-in-the-dark stars on her ceiling. The tingling sensation she had felt when she first opened up the book was back. Her bed started to vibrate ever so lightly and then stopped. She felt weak and a little dizzy, like Sha'kona had felt when her "other eyes" were opening. A powerful force pulled her out of bed and propelled her to the window that overlooked the backyard. Looking out, her heart nearly stopped. There wasn't a flake of snow or ice to be found. It was a warm, clear, normal September night.

As she searched for some possible explanation, her eyes were drawn to the old oak tree from which her childhood swing hung. The massive oak dominated the yard. Its trunk was topped with limbs that spread almost as wide as the house. From the size of it, it had to be several hundred years old. She remembered the count-less hours she and her friends had spent trying to climb all the way to the top. As they got older, they found other things to occupy their time and the fun with the tree became a memory. It had never really meant much more to her than something to play on.

Until now.

Halfway up the trunk, the tree branched out in different directions. She began to count the branches. There were seven.

A crazy thought came into her head. Was it possible this was the same tree Sha'kona had found, the same tree her people had lived next to so many years ago and the same tree where Sha'kona and Enapay had promised to keep the sacred eagle feather forever?

Taylor had to find out. She couldn't wait until morning. She couldn't wait another minute.

Slipping on her tennis shoes and her cousin's Davidson sweat-shirt, Taylor sneaked out the back door, hoping not to be heard by her mom or Nana. She knew her mom would go ballistic if she saw her daughter trying to climb that gigantic tree by herself. That was a chance the young girl was willing to take.

Quietly approaching the tree, she recognized what a monumental task climbing it was going to be, but there would be no stopping her. Pulling herself hand over hand up the massive trunk, she inched her way toward the place where it divided into the seven branches. Using all of her strength for what seemed like hours, she finally reached the spot. She struggled into the crook of one of the enormous branches and sat down, her legs dangling frightfully high above the ground. It took her a moment to catch her breath. The magnificent view of the fields below and the white-capped Atlantic

Ocean beyond nearly took her breath away again.

A dark section of one of the limbs to her left caught her eye. It looked like a shadow but there was no moonlight to cast it. She cautiously maneuvered herself closer to investigate. That's when she saw it.

Cradled within a small, oval opening between two thick branches was a weathered, but intact, brown and white eagle feather. Taylor slipped her hand into the small space and picked it up by its quill, holding the fragile plume as Sha'kona was told to do; high above her head like an eagle would fly. Taylor was overcome with emotion. In her hand was the same sacred feather Sha'kona once held. Taylor stayed there for quite some time, silent, her mind at peace. Before she left, she carefully placed the feather back exactly as she had found it. It was meant to remain there forever.

At that moment, Taylor understood.

# Characters' Names, Phonetic Spellings and Meanings

1. Sha'kona - **Shah** kone ah - Derivative - Oneida meaning "a gift"
2. Taylor Mashonee - **Tay** lur / Mah **shone** ee - Siouan meaning "trading belt"
3. Wowoka - Wo **wo** kah - Paiute meaning "wood cutter" - inventor of the ghost dance (Wovoka)
4. Tokanosh - **Tah** kah nahsh - Wampanoag
5. Kewa - **Keh** wah - Roanoke meaning "image of a god"
6. Makawee - **Mah** Kah wee - Sioux meaning "mothering"
7. Hakan - **Hah** kahn - meaning "fire"
8. Liwanu - **Lee** wah noo - Miwok meaning "growl of a bear"
9. Chepi - **Cheh** pee - Algonquian meaning "fairy"
10. Migisi - **Mee** gee see - Cheyenne meaning "eagle"
11. Mingan - **Meen** gan - meaning "grey wolf"
12. Tasunke - Tah **soon** keh - Dakota meaning "horse"
13. Nanuk - **Nah** nook - Inuktitut meaning "polar bear"
14. Enapay: Eh **nah** pay - Sioux meaning "brave"
15. Ohanko- O **hahn** ko - meaning "reckless"
16. Wa'kanda - Wah **kahn** dah - Sioux meaning "possesses magical power"
17. Achak - **Ah** chock - Algonquian meaning "spirit"
18. Niichaad - **Nih** ih chahd - Navajo meaning "swollen"
19. Tatanka – Tah **than** kah – Lakota/Dakota meaning "buffalo"
20. Weeko – **Wee** koh – Sioux meaning "pretty"

# *Jana Mashonee*

GRAMMY nominated, eight-time Native American Music award winner Jana Mashonee, a Native American singer/songwriter, actress and author, is one of the most well-known and recognized Native artists today. Her groundbreaking albums and concerts have been met with critical acclaim and commercial success around the world. Jana releases her music through her own label, Miss Molly Records, the first Native-owned label distributed by Sony/RED Music. The videos for her songs have won awards at festivals across the country. Despite her fast-paced career, Jana has still found time to give back by way of her non-profit organization, Jana's Kids. She helps Native American Youth achieve their dreams by awarding scholarships in academic, athletic and artistic categories and through the many programs offered by her foundation. American Indian Story – The Adventures of Sha'kona is her first book, co-written with Stephan Galfas, her long-time songwriting partner and a renowned music producer. It is based on Jana's best-selling, GRAMMY nominated album of the same name.

Visit her at: www.janamashonee.com or
www.facebook.com/janamashonee
Write her at jm@janamashonee.com

Also available from Jana Mashonee

# New Moon Born

*The new album from Native American sensation Jana Mashonee*
*Featuring "A Change is Gonna Come" and "Solid Ground."*

*To get yours now, visit*
*www.janamashonee.com*

*Or email*
*orders@janamashonee.com*

Also available from Jana Mashonee

# American Indian Story

*The GRAMMY nominated album, now an epic novel!*

*To get yours now, visit*
*www.janamashonee.com*

*Or email*
*orders@janamashonee.com*

Also available from Wampum Books

### Goddess of the Waters
# Poneasequa
*Stephanie A. Duckworth-Elliott*

## 2010 Mom's Choice Award winner

McKenzie embarks upon a journey of self-discovery after being asked by her teacher to do a presentation in front of the class. Having never taken her Wampanoag heritage very seriously, she discovers that it may not be so bad to be "different".

ISBN 978-0-9842012-1-1

90000

9 780984 201211

Breinigsville, PA USA
25 September 2010
246054BV00002B/2/P